PIECES OF US

CARRIE ELKS

Edited by Rose David

Proofread by Proofreading by Mich

Cover Designed by Najla Qamber Designs (www. najlaqamberdesigns.com)

I

"One more signature," Meg Ryker said, sliding yet another slip of paper full of tiny black print across the table. "Don't look so worried. It's your last one as Autumn Garner."

Autumn took the paper from her lawyer and scrawled her name – her soon to be old name – across it. How many times had she practiced this signature until it was exactly how she wanted it? With just the right amount of swirl and loops without looking too forced. And she'd never need it again.

She was Autumn Paxton now. Back to the name she thought she'd given up for good. It felt strange, like putting on a sweater you'd grown out of. The arms were too short, the knit too tight against her bust.

She glanced again at the piece of paper, with *Non-Disclosure Agreement* printed across the top. It was the final piece of the settlement, and it had taken her and Josh almost twelve months to negotiate.

Twelve months of feeling in limbo. Of wanting to be done with the marriage she never should have agreed to in the first place.

Now she was free, and she had no idea what to do.

"So that's it?" she asked, passing the agreement back to Meg.

"That's it." Meg laid it on top of all the other papers Autumn had to sign since Judge Benedict had given the go-ahead to dissolve the marriage. "I just need to exchange these with your husband—" she laughed, correcting herself, "I mean your ex-husband's lawyer and then it's all complete. You're a free woman."

"Without a home or a job." Autumn chewed her lip.

"Ah, but with more than enough money to buy both. This is a good thing, Autumn. You got almost everything you wanted. Now you get to decide what to do with the rest of your life."

"You're right." Autumn smiled at her. She'd spent enough time mourning her failed marriage. "And at least I got to keep the shoe collection."

Meg laughed. "I noticed the ones you're wearing today. They're beautiful."

Autumn lifted her foot to admire the yellow patent pumps she was wearing, with sky-high heels and a familiar red sole. Pretty shoes were her one weakness. Ever since her mom bought her first pair of sparkly pink glitter shoes when she could barely walk five steps.

"I guess these are my divorce shoes," she said, twirling her ankles.

Her sister, Lydia had put it a little more crudely, squealing loudly and clapping with glee when she saw them. "They're screw-you-Josh shoes. I love them!" she'd said. "Promise me you'll wear them to court."

And so she had, teaming them with a sober grey skirt suit with yellow piping, and hoping to heck the Judge didn't have something against bright yellow shoes.

"So what are you and your shoes planning to do next?" Meg asked, pressing the intercom button on her desk.

"I've no idea." And it felt weird. In spite of the crazy shoes, her life had always been regimented. Studying hard at school, then at college before finally getting her MBA. Then she'd done it all again in business, working for a huge Manhattan real estate firm before starting her own with her husband, building it until they were one of the movers and shakers in the Manhattan office space business.

And now that firm was her ex-husband's, thanks to the sheaves of paper she'd just signed. She'd been generously compensated for letting him buy her out, but it still felt strange. For the first time in her adult life she was unemployed.

Like her change in name, it didn't seem to fit.

"Well while you're thinking about it, let's drink to your future." Meg beckoned her assistant in. He was carrying a tray with two glasses of champagne, which he handed to Meg and Autumn before quietly walking away. "To new horizons," Meg said, lifting the glass up. "Good luck with wherever life takes you."

Autumn clinked her glass against her lawyer's and took the smallest of sips. It was delicious. If Lydia were here, she'd say it should be, thanks to the small fortune Autumn had paid for Meg's services. But it was worth it. That much she knew.

"New horizons," Autumn said, taking another, longer, sip. "Whatever they might be."

"This calls for tequila," Lydia said later that night, beckoning the bartender over to the table where she and Autumn were sitting. "Four shots," she said, her voice slurring ever-so-slightly. "And another bowl of those nuts. They're delicious."

"Where the heck do you put all that food?" Autumn asked her sister, looking up and down her tiny form. She was wearing a flowy white dress, completely inappropriate for the cool New York spring, yet so very Lydia.

"Same place you do. We were born with good genes." Lydia grinned at her. "How does it feel to be a Paxton again?"

"I've always been a Paxton," Autumn reminded her, ignoring Lydia's eye roll. "Well I have! I changed my name, not my gene pool."

"I'm glad you're not a Garner anymore. Josh didn't deserve you."

"I'll agree with you on that." Autumn finished the mojito Lydia had ordered earlier for her. "And I'm happy to be a Paxton again, I guess."

"Dad's happy, I bet."

"Not really." Autumn shook her head. "He's still upset about the divorce."

"He called me yesterday, asking why you gave up the business so easily. He wanted me to persuade you to let him help with money." Lydia's eyes softened. "I know how much the business means to you. We both do. I'm sorry you lost it."

"It was meant to be." Autumn smiled at her, determined not to get upset. She'd shed too many tears already. Josh didn't deserve more. "This way it's a clean break. I don't have to use his last name for anything." Garner Real Estates was all Josh's now.

The bartender brought over the tequila shots, and Lydia passed two to Autumn. "Okay, we have to do this properly. Lick, salt, tequila, and lime. You got it?"

"I know how to do a tequila shot," Autumn told her, amused at Lydia's shocked expression.

"You do? When did you learn that?"

"At college."

Lydia wrinkled her nose. "That's like learning about champagne at school. You should go to Mexico and drink tequila there. It's delicious."

"Maybe I will," Autumn said, though they both knew she wouldn't. Where Lydia was the free spirit, Autumn was the sensible one, doing exactly what her father expected of her. It had been that way for as long as she could remember.

A shrink would probably say it was their reaction to their mom's death when Autumn was five and Lydia was only a toddler. Not that it mattered. She liked who she was.

"Okay, then. Let's do it." Lydia dragged her tongue across the back of her hand and sprinkled salt along the moistened skin, passing the shaker to Autumn to do the same. Licking it off, they banged their shot glasses on the table, swallowing the tequila in one go before sucking on the limes.

"Oh god," Autumn said, already feeling the alcohol rush to her head. "That's strong."

"It's José Cuervo. You should try the good stuff." Lydia wiggled her eyebrows.

"I have two more shots for you," the bartender said once they'd finished the second they'd ordered. "Courtesy of the gentlemen over there."

Autumn followed his gaze to the bar, where two suited guys were leaning on the counter, smiling at her and Lydia. She shot a pleading look at the server. "Please tell them thank you, but we're not interested."

"Who said *we're* not interested?" Lydia asked, her eyes sparkling. "They're pretty cute."

"Okay, *I'm* not interested." She grimaced. "I got divorced today, remember?"

The bartender blinked as though a pair of headlights were trained at his eyes. Autumn tried not to laugh. "It's okay, I initiated it."

"In that case, congratulations." He set the shots on their

table. "I'll pass the message back to the gentlemen. I'm sure they'll understand."

"You're going to have to get back in the saddle sometime," Lydia said when they finished the third shot.

"No way." It came out more slurred than Autumn intended. "I'm not interested in guys. Maybe I'll stay single. It's safer that way."

"You're twenty-nine. You've got your whole life ahead of you. You don't want to spend it alone. Not every guy is like Josh."

The two suits walked over to the table they were sitting at, and gave them a dazzling smile. "Ladies," one of them said, the ring on his wedding finger catching the light. "Can we join you?"

"Not every guy?" Autumn said to Lydia.

Lydia laughed then looked at the suit who'd asked to sit with them. "I'm so sorry, but my sister here is swearing off guys."

The suit's smile widened. "Let me give you my number, anyway. Call me if you change your mind." He passed them both a business card, as though they were at the office rather than in a bar.

When they'd gone, Autumn turned to Lydia and raised her eyebrows. "I think I need another drink."

Lydia grinned. "I thought you'd never ask. Come on, let's find another bar and celebrate properly. It's not every day you get divorced."

She couldn't see out of her left eye. And if she was being honest, the right one was blurry, too. Add that to the fact her mouth tastes as furry as a monkey's behind, and it didn't take a genius to realize she was hungover.

Ouch! Yep, there was the banging headache to remind her that she and tequila definitely didn't mix. Why, oh why had she drunk that last shot?

And the five before that...

Today was supposed to be the first day of the rest of her life. She'd planned to spend the morning going through her closet a la Marie Kondo, throwing out anything that didn't give her joy. And then working out what the hell *would* give her joy post-divorce.

Finally, her left eyelid unstuck and the light came flooding in. Slowly, she sat up and took in her surroundings. Her bedside table was strewn with papers, which on closer inspection looked like her divorce agreement. Her laptop was open, though at least she'd changed the stupid screensaver picture of her wedding day on a beach in the Bahamas to a less emotive image of the desert at night. She didn't need a reminder of what she'd lost every time she opened it.

Leaning to grab the laptop made her stomach turn a double somersault, and she had to swallow down the nausea. This is why she didn't drink. That and the fact that the last time she'd gotten drunk in Grad School she'd ended up texting her professor to tell him his wire-frame glasses were very sexy, and to see if he would be interested in a date.

Oh god. She hadn't drunk texted anybody last night, had she? Please don't say she messaged Josh. Her heart galloped in her chest as she rooted around for her cellphone, unable to locate it on the mattress or the table or anywhere else she would have put it.

Then she remembered she had to surrender it as part of the divorce settlement. Company property. She was husbandless, jobless, and phoneless. Maybe that was a blessing.

As if it could read her mind, the landline phone that she never used began to ring next to her, dancing on the table as though it couldn't believe its luck. Autumn lifted it and gingerly placed it to her ear, pausing for a moment to remember her telephone etiquette.

"Hello?" Her voice sounded like her throat was full of gravel.

"Hey, tequila girl. How's the hangover?" Lydia's voice was way too cheery for Autumn's liking.

"It's brutal. I'm never drinking again." She turned her head too quickly and winced at the sudden shot of pain.

"I kind of like you when you're drunk," Lydia continued, her voice full of humor. "And when you're single, too. Remember the karaoke bar we went to? At least five more guys asked me for your phone number. I told them you didn't have one, so I took theirs instead. Do you want me to email them over?"

"Stop teasing me. I'm dying." Autumn leaned her head back onto the padded leather headboard, her eyes still firmly closed. It felt better that way. Maybe she'd go back to sleep. Hopefully when she woke up this would all turn out to be a bad dream.

"I'm not teasing. You sang a fabulous version of *I Will Survive*. Then you told everybody you were going to spend your divorce settlement on something stupid and frivolous, just like your marriage." Lydia laughed. "Come on, you remember that, don't you? I can probably find a video of it. Lots of people had their phones held up."

The worst thing was, Autumn *could* remember it. Or at least she was beginning to. Hazy visions of that bar danced behind her eyelids. Fleeting ones of her grabbing the microphone and how everybody laughed when she told them she was a divorcee at the age of twenty-nine, and open to offers from Mr. Right-Now.

She was *definitely* never drinking again.

"Anyway, that's not why I called," Lydia said. "I was just

returning the message you left me last night. I must have been asleep when you called."

"I left you a message?" Autumn blinked. "When?"

"Lemme check..." Lydia paused. "Okay, it looks like it was at three in the morning. You sounded so excited, but I couldn't quite make out what you were saying. It sounded like you bought something with your name on it, but I've no idea what."

That pulling at the base of her stomach turned into full blown nausea as Autumn tapped her password into her laptop. Her screensaver was replaced by a web page with a photograph of a long pleasure pier stretched into a sparkling blue ocean, complete with a big restaurant halfway down, a large boat parked at the end. Autumn scanned down, her eyes swimming as she tried to take in the small black print describing the pier and the small town of Angel Sands where it stood, followed by an email address for interested parties to submit a bid.

With her breath caught in her throat, Autumn pulled up her sent emails. Of course, there was one sent at three that morning. And naturally, it was to the real estate company listed on the web page, offering the full asking price and telling them she was able to pay cash and close very fast.

She'd even given them her attorney's contact details.

"Autumn?" Lydia said. "Are you okay?"

"No," she said, her voice thin. "Not really. I think I bought a pier in California."

2

Griffin Lambert lifted his board out of the surf, tiny droplets of water clinging to his suit and tanned body. He shook his thick brown hair and spray launched in all directions, like a dog drying itself after a swim.

At six-five, he was taller than anybody he knew. His first teenage growth spurt had come at the tender age of thirteen and hadn't stopped until he was almost twenty-years-old. But it wasn't just his height that drew looks as he pitched his surf board into the sand and unzipped his neoprene half suit. It was the bulk he'd built up over years of working and surfing. The kind of muscles that the gym could never give you.

"Hey!" a voice called out.

He looked up to see Lorne Daniels approaching. The seventy-year-old man was wearing bleached cut-off denims and a lurid pink-and-orange hibiscus shirt, unbuttoned to his mid-chest.

"Hey, Lorne." Griff smiled. "How's it going?"

"Did you see that?" Lorne asked, nodding his head toward Paxton's Pier. "Looks like they've found a chump to buy the old wreck."

Griff turned his head to look for the sign that had been hanging from the pier for the last year or so. It hadn't weathered well. The white paint was peeling from the wooden board, and some kids had drawn comically inaccurate pictures of male genitalia with black sharpies all over it. But Lorne was right, there was something new on there. Where the painted red letters that proclaimed the old pier was *'For Sale'* was covered with brand sparkling new lettering.

Sold

"You know who bought it?" Griff asked, two tiny lines appearing between his brows as his gaze scanned along the old Victorian pleasure pier. Halfway along the wooden boarded walkway was the bright blue painted building housing Delmonico's, an Italian restaurant much loved by the inhabitants of Angel Sands. It was closed up right now – but like everything else in Angel Sands, it would be bustling by lunchtime. At the end of the pier was a boat – Griff's boat. The Ocean Explorer was a sixty foot ex-fishing boat, adapted by his father back in the '90s for whale watching expeditions. His dad had long since retired, and Griff bought him out, taking over as captain of the white painted vessel.

"No idea." Lorne shrugged. "But I'm thinking maybe it's that guy who bought London Bridge and moved it brick by brick to Lake Havasu. If not him, somebody just as crazy."

Griff's lips twitched as he grabbed his board.

As the two of them walked up the sand toward Lorne's surf shop, the older man asked, "How are your folks?" Lorne was in the process of opening up, the canopy that covered the surfboards and racks of clothes already extended. Next door was Déjà Brew, the coffee shop owned by Griff's friends, Ally and Nate. They were outside unstacking chairs. When they saw him and Lorne, they lifted their hands in a wave.

"Good, I think." Griff shrugged. Since his mom and dad retired and moved to a community in Florida, he only heard from them occasionally. That was the way he liked it. He'd suffered too many years of their on-again off-again relationship to want any more communication than that.

"Tell them I say hi when you speak to them next."

"I will." Griff nodded, and headed along the golden sand toward the pier.

After washing himself off in the showers by the boardwalk, and storing his board and suit in the lock up shed that came with his boat mooring, Griff ambled up the wooden pier, the smile slipping from his face when he saw a woman outside of Delmonico's.

Not any woman. *Carla*. The daughter of the owner, and the woman he'd made the mistake of having a fling with a while ago.

Except she'd thought it was more than a fling. He felt the skin at the back of his neck prickle.

"Hey." Griff forced his face into a smile. "I didn't know you were back in town."

"I got back last week." Carla had left Angel Sands suddenly last year, a few weeks after Griff had told her he didn't want to be anything more than friends. According to local gossip, she'd spent some time with family in Sicily, then stayed with her brother a few towns over, in White City, for a while.

It had been a welcome relief not to see her accusing eyes wherever he went in town. Now it looked as though they were back.

Never mix business and pleasure. He'd learned that lesson well.

"Yeah, I'm back." She didn't return his smile. "Dad asked me to open up for him. He's upset about the pier. Do you know anything about it?"

"Just what you do. I saw the sign." He shrugged. "I guess we'll find out more in due time."

"That's so typical of you." She shook her head. "Mr. Happy-Go-Lucky. Maybe you should be more like Dad and be calling around, trying to find out who bought the place."

"It'll be some investment firm." Griff tried to ignore the dirty look she was sending him. He knew it had nothing to do with the pier or her dad and everything to do with the fact he'd tried to let her down gently when she asked to be his girlfriend. Yeah, he'd hurt her, but he hadn't meant to. He'd believed her when she agreed that they weren't going to be anything more than casual.

Relationships were complicated and he was an easy-going man.

"I'll call your dad later," he told Carla, backing up toward his boat. "I'm sure it'll be fine."

"Whatever," she snapped, and turned on her high heels. "Go play with the fish like you always do."

Griff bit down a grin at her description of his job. The fish he chased weighed about ten thousand pounds and could kill a human with ease. But if it made her feel better to have the last word, he was good with that.

Life was too short to worry about things. Or to spend time with people you didn't want to.

He just wished everybody else felt the same way.

"So you're really going through with it?" Lydia asked Autumn as they waited for their father to join them for lunch a week later. The restaurant his assistant, Annabelle, had booked was crammed full of office workers, situated in the heart of the financial district of New York.

"I really am." Autumn nodded. "Do you think I'm crazy?"

"Hell yes. But in the best kind of way." Lydia grinned. "It's meant to be, right? You get rid of a business with your ex's name on it, then buy one with your own name. Paxton's Pier. It's perfect. And completely unlike you." Her eyes sparkled. "Dad's gonna have a fit."

"That's why you're here, for protection," Autumn said dryly.

"Nope. I'm here to see his face." Lydia took a sip of her sparkling water. "I should take a photo for posterity."

Lydia was right. Making an investment like this without thinking through all the consequences was completely the opposite to something Autumn would usually do. She was the sensible older sister. A businesswoman. Not somebody who'd buy a pier on the other side of the country without even seeing it.

Yet, since she'd kicked the hangover last week, and then spoke to the owners, she'd felt a fire in the pit of her belly that hadn't been there for years. Excitement mixed with trepidation, but more than anything, she felt alive. Ready to start this new life everybody kept talking about.

"Here, take a look at it," Autumn said, passing her phone to Lydia. She'd spent the last week researching the area, talking to her lawyer, and making plans. The pier was situated in a small beach town on the Pacific Coast, around a two hour drive from Los Angeles. And it had recently benefited from a lot of investment, including a new resort being built less than a mile to the north.

The pier itself was a little run down, but with the cash injection and a good business plan she knew she could make it profitable.

"And you're moving there?"

"That's the plan. Until I get it up and running, at least. Then I'll bring in a manager." Another thing it had going for it. Twenty-eight hundred miles away from Manhattan. And since she'd spent the last week either bumping into Josh, or mutual friends who'd decided to be on his side, moving seemed like a good thing right now.

"I'm late," their dad said, breezing into the restaurant. He didn't look the least bit sorry about it. People turned to stare as he made his way to their table, his hair perfectly coiffed, his suit expertly tailored. He'd always been the kind of man to turn heads. "Just ice water and a salad for me," he said to the waiter before he even sat down. "And can you bring it out quickly? I have another meeting in half an hour."

Lydia's eyes met Autumn's, and she bit down a smile. "I guess we should order, too," she said. "And since there isn't much time, Autumn has something to tell you."

"She does?" He frowned. "Is it about Josh?"

Lydia kicked Autumn under the table. "No, it's not about Josh," she said, grinning.

"Then what is it?"

Autumn ran the tip of her tongue along her dry lips, then took a deep breath in. "The thing is, Dad, I've decided to buy a pier."

It took a full thirty seconds for him to regain his composure. Not that she'd ever expected anything less. Richard Paxton was way too controlled to shout or make a scene.

"I'm sorry?" he said slowly. "Can you repeat that?"

"She said she bought a pier." Lydia couldn't hide her exasperation. "In California. Isn't that great?"

He ignored his younger daughter, training his eyes on Autumn. "You can't be serious."

Autumn slipped her hands beneath the table and adjusted her napkin, rubbing the expensive linen between her fingers. "I've already signed the contract and arranged for the money to be wired. There's no pulling out."

"Have you looked at the projected income? At the zoning regulations? How long has it been on the market? Let me call my lawyer and get you out of the contract. I have a list as long as your arm on potential investments around here. Why would you buy a pier in California?"

She thought about telling him the truth. That she'd done it when falling down drunk. But that would only make him even angrier.

"I wanted a fresh start," she told him. "Away from New York and Josh and everything that's happened here. Angel Sands is a beautiful little town." She brought another website up on her phone. "Here, look at it. Doesn't it look pretty?" she asked, shoving the phone beneath his nose.

"It looks about three thousand miles away." He pushed the phone away. "This isn't like you. Was it your idea?" he asked, turning to Lydia with an accusing stare.

"It has nothing to do with me." Lydia held her hands up.

Autumn felt herself bristle at his insinuation. "I came up with the idea on my own and I'm glad I did," she told him. "It has a lot of potential."

"It's a pier," he said, his nostrils flaring. "It's a bit different than the office buildings you're used to managing. Send the contract over to me and I'll take a look. I'm sure we can get you out of this."

"I don't want to get out of it," Autumn told him, her voice sure. She could see Lydia's amused smile from the corner of her eye. "And I don't need your help with it. I just wanted you to know before I go."

"You're going soon?" he blinked. "To California?"

"Yes," she said patiently. "That's the plan."

"But it's thousands of miles away. Your home is here." He almost looked panicked. "With us. Your family."

"Take a chill pill, Dad," Lydia said. "She's moving to California, not Siberia. And it's only until she has the pier up and running. It's good for her. Look how excited she is."

"But you're coming back, right?" He trained his eyes on Autumn's.

Maybe. "Yeah, I am. Probably."

"This is so unlike you. I don't know what to say." He leaned in, lowering his voice. "Have you talked to a therapist?"

Lydia started to laugh. Autumn shook her head, trying to push down her smile. "No, Dad, I don't need a therapist. I'm okay, I promise."

The waiter came over with their lunches, sliding the plates carefully in front of them before filling up their water glasses. Autumn welcomed the silence his presence had enforced.

Whether her dad liked it or not, she was going to California. And if it turned out to be a bad decision, it would still be okay.

It couldn't be any worse than marrying Josh, after all. And she'd somehow managed to get herself out of that.

It was time to grab the bull by the horns and head to California.

It was almost nine that evening by the time the last of Griff's customers stepped off the boat. It took another hour for him and his assistant, Brett, to wash down the deck, sort through the lifejackets, and make sure everything was shipshape ready for the next day's excursion. Griff rolled his shoulders as he locked up, his body aching. Not only from eight hours on the boat, but also his early morning surfing.

"Those corporate guys were something else," Brett said as they made their way onto the pier. "They think they know everything. Can you believe they brought beer on board?"

Griff had confiscated all the alcohol he could find, and gave it back to the group of management consultants when they left. They'd been on a team-building trip, which actually meant they'd spent most of their time begging him to get closer to the Orcas, asking to steer the ship, and generally making a nuisance of themselves.

The problem was, corporate hires were lucrative. Especially at this time of the year when the tourist season hadn't ramped up. And it *had* been amusing when at least half of them had started to feel seasick as soon as they reached the open water. It was choppy as hell out there today. Great for surfing, not so good for city-boy stomachs.

Just as they reached the glass and wooden structure of Delmonico's, Griff's phone rang. He pulled it from his pocket and glanced at the screen. *Ember.*

She was his best friend's wife, and had become one of his best friends, too. She and Lucas would have been his couple goals, if he'd had any.

"You go ahead," Griff said to Brett, nodding at his phone. "I gotta take this."

"Okay. I'll see you on Saturday." Like nearly all Griff's staff, Brett was a part-time Oceanography student at the local college. "Have a good evening."

"You too." Griff watched Brett walk, his fingers sliding along the wooden rail at the edge of the pier, then answered his still-vibrating phone.

"Hey. Everything okay?" he asked Ember.

"I need you to sing for me," she pleaded.

He shook his head. "Not again. Where's Lucas?"

"He's working. And I can't get ahold of Jack or Breck. You're the only one who can help."

"Why can't you sing?" Griff asked. "You have to know the words by now."

"Because Arthur only calms down when a male voice sings to him," Ember said, her voice tight. "And he's been screaming all night."

Now that she said it, Griff could hear the muffled wails of

his godson through the phone line. And damn if he didn't have a soft spot for that little kid. At eight months old, Arthur always grinned toothily whenever Griff was around.

"Okay. Put the phone to his ear." Griff sighed.

"Thank you," Ember breathed. "Did I say you're my favorite guy?"

There was an abrupt change in sound, as Arthur's sobs and sniffles increased. "Hey buddy, you teething again?"

There was a brief moment of silence, followed by another loud cry.

"Please start singing," Ember begged.

Griff leaned on the wooden rail and looked out across the bay, his phone at his ear. To the right, the lights of Angel Sands were sparkling in the night air. To the left was the dark abyss of the Pacific Ocean, lit by a sliver of the moon.

He couldn't remember which of them had first discovered that Arthur stopped crying every time he heard "Baby Shark". But he did remember that each of them had tried it, and Arthur had only fallen asleep when a man sang it.

Usually it would be Lucas who had to look like an ass and sing that song. It was only right – he was Arthur's dad, after all. But when he was on duty as the captain of the local fire station, one of Arthur's godfathers had to step in.

Tonight was his lucky night.

"Baby Shark, doo-doo-de-doo-doo-doo," Griff sang softly down the phone. "Baby Shark, doo-doo-de-doo-doo-doo." Arthur's sobs quieted, but didn't stop altogether.

"Try a little louder," Ember encouraged him.

Griff shook his head and continued, his voice picking up volume, and Arthur started to babble softly.

"That's it. Keep going," Ember encouraged again.

"Mommy Shark, doo-doo-de-doo-doo-doo," Griff continued.

"A bit louder. It's doing the trick," Ember told him.

"Daddy Shark..." To his right, Griff saw some movement. Somebody – a woman – was walking past Delmonico's and was heading his way.

"Don't stop now," Ember urged. "Come on, keep singing."

"Grandma Shark, doo-doo-de-doo-doo-doo." He felt like a fool.

The woman turned to look at him, her eyebrows rising with amusement. Jesus, she was pretty. And overdressed, too, for Angel Sands, in a pair of tight designer jeans and a blouse, a short navy wool jacket over the top. But it was her shoes that drew him in. Most women around here wore sandals or flip flops, but she was wearing black patent pumps with a red sole and heels that seemed to go on forever.

"Are you okay?" Griff asked her, covering the mouthpiece. "The exit is that way." He inclined his head toward the beach.

"I'm fine." Her voice was clipped. She blinked as she looked at him, her gaze taking him in.

Arthur began to wail again. *Shit.* "I... ah... I gotta keep singing," he said, pointing at his phone. Damn, he was lame.

Her lips twitched. "Sure. It's a good song." He watched for a moment as she walked up the pier and disappeared behind Delmonico's, before he started to sing again. It usually took a couple of minutes to get Arthur back to sleep, and most of the time he didn't mind helping. But right now he'd rather be following those lithe legs and peachy behind than singing about goddamn sharks.

A minute later, she was walking back, just as he heard Arthur's breathing settle into a gentle rhythm. By the time Ember ended the call, the woman with the sexy heels was almost at the end of the pier, too far away for him to catch up with, unless he wanted to look like he was trying too hard.

And he never wanted to look like that.

3

Parking her rental car, Autumn climbed out and walked across the parking lot to the coffee shop that overlooked the beach.

It was her first full day in Angel Sands, and she was still getting used to how different everything was here. The brightness of the sun, the crashing of the waves against the ocean. Even the smells were completely alien to her New York nose. Instead of gasoline and overheated concrete, the air was full of salt and ozone, and the gorgeous smell of caffeine drifting from the café before her.

"What can I get you?" the barista asked as Autumn wandered up to the counter.

"A large decaf latte with no foam, please," Autumn said, leaning on the counter and looking around.

"You're new around here, right?"

She glanced up at the barista as she was reaching for an oversized mug.

"I am." Autumn wrinkled her nose. "What gave me away? Was it my order? My accent?"

"Nope. I've lived here for all my life, worked in this place for the last ten years, and I don't recognize your face." The woman shrugged. "Though I don't get many no foam orders around here. I'm Ally," she said reaching her hand out for Autumn to shake.

"Autumn." She shook it quickly.

"Are you here on vacation?" Ally asked as she poured the milk into a stainless steel jug.

"Not really. I just bought the pier."

Ally's mouth fell open as she slowly put the jug down. "You're the one who bought Paxton's Pier?"

Her shock would have been funny if Autumn didn't still feel the same way herself. "Um, yeah. That'd be me."

"Do you work for a real estate company?" Ally asked, filling an espresso cup with a double shot, then pouring it into the milk.

"No company. Just me." Autumn took the coffee from Ally and pulled her wallet out.

"Oh no. This one's on the house," Ally told her. "So what are your plans for the pier?" She shook her head. "Sorry, that's really nosy of me. It's just been for sale for the longest time. It needs so much work."

"Yeah. I can see that," Autumn said dryly. "And to be honest, I'm not sure what I'm going to do yet. I've called a meeting for all the interested parties tonight to try and get started."

"Are you planning to stay in town for a while?"

"I guess. I need to find somewhere a little more permanent. The Silver Sands Resort is nice, but I can't live in a hotel room forever."

"Hmmm." Ally tapped her finger against her lips. "You know what, I've got a friend with an empty, fully furnished cottage. They were talking about renting it out. I can call them for you if you like? It's little, but it's walking distance from the pier, and it's been completely modernized."

"But you don't know me." Autumn frowned.

"You just bought our pier. You're practically part of the community." Ally shrugged. "And you have references, right? And can pay a deposit up front?"

"Well... yeah." This was so surreal. Like walking onto the set of a TV show where everybody knew everyone else.

"Great," Ally said, passing her the cup of coffee. "I'll call Ember and see if she can bring the keys over later."

"You've not even been there a day and the locals are already giving you free drinks and offering you somewhere to live?" Lydia said through the phone line as Autumn sat on the deck of the coffee shop and made some notes for tonight's meeting. "Where the heck is this pier again, Stepford?"

"Hey, you're the one who keeps telling me to take the stick out of my ass and take life as it comes," Autumn reminded her sister. "I'm just following your advice."

"And I'm very glad you did." There was a grin in Lydia's voice. "Now you just need to have some unbridled sex with a handsome stud, and all my dreams for you will be complete.

For some reason, Autumn's mind turned to the man she'd seen on the pier last night as she was delivering letters to her new tenants, informing them of tonight's meeting. He wasn't her type at all. She liked them neat, lean, and dressed in designer suits. Not Aquaman wannabes with shaggy hair and hands that could crush you without trying.

Even if he was singing the cutest song to his kid over the phone.

"So what's next?"

"I meet with the pier's tenants tonight at six."

"What are you gonna say?" Lydia asked, her voice hushed.

Autumn had absolutely no idea. Telling them that she'd

bought the pier while under the influence of tequila, thanks to her recent divorce, wasn't going to be the best way of getting them on her side. They were going to want her to have a solid plan and reassurances and everything else a new owner would give them.

"I'll tell them it's business as usual."

"Dad's throwing a fit. You know that, right?"

Autumn pressed her lips together. Yeah, ten missed phone calls and five texts she couldn't bring herself to read told her that. But she wasn't ready to let him rain on her parade.

"Autumn?"

She looked up from her notepad to see Ally looking at her, smiling. Smiling back, she covered the phone. "Yes?"

"I just heard from my friend, Ember. The beach cottage is yours if you want it. She can meet you there during her lunch break if you want to look around?"

Autumn nodded fast. "That would be wonderful. Thank you so much." She removed her hand from the mouthpiece. "I gotta go," she told Lydia.

"Okay, but call me tonight. I need to know how the meeting goes."

"If I'm still alive, I'll call."

"Love ya, sis," Lydia said.

"Love you too. Now go do something crazy to get Dad off my back."

The cottage was beautiful. Okay, it was tinier than her apartment in New York, and any more than two people in it would be a squeeze, but you could sit on the sofa, have the front door open, and hear the waves as they lapped against the beach.

"Are you certain you want to rent this out?" Autumn asked

the owner, as she showed her the expensively shiny appliances and sparkling bathroom. "I'm not sure I could if I owned this place."

Ember nodded. "We lived here for a little while after my husband, Lucas, renovated the place," she told Autumn. "It used to belong to his grandparents, and when they died they left it to him and his sister. But it's really only big enough for one person, and Caitie hates the water, and lives with her boyfriend, so it's either rent it out or put it up for sale, and I don't think Lucas could bear to do that."

"What kind of deposit are you looking for?"

"Don't worry about that." Ember shrugged. "Ally recommended you and that's security enough for me."

"I only met Ally today." Autumn's eyes widened. Was this really how they did business around here? "She doesn't know me from Adam."

Ember grinned. "I trust her judgment. Plus she said you bought the pier, which makes you one of us." She tipped her head to the side, her warm eyes catching Autumn's. "Have you owned a pier before?"

Autumn had to bite down her laugh. "Um, no. But I used to run a business buying and managing commercial property in New York City. Office buildings, nightclubs, that sort of thing."

"So it's part of your portfolio?"

"No, not really. I sold that company." It wasn't a complete lie. She really didn't want to talk about her divorce. "And I bought the pier with the proceeds."

Ember's face was a picture.

"You think I'm crazy, don't you?" Autumn asked her.

"I've done some crazy things myself." Ember shrugged. "And it's really none of my business. You have the experience to make things work, which is more than most people around here. The pier's been neglected for too long. I'm glad somebody's finally going to do something with it." She grabbed her notepad from her bag. "I'll get a contract written up this evening when I get home from work. What's your last name?"

"It's Paxton."

Ember's head shot up. "Really? Are you any relation to the original Paxtons?"

"I don't think so. It's just a coincidence." A flash of humor crossed her face. "Or maybe it was meant to be."

"You know that Captain Paxton founded this town? That's who the pier is named after. The story goes that he was sailing past the coast, saw an angel descend, and it pointed at the bay. So he moored his ship up, rowed his crew over to the sands, and that's how the town got it's name."

"An angel?" Autumn lifted an eyebrow.

"Rumor has it he was drinking a lot of rum in those days."

Autumn couldn't help but laugh. Maybe she and Captain Paxton had more in common than just a name. They both made strange decisions while under the influence of alcohol. "As far as I know my family's lived on the east coast for generations."

"I like the idea of it being fate," Ember said warmly. "And by the way, most people I know who come here never want to leave."

"I can see why." Autumn looked at that view again. Clear blue skies, golden sand, and a horizon that seemed to stretch on forever.

"How about you? Are you planning on staying long?" Ember grimaced. "I should have asked you that right away, shouldn't I? I'm a terrible landlord."

"I get the feeling you're going to be a great landlord. And if possible, I'd like a six month lease with the option of extending. It'll take at least that long to get everything straight with the pier, and even if I'm back in New York for some of the time, I'll need to travel here."

"Six months it is." Ember passed her the keys. "Feel free to move in whenever you're ready. And welcome to Angel Sands, I hope you'll be happy here."

Autumn hoped she would, too. For the last year, happiness had been a very rare thing.

She could taste the worried atmosphere as soon as she walked onto the pier. Autumn had arranged for three rows of seats to be set up there, and they were already full of people, which was crazy considering there were only a few businesses operating along Paxton's Pier.

Every one of them looked up as she walked to the front, her heels clacking loudly against the wooden planks. After she left Ember's beach cottage, she had her hair done at the hotel's salon then put on a designer skirt suit and 'don't mess with me' heels. She felt like a warrior going into battle.

Although, she wasn't sure *who* she was fighting. Her dad's opinions? Herself? Or the rows of people eyeing her suspiciously as she smiled with confidence.

"Good evening, everybody. I'm Autumn Paxton, the new owner of the pier."

"Paxton?" one of the women in the seats called out. "Any relation to Captain Paxton?"

"No. It's just a coincidence." She was going to have to get used to that question. "Maybe we can start by all of you introducing yourselves so I know your names and where you work here on the pier." She looked at the man at the end of the front row. "How about you start?"

"I'm Pietro Delmonico. Owner of Delmonico's. And this is my family." He gestured at the women next to him.

"It's a pleasure to meet you, Pietro. Who else do we have here?" She looked along the seats.

"I'm a Delmonico," the woman halfway along the seats said, as she gestured to the rest of her companions. "We all are." She gestured at the rest of the people in the chairs. "Apart from Ricky at the back who owns the watersports rental company."

He lifted up a hand, looking distinctly uninterested.

"And me," a deep voice called out.

Autumn looked up to see the man from last night ambling down the pier, his hands pushed into the pockets of his jeans, the ocean breeze lifting his thick brown hair. Damn if her heart didn't do a flip at the sight of him.

Not her type. Not at all.

Yeah, tell that to her libido.

A half-smile pulled at his lips as he leaned on the rail and looked at her. "Sorry I'm late. We were delayed coming back from a trip. I'm Griffin Lambert." He pushed himself off the rail and held his hand out to her. "But most people call me Griff."

Griff. It was the perfect name for him. Strong and gruff and maybe more than a little bit rough. It took everything she had not to shiver. "Hi. I'm Autumn Paxton." She slid her palm into his, feeling the warmth of his skin as his fingers folded around hers. It was absurd how tiny her hand looked in his.

With one squeeze he could probably break every bone.

"Shall I... ah... let go now?" Griff asked. She looked down to see her fingers still curled tightly around his hand, even though he'd relaxed his grip. She quickly pulled her hand away.

It took her a moment to regain her equilibrium. And in that moment she blamed the divorce, the ocean air, and even that damn angel Captain Paxton saw centuries ago. Because this was so unlike her.

She didn't get flustered, especially not by a guy. She was Autumn Paxton. She was in control.

She took a deep breath. "Okay, so I just wanted to introduce myself, tell you a little about my plans for the next few weeks, and then answer any questions you might have." She turned to the assembled crowd and smiled again.

"Let me start by telling you a bit about my background. I'm a real estate professional from New York, and have been involved with commercial property since I graduated. I have a Masters in Business Administration, and for the past six years I've owned and run my own business. When I saw the listing for Paxton's Pier, I knew that I could make it work. I've taken a look at the books and have also spoken to a lot of locals. I understand that for years the pier has been underfunded, neglected, and most importantly for me, running at a loss." She gave them a rueful grin. "I know that all of you have been running businesses on the pier for a long time, and you're understandably nervous about what's going to happen with them. But I can tell you that I always work with my tenants, not against them. I believe my success comes from your success."

The front row looked singularly unimpressed. She glanced beyond them at Griff, who was still leaning on the rail, his expression placid, and his substantial arms folded across his chest.

His gaze caught hers and it threatened to throw her off her game. She quickly pulled her eyes away.

"I plan on spending time with each of you over the next couple of weeks. I want to learn about your business, about your history. And maybe I can give you some suggestions for improvement."

A woman in the front rolled her eyes, muttering something unintelligible.

"I'll also be looking at some of the underutilized space on

the pier. To make more money, I either have to reduce costs, up the rent, or find more tenants. I'd prefer the latter option."

At last somebody nodded. It felt like she'd won a marathon.

She took a deep breath. "Okay, who has any questions?"

At least ten hands shot up. She spent the next twenty minutes answering each one, taking her time to make sure they were content with her answer, or occasionally promising to get back to them once she knew more.

"For any questions you might think of later, I will be working in the office at the top of the pier. My door is always open if you need me," Autumn added before she ended the meeting.

At that time, most of the Delmonico family headed to the restaurant which was already filling with guests, while Ricky, the watersports rental owner, gave them a nod and ambled back to his shack by the beach. Autumn grabbed her phone to call the Beach Club, who'd kindly loaned her the chairs.

"You did good."

She looked up to see Griff towering over her.

"Thanks." She gave him a smile. "I know it must be disconcerting for everyone having an outsider buy this place."

He shrugged. "I'm just glad *somebody* bought it. The last owners weren't exactly responsive to the problems. A few years ago, they used to have a general manager working out of the office, but once he retired they never replaced him."

That explained the thick dust on the furniture in there. And the fact that nothing worked – not the phone line or the electricity, and of course there was no internet. She'd already arranged for a cleaning company to come to do their magic the next day, along with an electrician and the cable company.

"How long have you worked here?" she asked Griff.

He shrugged. "Ever since I can remember. I started off

helping my grandpa when The Ocean Explorer was a fishing trawler. When he died, my dad converted it into a whale watching boat, and I used to crew every weekend for him. I took over as captain about six years ago." His voice was deep and smooth.

"I see the rent hasn't gone up in around ten years," she said. "According to the records, at least."

"That sounds right." He raised an eyebrow.

"I'm afraid that might have to change. I'll be doing some market comparisons to see what a fair level will be."

He tipped his head to the side as though sizing her up. "I'll be interested to hear what that might be." He didn't sound pissed, but then she didn't know him. Maybe he was one of those guys who seethed silently. All she knew was that nobody liked rent increases.

"And I'd like to come out on your next cruise, if that's okay?" she added. "Just to learn a little more about what you do."

"If you come out on my boat, I'll put you to work. We don't take any freeloaders on the Explorer."

She bit down a smile. "I'm not afraid of work."

Griff nodded. "We leave at eight on Saturdays. But the crew starts at six. That's when I'll expect you." He gave her a nod, and turned to walk away, not waiting for her reply.

It was only when he was halfway up the pier that he turned around and called out to her.

"And Miss Paxton?"

"It's Autumn."

The hint of a smile crossed his lips. "Autumn, then. As delightful as those shoes are, I suggest you wear flats tomorrow. Unless you want to end up as shark bait."

4

"So there's a new woman in town and neither of you thought to give her my number?" Jackson asked as Lucas slid a tray of beers on the table. "At least I know where she lives." Griff and his two friends were at the local bar for a rare guys' night out. He watched, amused, as Jackson swallowed a mouthful of cold beer.

"Don't harass my tenants." Lucas shot Jackson a warning glance. "And anyway, I thought you were seeing that programmer from White City."

Jackson shrugged. "We ended things last month. So I'm free and single. And we all know that Griff would never date somebody he works with. Not after the Carla fiasco." He grinned at Griff. "I bet you were delighted to see she's back."

"Over the moon," Griff said, deadpan.

"That'll teach you to date so close to home."

"Griff never dates anybody all out," Lucas pointed out. "He just breaks hearts all around town."

"Guys, I'm sitting right here." Griff took a sip of beer and glanced at Jack. "And leave Autumn alone. She's too nice for you."

Jack's eyebrows lifted. "Oh yeah. How nice?"

Lucas leaned back in his chair, glancing with amusement at the two of them. "Ember says she's pretty. And that she has great shoes, whatever that means."

"What kind of shoes?" Jackson leaned in. "I need details here."

Lucas's phone rang and he grimaced as he glanced at the screen. "Gimme a sec. It's Ember. I gotta take this."

Jackson looked at him with amusement. "You only just left her. What the hell could you two have to talk about?"

Lucas shrugged and took the call. "Hey, baby." There was a pause. "Are you sure? I'm at the bar." Another pause. "Okay." He sighed, glancing at Jackson and Griff. "I need to sing to Arthur."

Griff coughed out a laugh.

"Hey. Any more of that and we're doing a duet," Lucas warned him.

Griff held his hands up. "I did my duties the other night. This one's all on you."

"Well, I'm not doing it with an audience. I'm heading outside." Lucas sighed and exited through the door, leaving Jackson and Griff.

It wasn't often that the three of them got together. With Lucas's family and Jack's thriving business, the two of them were hard to pin down. And on the occasional time that they did manage to meet, they were often joined by their friend Breck, as well as Nate and Aiden, partners of Ember's friends.

Griff never minded who joined them. But it was nice catching up with his two oldest friends.

Even if one of them was singing "Baby Shark" in the floodlights outside the bar right now.

"Seriously, though. This Autumn. She's single, right?" Jackson asked as the door closed behind Lucas.

Griff shrugged. "I've got no idea. I didn't ask about her marital status when she was telling me about raising my rent."

Jackson laughed. "Did she have a ring on her finger?"

"What am I? Some kind of stalker?" Griff shook his head. "She's from New York, she's pretty, smart, and successful. That's all I got, except she's too smart to date a loser like you." He grinned at Jackson's outraged expression.

"Takes one to know one."

"Yup." Griff took another mouthful of beer.

"So what else do you know?"

"About Autumn?"

"Yeah?"

"Stop asking. I know nothing." Apart from the fact he couldn't stop thinking about those heels. Nor about the way his skin heated up when she slid her delicate hand into his.

Or the way he'd spent last night thinking about her after seeing her on the pier, and how most of those thoughts carried an *R* rating.

"Well tomorrow's the perfect chance to find out," Jackson told him. "A whole day at sea with the woman who has sexy shoes. I'm almost jealous."

Griff sighed loudly. "I told her not to wear the shoes."

The early morning sun was beating down on the vivid blue ocean as Autumn made her way along Paxton's Pier toward the large boat moored at the end. Everything she was wearing she'd picked up from Lorne's Surf Shop yesterday. White tennis shoes and cut-off shorts, along with a tight grey tank beneath a cropped navy hoodie. Nothing she'd ever think of wearing in New York, not even in the blistering heat.

She hadn't bothered to straighten her long, dark hair, either, figuring it would get blown into a frizzy mess anyway.

Instead, she'd pulled it into a messy bun, with tendrils trailing down her slender neck.

Her dad would have a fit if he saw her like this. Lydia, on the other hand, would be jumping for joy.

There was already activity at the boat when she reached the metal gangplank that led from the pier to the boat deck. A young guy was carrying boxes of supplies onboard, and a teenage girl was scrubbing the wooden planks of the deck with a thick brush. Griff was nowhere to be seen. Autumn rolled her shoulders back and pinned a smile on her face before she stepped onto the mesh of the gangplank, trying not to feel completely out of place.

It was just for one day. To learn more about the whale watching business. Maybe she'd even be able to help.

"You okay there?" the guy asked as she stepped onto the deck. He was walking out of what looked like a cabin on the far end, his head tipped to the side as he took her in. "You're a little early for the excursion. We don't set off for a while yet."

"I'm looking for Griff," she told him. "I'm Autumn Paxton, I'm helping out today."

The guy nodded his head. "Oh sure. He's in the wheelhouse."

The last time she'd stepped foot on a boat was for her friend's wedding reception in Manhattan. That had been more of a cruiser, complete with waiters in white jackets and glasses of champagne as soon as she was onboard.

She hadn't been wearing cut-offs and tennis shoes then, either. But she still had no idea where the wheelhouse was.

"Can you point me in the right direction?" she asked him, looking around the boat. It was bigger than it looked from afar.

"Up the ladder on the starboard side," he told her, pointing at a wooden ladder that ran up the side of the cabin.

"Hey, Griff," he called out. "There's somebody here to see you."

Griff climbed down the ladder and Autumn swallowed hard. There was something so easy about him. It was like watching an animal in its natural habitat. There was no guile or false machismo. But you only had to look at him to know who was in charge.

And yeah, that thought sent a shiver down her spine.

His long, thick legs were clad in denim, right to the ankles, unlike her own cut-offs. A black t-shirt stretched across his muscled torso, with Angel Sands Whale Watching printed on the back. And a pair of sunglasses were casually atop his head. But it was the way he was smiling at her that made Autumn's breath catch.

It felt like she was staring straight into the sun.

"Hey. I wasn't sure you'd come," he called out, pulling his shades over his eyes.

She pushed down the stupid attraction that rose up every time she saw him. "I said I would. And look," she said, lifting a foot, "flat shoes."

"And very short shorts," he pointed out with a grin.

"I figured it might get warm." Was it wrong that she liked the way he was looking at her legs?

"Welcome onboard," he said when he was only a few feet away from her. "I see you've met Brett. And that's Ellie up there," he said, pointing to the girl on the deck. "Mike's my second in command, and should be here any minute. And along with you, that's the crew."

"Are they all full time?"

"Nope. Only me and Mike are permanent. The rest of the staff are seasonal. Students from the oceanography course at the local college. They're full of enthusiasm and knowledge about the whales and dolphins."

She suspected Griff knew more about the marine life than

anybody in an academic course. "Do you take excursions out year round?" she asked him, after she'd shaken Brett and Ellie's hands.

"You're full of questions, aren't you?" The warmth of his smile echoed in his voice.

"Sorry. I've never been on a boat like this before. It's all new to me."

"I've got a few more things to get ready before the passengers arrive. Let's work and talk at the same time." He inclined his head. "It'll be crazy for an hour or so once we set off, and then things will calm down again. On the way back, Ellie or Brett will give a talk about the marine life we've spotted, and knowing them they'll lecture the passengers about reducing plastic waste and environmental harm, too."

By the time they were out in the open waters, Autumn felt like she was aching all over. Griff hadn't gone easy on her, and she appreciated that. He'd made her feel part of the team, not somebody just along for the ride.

Twenty minutes into the cruise, someone shouted that they'd spotted a pod of short beaked dolphins. According to Ellie, they were common around the coast. Listening to her explaining the different types of dolphins to a group of passengers was fascinating. Autumn had no idea that at least five different types of them swam around these shores alone.

"Do you like working here?" she asked Ellie.

"I love it. No two days are the same." Ellie grinned. "Most of my friends are working their way through college in shops or restaurants, but I get to see dolphins and whales and a hundred different types of birds.

"How long have you worked here?"

"This is my second year. I'll be graduating in the fall, then onto study my masters in Baltimore. I'm going to miss this place." She wrinkled her nose. "Some of the freshmen are already begging me to introduce them to Griff so they can take my spot."

"Is he a good boss?" Autumn asked.

"He's great," Ellie said, smiling. "I mean, he's a good guy and all, but what impresses me the most is how much he knows about the marine life out here. I swear he knows more about some of the whales than my professors. I guess he's been studying some of them for years."

"Like Ahab and Moby Dick?" Autumn asked.

Ellie burst out laughing. "Not quite. For a start, Griff isn't a sociopath, and he never wants to harm any animals. In fact, I'd say some of the whales really love him. When they see the boat they'll start performing like they know he's watching. A bit like they're flirting with him or something."

"Is it wrong that I want to see that?" Autumn grinned.

"There's nothing wrong with that at all."

5

Griff was intensely aware of Autumn's proximity as he restarted the engines and sailed further out into the ocean. After she'd spent some time with Brett and Ellie, and they'd spotted some razorbacks, he'd suggested she join him in the cramped wheelhouse, while they went searching for an elusive blue whale.

For the most part, she was silent, staring out of the windshield in front of them as he steered toward the place he'd last seen the baleen.

The wheelhouse was built for use, not comfort. He was used to sharing it with Mike, or being on his own. Having Autumn Paxton with her tiny cut off shorts and long, lean legs next to him felt different. As though the room had shrunk.

"It's hot in here," she said, pulling her cropped hoodie over her head. From the corner of his eye he could see her tank rise up, revealing her taut, pale abdomen.

Eyes straight ahead, skipper.

"This room's a sun trap," he told her. "It's all the glass. It's like a hothouse."

"But you're still wearing jeans."

"I save shorts for warmer months. Otherwise I've got nowhere to go."

She laughed. "The same way I won't wear a coat in New York until the temperature dips below forty degrees."

"Do you have family in New York?" he asked her, keeping his hands steady on the wheel.

"My dad lives there. And my sister has an apartment there, but she's often traveling."

"What does your dad do?"

"He's a real estate lawyer. He works in Manhattan," she told him.

"Sounds lucrative." He raised an eyebrow.

"It is. He was disappointed I didn't follow in his footsteps and study law."

There was a wry smile on her face. Strange how different she looked today. At the pier meeting she was all business, with a designer suit and immaculate heels. But now she was wilder, her curvy body on display in those shorts and top, and he really liked what it did for her.

Yeah, well you can like all you want. Just don't touch, my friend.

"You don't seem to be doing too badly as a real estate investor."

"I'll let you know after a few months of owning this place." She tied her hoodie around her waist and fixed the tendrils of hair that had fallen from her ponytail. Griff slowed the boat as they approached the spot he was looking for. From below he could hear Brett telling the passengers to look out for more whales – blue ones this time.

"Do you plan on staying here permanently?" he asked her.

"In Angel Sands?" She tipped her head to the side. "I'm not sure. I have a few decisions to make, and I'm hoping being here can give me some clarity."

He opened his mouth to ask what kind of decisions, then

closed it again. It was none of his damn business. One of the passengers shouted when they spotted a blow hole, and Brett radioed up to the wheelhouse, asking Griff to cut the engines for a moment.

"That's a blue whale up ahead," he said softly to Autumn. "You might want to go down and look."

"Are you coming?"

"No, I'll stay here and watch."

"Then I'll stay here, too."

It was stupid how much those few words warmed him.

"Oh my god, is that it?" Autumn said, leaning forward until her nose was practically touching the glass in front of them. "Is that the blue whale blowing water up?"

He bit down a grin at her enthusiasm. His hands tingled with the need to touch her. "Yeah. You see how straight and high the water is going?" he said, pointing. "And if you look on its back, you can see a really small dorsal fin. That and the color of the skin makes it different to the fin whale we saw earlier."

She looked over her shoulder at him, her lips parted. "You know a lot about them, don't you."

He shrugged. "It's my job."

"It's huge," she whispered as the whale dove below the surface, its tail flipping into the air before disappearing. She lifted her hand to her hair, and he automatically glanced at her ring finger. It was empty. He filed that away with other things he wouldn't be telling Jackson.

"Do you get many returning passengers?" she asked him.

"Some come out a few times while they're on vacation. Others return year after year. But most of our passengers are a one time shot. People who get tired of sitting on the beach all day, or hiking in the hills."

"How about off season? What's your income stream then?"

His lips twitched. They were back to the questions. "We do executive charters, school trips, that kind of thing. And we try to maximize the in-season income to ride out the downtime. Expenses drop in off season, too. The students are seasonal workers, and Mike takes on other jobs. Plus I only use fuel when I take out the boat."

"But the pier rental has to be paid."

"Yep."

"So if it went up things would get tight in the winter?" she asked, glancing at him from the corner of her eye.

"Yeah, but everything's tight in the winter. We've always survived."

"Have you thought about diversifying?" she asked him. "You could run evening cruises. Offer dinner and dancing or something?"

"Have you seen the galley?" he asked her. "It fits one person in at a squeeze. You couldn't cater for people on there."

"You could get Delmonico's to cater."

"And have them accuse me of stealing their customers?" Carla would be on him like a screaming banshee. He shuddered at the thought. "I'm thinking that might not work."

"When was the last time you raised your prices?" she asked, changing tack.

He lifted an eyebrow. "Are you worried about me being able to pay the rent? Because it gets paid on time every month."

She blinked. "I'm sorry. I just..." She took a deep breath. "I know I'm an outsider and I'm a woman, which is a double cross in the box. But I understand business and I want this to work for us all." She shook her head. "I came on too strong."

He immediately felt like an ass. "No, you didn't. I reacted badly. *I'm* sorry."

She nodded, but he could already sense the change in her.

Like she'd pulled the shutters down. Her previous ease was replaced by tension that held her back ramrod straight.

"Maybe I'll go and listen to Brett after all," she said softly, giving him a brief smile. "It's not every day you get to learn about blue whales while one's darting around in front of you."

"Sure." He nodded. "Brett's a mine of information. Go and listen while you can."

Twilight had painted the sky and clouds in orange and peach hues, contrasting with the dark blue of the ocean. Autumn climbed off the gangway that led to the pier, and thanked the crew for their welcoming support.

"Anytime," Brett told her, as Ellie leaned in to give her a hug.

"And we'll see you around, right?" Ellie asked. "Since you work here and all."

"Almost certainly." Autumn smiled.

Mike nodded at her and slung his bag over his shoulder. "Have a good evening."

"You too."

Behind her, Griff was closing up the boat and locking the gangplank. "You heading home?" he asked her as the other three left.

"Yeah. There's a shower and a glass of wine with my name on them."

"I'll walk you up there. My truck's parked at the coffee shop."

"How do you know where I live?" she asked, two tiny lines appearing between her brows.

"Because your landlord's my best friend. Lucas Russell. He told me you moved in yesterday."

"Oh." She gave a half-laugh. "I guess this really is a small town."

"Yeah. Sometimes it's good, sometimes it drives you crazy."

"Lucas seems nice. Ember does, too," Autumn said, as they passed Delmonico's. It was already full, with diners spilling out onto the terrace. "And they have a little boy, right?"

"Arthur." Griff nodded. "He's my godson."

She glanced at him from the corner of her eye. "And you? Do you have children?"

Griff laughed. "No. No kids, no wife. Just me."

There was a little flutter in her chest. "So you were singing to Arthur the first night I saw you?"

"Yep. Sorry if I burst your eardrums. How about you?" he asked. "Did you leave a brood back in New York?"

She shook her head. "I didn't leave anything in New York except a closet full of shoes."

"Interesting."

The flutter increased. He was so damn attractive. And she was lonely, and it had been way too long since she'd even laughed with a guy let alone done anything else. And then there was the way her body reacted every time he was close. It was like he was sparking off a chemical reaction.

One she liked too much.

They reached the boardwalk, and turned left toward the row of cottages that lined the sand. Autumn pushed her hands into her pockets, and willed herself to be an adult.

She wasn't in Angel Sands on vacation, she was here for work. A clean slate. Maybe even a chance to show her father and Josh and the whole damn world that she could make good decisions.

And good decisions didn't involve sleeping with one of

your tenants just because your body felt electric every time he was close.

They reached the pretty little cottage that had been her home for almost thirty-six hours. She pulled her keys from her pocket and turned to him with a smile.

"So this is me."

"Yeah, I know. I helped renovate the place." He leaned on the wall beside the door as she slid her key into the lock. A little step to the left and her body would press against his.

Not a good idea. Not at all.

"Thank you for letting me come out on the boat today," she said, pushing the door open. "I had a really good time."

"It was a pleasure." He was still leaning on the wall.

"Well, good night."

"Sleep tight." He winked.

"With all that fresh ocean air, I'm bound to."

It felt like a lie. She had a feeling she wasn't going to sleep that night at all.

6

She was halfway through brushing her teeth the next morning when somebody knocked on the cottage door. Luckily she was decent – if you counted jeans and a tank as decent – so she spat out the toothpaste and wiped her lips on a towel before running to the front door.

"Hey." Ember smiled at her as the door opened. She was holding Arthur on her hip, a huge baby bag slung over her other shoulder. It looked like a full body workout. "I hope you don't mind me popping over, but I'm meeting a few friends for coffee, and since you're new around here I thought you might like to join us."

"That sounds great," Autumn agreed with a smile. "When are you meeting?"

"Um, now?" Ember wrinkled her nose. "I meant to text you last night, but Arthur's been teething and I completely forgot. It's just a casual thing, coffee on the beach with the girls. They're all lovely and I know they're dying to meet you."

"They are?" Autumn pretended to grimace. "Why does that make me feel like I'm the new kid at school?"

Ember laughed. "Don't worry. It's just a small town and you're big news. Come for coffee and they'll soon find something else to talk about."

"Okay. Give me ten minutes and I'll be there. Where shall I meet you?"

"We'll be on some blankets in front of Déjà Brew. I'll put your order in. How do you like your coffee?"

"A no foam latte would be great."

Ten minutes later, Autumn was walking down the beach toward the group of women and children sitting on overlapping blankets. At the last minute she'd decided to change into a pair of shorts. It didn't seem right to be wearing jeans on the beach.

"Hey." She smiled at Ember as she reached the group.

"Hey." Ember sat Arthur on the blanket and scrambled to her feet. "You found us. Everybody, this is Autumn Paxton, new owner of the pier, and new tenant in our cottage." Arthur started to crawl away, and she reached out to lift him back on the blanket again. The little guy giggled, his long eyelashes sweeping over his face.

"Hey," a familiar voice greeted her. "We met at the coffee shop. I'm Ally, and that girl over there is my stepdaughter, Riley."

"And I'm Brooke, and the boy she's playing with is my son, Nicholas," the cool blonde said, offering Autumn her hand. "I think you might have met my husband. He runs the Silver Sands Resort."

"Um yeah, I might have while I was staying there." Autumn desperately tried to remember his name.

"Aiden Black," Brooke said helpfully, her face full of kindness. "He's in the coffee shop talking to Ally's fiancé, Nate."

"I'm Caitie," the brunette next to Autumn held out her hand, and Autumn shook it. "I used to live in New York, too. And so did Harper." She pointed at a petite blonde-

and-pink haired woman holding a baby. "But now she lives here with that cute little baby of hers and her boyfriend, James."

"You'll meet him later, I'm sure. He's a doctor, so he seems to always be working," Harper said, grinning. "And Hi. It's great to meet you. And don't mind Caitie's pained expression. It has nothing to do with you. She's had a water phobia for years, but she's trying to beat it."

Autumn was desperately trying to remember everything they said, but it was a losing battle. There were just too many of them, and too much information flying about. She felt like she was watching a tennis match, her head moving from side to side every time somebody said something.

She took a deep breath, and smiled.

"You have a water phobia?" She asked Caitie. At least she could remember that. "That's really brave," Autumn said, glancing at Caitie, whose lips were tightly closed. "My mom had a phobia about flying, so I know how bad it can be to face them."

"Thank you." Caitie's expression softened. "I'm getting there."

"And I love your baby's dress," Autumn said to Harper, whose little girl was bouncing around on her lap in a frothy yellow and white sundress. "It's so pretty."

"She makes all of her own baby clothes," Ember told her. "And a lot of Arthur's too."

Harper kissed her baby's downy head. "Do you have children?" she asked.

Autumn shook her head. "No kids." She took a deep breath. They were all being so friendly. She didn't want to be the one to clam up. "I'm recently divorced, so no prospect of them in the near future either."

"I'm really sorry." Ember's expression was thoughtful. "I know how hard breakups can be."

"Here's your coffee," Ally passed it to her. "And help yourself to pastries. Freshly made."

Autumn sat on the blanket and sipped her latte, listening to the other women as they talked about work, boyfriends, and families. They asked her questions and she answered them openly, but for the most part she was happy to sit and observe. Ally reminded her a little of her sister, Lydia. She was forthright and funny and a little bit wild. Brooke was motherly and calm, always making sure everybody was happy. And Ember was friendly and welcoming, or as much as she could be when Arthur was constantly crawling everywhere and she had to chase him.

"Have you been invited to join the Angel Sands Chamber of Commerce yet?" Caitie asked her.

"Not yet. Should I be happy about that?"

Caitie shrugged. "It's not so bad. It's run by Frank Megassey. He owns Megassey's Hardware store on Main Street. I think he's been running the chamber for the last two hundred years."

Autumn laughed.

"Don't let him suck you in," Ally warned. "Before you know it you'll be running the Angel Day Fair and organizing for the Christmas lights to be strung along the boardwalk. If you see him coming, run."

"Frank's okay," Caitie told her. "Apart from the fact he talks a lot."

"You can sit in the back with Caitie and me," Ally reassured her. "We just eat cupcakes and heckle."

"*You* heckle," Caitie pointed out. "I sit there and look pretty."

"Who's pretty?" a deep voice asked. Autumn looked up to see a tall, dark-haired man grinning down at them. His hair and body were wet, droplets clinging to his skin, and he was holding a surf board in his hands.

"I am," Caitie told him, grinning. "Or at least I should be to you."

"And you are." He leaned down to kiss her nose. "How are you holding up, baby?"

"I'm good. Autumn's been distracting me. Autumn, this is Breck, my fiancé."

Autumn reached her hand out. "It's good to meet you."

"You too. I've heard a lot about you."

"You have?" She should be used to the small-town talk by now. But it still shocked how everybody knew each others' business.

Then she saw Lucas walk up behind him and recognized her new landlord immediately, from when he and Ember helped her move into the cottage.

And behind him was Griff, wearing a half-wetsuit unzipped and hanging from his waist, exposing his tan, muscular chest and oh-so-broad shoulders. She felt her stomach do a flip.

"Hey, Autumn." Lucas gave her a wave, and she grinned back.

Griff's eyes locked with hers, and her lips curled up. "Hi," he said with a smile that sent her pulse racing.

"Hey."

"This is Autumn?" Another man joined Griff and Lucas, slapping them both on the backs. "Hey, it's good to finally meet you. I'm Jackson." He wasn't as tall or as broad as Griff, but he was still a good looking guy. "How are you settling in?"

"Really well." She smiled at him as he sat down on the sand next to her, being careful not to get her wet. "I'm loving Lucas and Ember's beach cottage. I used to play white noise to get to sleep in New York, but now I get to nod off to the sound of the waves."

"And you're planning on being here for a while?"

"I think so. I'm still hashing out the details, but if the weather is always like this, then I'm in."

"It really is," Jackson told her. "The best thing about living here is the climate."

"And the ocean," Breck pointed out.

"Well, yeah."

"And the mountains," Lucas said. "If you like hiking."

"I *do* like hiking," Autumn told them. "I didn't get to do a lot of it in New York, but I'd try to get to the Catskills at least once a year to climb some hills."

"You got your hiking boots with you?" Griff asked.

"Um, yeah. They're somewhere in the cottage." Still in the box she'd packed them in.

"I can show you a trail later if you want," he said, his voice nonchalant.

"Today?" Autumn blinked. It was a simple friendly offer. Her skin didn't need to heat up like it was on fire.

"Yeah. If you're not busy."

"I'm not busy," she said quickly. "And I'd love to check out some trails."

Jackson looked from Autumn to Griff, a bemused smile on his face.

"Okay, then," Griff said, ignoring his friend's questioning gaze. "I need to go home and wash up. I'll pick you up at your place at one."

7

"What's with the caveman attitude over the new girl?" Jackson asked as they carried their boards up the beach. "Me Griff, you Autumn. You were practically beating your chest, man."

"I have no idea what you're talking about." Griff felt his jaw twitch.

"Come on. I was shooting the breeze with her and you jumped in so fast it took my breath away. You like her, right?"

"She's my landlord. A colleague. And she's new in town. I just didn't think you should be hitting on her like that."

The corner of Jackson's mouth quirked up. "So if I ask her out on a date you'll get angry."

"I don't want to deal with the fallout when you mess it up," Griff said, raising an eyebrow. "I have to work with her."

"But what if I don't mess it up?" Jackson tipped his head to the side. "What if I like her and she likes me. You'd be okay with that?"

The thought of it made Griff feel weird. And he had no idea why. Yeah, she was pretty, and clever as hell. But he knew better than to date somebody he had to work closely with. Look at what happened with him and Carla.

"I don't think she's planning on sticking around forever," he finally said, avoiding Jackson's question altogether. "Just until she has the pier under control. Then she'll head back to New York."

"So we could have a fling." Jackson shrugged. "Suits me."

Griff's fingers tightened on his board, his knuckles blanching. "Leave her out of it."

Jackson started to laugh. "Oh man, you've got it bad."

"Shut up."

"You like her, don't you?" Jackson persisted.

"It doesn't matter," Griff said through gritted teeth. "It's not happening."

"Look, I know what happened with you and Carla was bad. That she made your life hell when things were over, but you've got to get back on the wagon, my friend. Not all women expect you to put a ring on it after the second date. If you feel something for Autumn, then go for it." Jackson raised an eyebrow. "Or somebody else will."

They'd reached the showers in front of the parking lot, and Griff pressed the lever down, letting the cold spray wash over him and rinse the salty ocean water away. He closed his eyes and shook his hair, water flying everywhere. Then he washed his board off before grabbing a towel from the flatbed of his truck.

"I'm not interested," he said roughly, rubbing the towel over his hair and neck.

"Sure you're not," Jackson said grinning. "That's why you're spending the afternoon with her."

"As friends."

"Whatever you say. Good luck with keeping it at that."

"Dad wants to know why you're not answering your phone."

Autumn could hear the amusement in Lydia's tone. Wedging her phone between her shoulder and her ear, Autumn pulled her hiking boots over the thick walking socks she'd bought last year but never used.

"He called once this morning and I was busy. I figured I'd call him tonight." Or tomorrow. Or maybe next week. Whenever she felt up to hearing how disappointed he was again.

"*But she always answers her phone, Lydia. Unlike you,*" Lydia said in a deep, gruff voice.

"Your impression of him is terrible," Autumn told her sister. "For a start your voice was too deep."

"Ouch! What a burn, and he wasn't even here to hear it. I'm going to tell him you said that the next time we talk. Anyway, what was so important that you didn't pick up the phone?"

"I was at the beach with some friends."

Lydia laughed. "Okay. Now what were you really doing?"

"I was at the beach. Honestly. The woman who owns the cottage I'm renting invited me to join her and her friends for coffee this morning. I figured why not."

"But you don't meet people for coffee. Or do anything but work on Sundays. Oh my god, Autumn, is Dad right? Have you lost your mind?" Lydia was loving this. Autumn could hear it in her voice. "Next thing we know you'll be hooking up with a guy without knowing his portfolio."

Autumn reminded herself to say nothing about Griff or the hike they had planned that afternoon.

"Autumn?" Lydia's voice was full of amusement.

"Yeah?"

"You haven't hooked up with anybody, have you?"

"No." She laughed. "Of course I haven't."

"Oh. My. God."

"What?" Autumn shook her head even though Lydia couldn't see her. "Stop it."

"I'm your sister. I know when you're lying. You do this stupid little laugh, the same way Dad does."

"I don't." Autumn grimaced. She knew exactly the laugh Lydia was talking about.

"You really do."

Did she? Autumn tried to think back, but her mind was blank. Whatever, she'd just never laugh again. That would work, right?

"So who is he?"

"Who?" Autumn frowned.

"The guy. The one you're *not* hooking up with."

"Even if there was a guy, which there isn't, I wouldn't be hooking up with him. I'm hardly divorced, I'm not looking to make any more mistakes."

"You got rid of an asshole," Lydia pointed out. "One you never should have married in the first place. And you probably wouldn't have if it hadn't been for Dad telling you how wonderful Josh was and that he'd be the perfect husband and business partner. Not all guys are like that, Autumn. There are good guys, too."

"Yeah, well they're like a needle in the haystack in New York. The single ones, anyway."

"But you're not in New York, are you?" Lydia said, her voice pointed. "And whoever this non-existent guy is, maybe he's just what you need right now."

Autumn finished lacing her boots and sat up. "I just bought a pier without looking at it. Don't you think I'm way out of my comfort zone already? I've made enough bad decisions this year."

"Maybe you should drink some more tequila and see what happens next?" Lydia suggested.

"And that's my cue to go," Autumn told her. "I'm never drinking tequila again."

"Wait! What shall I tell Dad if he calls again?"

Autumn laughed. "Tell him I've slept with half the town and now I'm setting my sights on the other half."

"It's a shame he wouldn't believe me." Lydia sighed. "Because I'd love to see you go wild."

It took just under an hour to reach the foothills in Griff's old Ford truck. He had the windows rolled down and rock music blasting from the stereo. Autumn leaned back on the brown leather seat and let the warm air wash over her as they made their way along the highway, enjoying the wide open space surrounding them. She rarely got to see the full horizon in New York.

They parked in the lot at the base of the trail, squeezing in between a shiny SUV and a Mustang. Climbing down from the car, Autumn felt the warm sun beating down on her as she took in the rocky trail, edged with verdant trees and thick, dry brush.

Griff pulled out a backpack and slid it over his shoulders. "You want to take the easy route, or the hard one?" he asked, glancing at her.

"How hard is the hard one?" she asked.

"Hard."

She laughed. "You're a real mine of information, you know that?"

"Why don't we take the easier route for today?" Griff suggested. "Especially if you haven't been hiking for a while. Save the tougher one for another day."

She liked the sound of *another day*.

"That's good with me." She coiled her hair in her hand, securing it with a tie. "Let's do it."

Ten minutes later they were on the trail, heading up into the foothills with the sun beating down on them. Thank god she'd kept up her fitness regime since filing for divorce last year, because Griff's strides were long and powerful.

A couple of times he asked if she wanted to slow down, but she shook her head.

"I like the pace," she told him. "I haven't found a gym yet, and I need the workout."

"A gym?" He raised an eyebrow.

"Yeah, you know," she teased him. "Indoors, full of equipment, and women in tight spandex?"

He grinned back at her. "I know of them. Never been to one though."

"You would if you lived in Manhattan. There aren't too many hiking trails there."

"Maybe that's why I don't live in Manhattan. There are so many better things to do around here than rot away on a treadmill. Not just hiking or surfing, but there's ocean swimming, beach running, and Angel Sands has its own cycling club, too. Why exercise indoors when you can be out in the sun?"

"I guess I've never really had the chance to do that before." She looked up at the bright blue sky, closing her eyes as the sun shone down on her. "By the time I finished work it was always dark, so it was easier to head to the gym after hours than do anything else. Or hit it at four-thirty a.m."

"It's a different kind of life, huh?" he asked softly.

"Yeah." She nodded, her eyes catching his. "I'm still getting used to this one. It feels like I'm on a permanent vacation right now."

"Apart from the fact you have to work here." He grinned.

She shrugged. "I usually work on vacation." She and Josh

had spent most of their honeymoon closing a deal. Ugh, she didn't want to think about that.

Griff quirked an eyebrow, his warm gaze bringing her back to the present. "Of course you do."

Autumn tipped her head to the side. "You don't strike me as the kind of guy who relaxes much, either."

"I relax all the time. My whole life is laid back." He shrugged.

"Apart from when you're working or surfing or hiking." She grinned at him. "Do you ever sit down and watch T.V.?"

"I watch it occasionally."

"What was the last thing you watched?" she asked him, enjoying the banter between them. Striding next to her, in his cargo shorts and t-shirt, he felt more like a force of nature than a man. She wasn't the lightest woman in the world – her ass could attest to that – but she had no doubt he could lift her up without even taking a breath.

"I watched the Backyardigans with Arthur yesterday," Griff told her.

She laughed. Could he be any more adorable? "What about TV for the over twenty-one crowd?"

"I can't remember the last time I switched my TV on." He shook his head. "I'm not sure if it even works."

Ahead of them was a field of rocks, inclining up to the base of a craggy hill. "Have you walked on scree uphill before?" Griff asked her, glancing down at her pristine boots.

Autumn looked at the incline ahead of them, covered with loose stone. "A couple of times."

"There are a few tricky areas," he told her, inclining his head toward the rocks. "But it's mostly okay. Take your time and put your weight in your feet to keep your balance. I know the easiest way through, so follow me."

"Okay." She watched as he scrambled over the rocks, the thick muscles in his back and legs contracting as he climbed.

His thighs were tight against the thin fabric of his shorts, and her gaze rose up to his ass.

His fine, tight, perfectly rounded ass. Was it getting hot up here?

"You okay?" He looked back at her, and she immediately blushed.

"Yeah." She nodded and gave herself a mental slap. *Stop ogling the sexy guy, Autumn.*

She stepped onto the loose stone, feeling it roll beneath her soles. She flexed her own muscles to keep herself steady, taking long slow steps to where Griff was waiting for her.

"The next bit is harder. Hold on to that rock for as long as you can," he said, pointing at a large boulder. "It won't move."

She did as he directed, circling around the rock behind him, feeling her body warm with the exertion.

"If this is the easy trail, what's the hard one like?" she called out to him.

"Hard," he said again, and she swallowed down a grin.

A thin sheen of perspiration covered her face as she let go of the boulder and stretched her right foot out for the next step. Moving her left foot forward to complete the stride, she felt the rocks sliding out from beneath her, and found herself windmilling her arms in a desperate attempt to find something to grab onto.

Her fingers closed around the cotton of Griff's t-shirt, bundling the gray fabric into her fist. Her knuckles pressed against his warm skin, and he turned immediately, reaching out for her wrist to stop her from sliding. He gently pulled her toward him, hooking his thick arms around her waist.

By instinct, she grabbed hold of his arms, feeling his iron-hard biceps beneath her palms. Her heart was hammering against her chest from a mixture of adrenaline and something else... something altogether more electrifying.

"You okay?" he murmured.

"Yeah," she said breathlessly, feeling her hair tumble down around her shoulders. "It's a rookie mistake. I stepped too far and lost my balance."

He reached out and tucked the loose hair behind her ear, his finger leaving a trail of fire on her skin. "Do you want to go back?" he asked her.

She shook her head. "It was just a little slide."

The corner of his lip quirked up. "We used to slide down this hill when we were young and stupid. Until Jackson fell over and broke his arm. Lucas's folks gave us hell over it. He and Jackson were grounded for a month."

"You slid down the scree?" Autumn asked, looking down the long slope they'd just climbed. "Are you crazy?"

He raised an eyebrow. "We were. Not so much anymore. Lucas is all about safety now."

"He's a fireman, right?"

They started to walk again, but this time Griff reached for her hand, sliding her palm into his.

"Yep. Captain of the Angel Sands Fire Station. We all give him hell for being cautious, but he's right."

"And how long were *you* grounded when your folks found out?" she asked him, trying to imagine a teenage Griff being forced to stay home. From the little she knew of him, that would be his worst nightmare.

"I wasn't."

"Why not?"

"I guess they didn't care about it." He shrugged.

They'd reached the crest of the hill, and Griff released her hand. She looked around at the view of the hills as they rose and dipped below them, the land stretching out to the coast, and the sparkling blue ocean.

"Come here," Griff said, "I want to show you something."

She raised an eyebrow, feeling flirtatious. "Oh yeah? What kind of thing?"

He laughed, the ease returning to his face. "It's over here," he said, walking along the hilltop to the other side. The air was cooler up here, enough for her to unknot her sweater from her waist and pull it over her head. As they came to a stop she could see a dilapidated two-story wooden building clinging to the side of the hill, with two large rusty metal chutes leading out of it to the valley below.

"What is that?" she asked, peering over.

"An old gold mine."

"You're kidding me." She wanted to laugh. "No way."

"It was one of the biggest producers of gold in its time. Back in the early 1900s, there were around fifty men working here. Most of them bunked in wooden cabins in the valley down there."

"Do you think there's any gold left?" she asked him. "We could get rich."

"If there is, it's probably buried far below the rocks. The mine's been abandoned for almost a century."

"Have you ever been inside?"

"Not that I'm telling." His face was straight, but there was humor in his eyes. "It's dangerous. See the signs?"

"So is pebble skiing."

He chuckled. "Touché."

She loved the way the skin at the corner of his eyes crinkled as he grinned at her. She could feel her heart race again, the way it always did when their gazes caught. A breeze ruffled his brown hair, revealing a jagged scar leading from his brow to his temple. Without thinking, she reached up to trace the silvery line.

"How'd you get this?" she asked.

He closed his eyes for a moment, then opened them again, his gaze fiery as he looked down at her.

"Surfing accident."

She couldn't bring herself to pull her hand away from his

face. It was too warm, too real, too *him*. She cupped her palm on his jaw, feeling the roughness of his beard growth on her palm. "It's hot," she said, the words spilling out before she could stop them.

He swallowed hard. "Autumn..."

"Yeah?"

"If you keep touching me like that, I'm going to touch you back."

His words sent a shot of electricity through her. Up here, it felt like they were the only two people in the world, and she liked it. It made her feel brave and strong and like a completely different person.

The sort of person who wanted this strong, tall guy to kiss her.

She lifted her head, her eyes challenging his. "Go ahead. Touch me."

His control had been hanging on a shoestring since he'd picked her up from the beach cottage. It wasn't just those tight shorts that molded perfectly to her ass, nor the thin tank that she'd *thankfully* covered up with her sweater. It was the way she'd grinned at him, laughed with him, been more carefree than he'd thought she had in her.

Now she was looking up at him, her full, pink lips parted, her warm eyes sparkling beneath the afternoon sun, self confidence-radiating off her. It was sexy as hell.

The atmosphere between them sparked and flashed, sending a jolt of desire through his body. He could feel himself respond to her, need making him ache. "You're beautiful," he whispered, his voice thick and raw.

With the pad of his thumb, he traced the line of her jaw, then slid it to those full lips. He softly brushed them, and she opened her mouth to suck him in to her warm, wet mouth.

"Jesus," he rasped.

The last vestige of control left him. Pulling his thumb from between her lips, he tucked it under her chin, angling her head before he leaned toward her to press his lips against hers.

Her breath was hot against his mouth as he pulled her against him, feeling the softness of her body press into his hard abdomen, the need pulsing inside him as he deepened the kiss. Their tongues slid together, and her arms hooked around his neck to steady herself.

But then she stepped away, her eyes wide with horror as she looked up at him. "I'm sorry, I don't know what came over me."

Griff blinked, the abrupt end to their kiss taking him by surprise. His skin felt cool at the loss of her body against his. "It's okay..."

"No, it's not. I'm an idiot. Blame the heat or something." She fanned herself as though it wasn't cool on the hilltop. "It was so inappropriate. You're my tenant, I'm new in town, and I'm newly divorced." Autumn attempted a smile. "Believe me when I tell you I'm a walking disaster right now."

He raised an eyebrow. "You don't look like a disaster." So she was divorced. He'd store that little gem away to think about later.

"You don't know the half of it. I'm making bad decisions left, right, and center at the moment."

Bad decisions? He swallowed down his reaction. "We should be heading back anyway. The sun's slipping away."

"Sure." She nodded. "That makes sense."

"And I'm sorry to hear about your divorce."

Her expression softened. "Another bad decision. Or a series of them."

"Let's head down that path," he suggested, pointing at a graveled trail winding down the other side of the hill. "I know a shortcut back to the parking lot from there. Should only take us half an hour or so."

She nodded, pulling her lips between her teeth. "Sounds good."

This time, they kept a distance between them as they walked, and Griff kept his hands firmly fisted at his sides. And if he was still feeling a little bit crazy about the way the afternoon had turned out? He could live with that. They'd stopped before things got serious. That was something to be glad about.

He and women didn't mix. He should have learned that by now.

8

Pouring herself a large glass of wine, Autumn swallowed a mouthful before draining the water from the pan and adding the creamy sauce. What the hell had she been thinking, kissing Griff Lambert?

She *hadn't* been thinking, that was the problem.

Laying her plate and glass in front of her on the small kitchen table, she twirled a forkful of spaghetti and lifted it to her mouth. She was under no illusion that Griff was devastated at her pulling away from him. Yeah, he'd looked surprised, and more than a little confused, but he'd been back to his easy-going self by the time they were halfway down the hill.

It was Autumn who could barely bring herself to look at him.

She took another large sip of wine, letting the cool Sauvignon slip down her throat. She'd bought it from an amazing little wine shop she'd discovered along the boardwalk, a few hundred yards from the pier. Was it only this morning when she'd walked in there and talked about the different grapes with the owner? It felt like a lifetime ago.

Her life was a disaster. That's all there was to it. She hadn't lied when she told Griff she'd been making one terrible decision after another.

First getting married to the wrong guy.

Then getting divorced.

Not to mention buying a damn pier on the other side of the country while drunk. And now she was throwing herself at tenants.

Her phone began to vibrate on the table in front of her and she sighed as she looked at the screen.

What was this, the tenth call? The eleventh? She couldn't avoid her dad forever.

Taking a quick glug of wine she swiped her finger to accept the call. She'd always been the kind of person to rip off a Band-Aid, rather than gingerly tug at it. She might as well find out what he had to say.

"Hey, Daddy."

He paused, as though surprised she'd answered. "I've been calling you for days," he said after a few seconds. "Where have you been?"

"I've been busy working."

He sighed. "I was on the verge of calling the local police department to ask them to do a wellness check."

"There's no need for that. I'm absolutely fine. Did Lydia not tell you we spoke?"

"She did. And I have to say I'm surprised that she's being the reliable one right now. I never thought I'd see the day." He huffed. "So how are things going with the pier? Do you have a business plan yet?"

"I'm still working on it. Things are a little slower here than in New York."

"When do you think you'll be coming home?"

"I don't know. A while." The thought of getting back on a plane to New York made her chest hurt. Yeah, she'd made an idiot of herself today on the trail, but she wasn't ready to leave. This morning on the beach she'd felt like she'd finally come home. Made friends. Laughed a lot. These were things that felt in short supply in New York.

"We miss you here, sweetheart. I just want to help you get back on track. Have you thought about putting the pier back on the market?"

"I've only just bought it," she said with a laugh.

"I could talk to people. Or you could. Maybe Josh could help," he suggested, sounding hopeful.

The thought of Josh having anything to do with the pier – *or her* – made her blood turn cold. "I have it under control, Daddy. Please don't talk to Josh."

Her dad sighed. "I don't know how to help you."

A smile played at her lips. "Maybe I don't need any help with the business," she said softly. "Though I'm glad that you care."

Something beeped on the line. "I have another call," he said abruptly. "But think about what I said. Your home is here with us." His voice turned business like. "I'll look into some options for us to work through."

She swallowed down a sigh. He always did this. She could protest and he simply wouldn't hear her. Sometimes it was better to say nothing at all.

"Goodbye, Daddy."

"Good night, Autumn. I'm looking forward to you coming home. This town isn't the same without you."

She ended the call and carried her plate over to the garbage disposal, letting it run extra long to enjoy the grinding noise.

Today hadn't turned out to be the best day in the world. But tomorrow was another one.

"So how'd your date go?" Jackson asked as the three guys carried their boards toward the water. It was early on Monday morning – the sun had barely begun to rise on the hills behind them, tingeing the darkness of the ocean with sparkling pink tips. The beach was empty and combed – the sand laying in perfect lines thanks to the *sandboni* that rumbled across the shore every morning, picking up the trash and sifting the grains.

The tide was slowly retreating, leaving a pink sheen on the wet sand behind it. Their bare feet sunk down as they reached the water's edge.

"It wasn't a date."

"Of course it was. You were alone with a girl on the trail. That's the definition of a date." Jackson rolled his eyes as he lay his board down in the foamy shore.

"Are we gonna gossip all day, or are we planning on surfing?" Lucas asked, glancing at Griff from the corner of his eye. "I have to be at work by nine, and I promised Ember I'd bring her coffee back before I go."

"That's because you're under the thumb," Jackson said, grinning.

Lucas looked unperturbed. "Exactly the way I like it."

Jackson paddled ahead of them, his eyes trained on the waves peaking to the south of the pier. There were only a handful of surfers out on the waves. It was too early for tourists, and most of Angel Sands' residents were either asleep or heading to work. Only the most dedicated of surfers – and those who'd received a hall pass from the wife – were out before the sun was above the skyline.

"You okay?" Lucas asked Griff as they slowly made their way out into the ocean.

"Yeah, why wouldn't I be?"

"You looked mad at Jackson. You're never mad at him. You always laugh when he needles us."

Griff sighed. "Ignore me. I'm in a shitty mood. Probably shouldn't have come out today."

"Did something happen with Autumn yesterday?"

Griff turned to look at Lucas. There was no sarcasm in his face, no judgment. Just the expression of one friend who was concerned for the other.

He couldn't remember a time when Lucas wasn't part of his life. The three of them had grown up together. From grade school all the way through to now. They'd ragged each other about girls, commiserated about Griff's shitty parents, been there when they'd gotten their final grades for school and launched into adulthood.

Most people tend to lose touch at that time. With Lucas heading to White City to become a firefighter, and Jackson studying at school, Griff had been the only one left in Angel Sands, working with his dad on the boat and surfing alone every morning.

Then one by one they'd come home. First Jackson to set up his business, then Lucas when he wanted to settle down with Ember. Griff knew he was lucky to be surrounded by his childhood friends. Most people didn't have those kind of relationships.

"Nothing happened," he said, spotting a wave coming in from the west. "We had a good afternoon and then I brought her home. That's all."

Maybe this was all he needed. His friends, the ocean, and his boat. He knew where he was with them. Even at his grumpiest, Jackson never caused him any pain. And that was exactly the way Griff liked it.

"How long has your restaurant been here?" Autumn asked

Carla as she cleared the tables of Delmonico's after the lunchtime rush.

It'd been two days since she'd gone on that hike with Griff, and Autumn had spent most of those forty-eight hours talking with business owners on the pier and along the nearby boardwalk. Today was Delmonico's turn. She'd arrived before they'd opened at twelve o'clock and watched the tables fill with couples and families and businessmen. It was clearly a local favorite, and when she was served a bowl of spaghetti putanesca she understood why.

It tasted heavenly. Better than anything she'd had in a upscale restaurant in New York. If she hadn't been promised the best cannoli outside of Italy for dessert, she'd have asked for a second helping.

"My Great-grandfather opened up the first restaurant in the nineteen-thirties. He emigrated here from Sicily, and worked in San Francisco. The family moved south after the Great Depression, and started selling food from a little shack on the beach." Carla walked as she spoke, and Autumn followed her, pushing the door to the kitchen open so Carla could walk through. "After the war, they built this place and it's been going ever since. Most of the family works here in one capacity or another." She nodded at the chef. "That's my cousin, Vincent. And those two chopping vegetables are Luca and Sophia. My brother, Matteo, used to work here, but he has his own restaurant in White City now."

"Have you ever thought of expanding the Delmonico's brand?" Autumn asked as they began to load the industrial dishwasher. "Maybe open up a delicatessen or have deliveries? I mentioned to Griff that you could work together on evening dinner cruises."

Carla blinked and looked away. "No. I don't think we'd want to do that."

Autumn shrugged. "Expansion isn't for everybody."

She glanced out of the window at the dock at the end of the pier. It was empty. Griff must have taken the boat out on a whale watching cruise.

She was going to have to face him sometime. They had to do business together, after all. And whatever plans she had for the pier would need his support.

"Hey Autumn, the cannoli are ready. You want one?" Vincent asked, holding out a plate. The crisp, golden pastry tubes were filled with piped, sweet ricotta, the ends dusted with chocolate shards and powdered sugar.

"I'd kill for one." Autumn grinned and took one from the top, biting into the delicious goodness. "Oh my god, this is amazing," she told him once she swallowed. "No wonder the restaurant is always full."

"Vincent trained in Sicily," Carla told her. "We try to make everything as authentic as we can. Great food without being pretentious."

"It's working."

Somebody was striding toward the end of the pier. Autumn blinked when she realized it was Griff. If he was here, why wasn't his boat?

She took a deep breath. It was time to face her demons. Better now than later.

"I need to talk to Griff for a second," she told Vincent when she'd finished the cannoli. "I'll be back to buy a box full of those."

The air outside was warm and salty. Waves hit the wooden pillars, sending up spray through the gaps in the planks. "Griff!" Autumn called out, walking fast to catch up with him. Damn, his strides were long.

He turned to see her, his expression quizzical. "Everything okay?"

"Yeah. Where's your boat?"

He grinned, and she let out a mouthful of air. "Mike took

it out for me today. I had a meeting in town. They should be back in an hour. Thought I'd come and meet them, finish everything up to thank him for doing me a favor."

"And there was me imagining it was stolen by pirates."

"We don't get a whole lot of pirates around here." Griff chuckled. "Is everything okay with you?"

"Yeah. I just wanted to say hi. And thanks for Sunday." She looked down at her hands. "And to check that things were okay between us."

"Things are okay." He blinked, as though he couldn't quite understand her.

Her lips curled into a wan smile. "I've only been here a few days, yet I've already made an ass out of myself with you." She looked up, her gaze catching his. "And I like you, I really do. I was hoping we could be friends."

Griff said nothing for a moment. His gaze roamed over her face, her neck, then back up to her eyes. "We *are* friends. What happened on the trail was a mistake. We both agreed on that. I'm not the kind of man who holds grudges."

She knew that from looking at him. And damn if that didn't add to his attraction. Standing there on the weather-worn pier, he looked like some kind of ancient god with the sun beating down on him. The sort that could fight a lion with his bare hands then ravish a maiden before breakfast.

"Thank you," she said softly. "I need all the friends I can get."

"Anything you want, just say the word. That goes for Lucas and Jackson, too. Hell, all our friends."

Her smile widened.

"Speaking of which, there's a party for Lucas's parents on Sunday. Why don't you come as my plus one? As a friend," Griff said, emphasizing the final word. She ignored the little tug in her chest at the word *friend.* It was what she wanted, after all.

"Won't they mind me tagging along?" She really wanted to go, but old habits died hard. She couldn't imagine dropping in uninvited to a party in Manhattan.

He laughed. "You need to live in Angel Sands for a while longer. Of course it's okay. Everyone will be pleased to see you."

"Then I'd be delighted to go."

"I'll pick you up at one. It's Deenie and Wallace's ruby wedding anniversary, in case you want to bring them a card."

"Deenie and Wallace?"

"The Russells. Lucas's parents. Caitie's, too." He grinned. "And Ember's in-laws."

"I'll never remember everybody's names."

"Don't sweat it. Just call everybody 'man' like I do. It saves a lot of time."

Her eyes met his once more, and those stupid fireworks went off in her chest.

They were friends again, and that was good. The fireworks could go take a hike.

"Okay, I'm heading off," Autumn said to the younger Delmonico's. "Thank you for being such gracious hosts today. And you know where I am if you need anything."

"Thanks for loving my food," Vincent said, grinning. "You're welcome back here at any time."

"Can I have a quick word?" Carla asked her, as Autumn reached for the handle of the kitchen door, the box of cannolis in her other hand. "In private."

"Sure." Autumn followed her to a little office at the back of the kitchen. Carla ushered her inside and closed the door behind them. She sat on the edge of the desk – pushing away some papers that were strewn across the surface, and sighed.

"I saw you talking to Griff earlier."

The back of Autumn's neck tingled. "Uh, yeah..." She trailed off, wary of where this was going.

"The two of you looked close. So I wanted to give you a warning, woman to woman. He's bad news, you should avoid him."

Autumn waited for Carla to laugh, but she looked deadly serious. "Griff's bad news?" she clarified, wondering if she was talking about someone else.

"Yeah. He can be charming as hell, but he's a player. An asshole." Carla spat the words out. "He leads people on, then breaks their hearts. And I could see the way he was looking at you while you were talking."

"You were watching us?" Autumn's eyes were wide.

Carla carried on, ignoring Autumn's question. "I know he seems like a nice guy. He takes people in. Hell, he took me in. Then he spat me out as soon as I asked for a commitment. He's happy as hell to get into your panties, but he'll drop you like a hot tamale if you want more."

"I don't want more," Autumn said, trying not to grimace at Carla's description. "And I certainly don't want him in my panties." She wrinkled her nose. The thought of Griff and Carla together made her stomach turn. "I'm just here to work. Nothing more. And I don't want any drama." God knew, she had enough back in New York.

"Okay. Good." Carla smiled at her, baring a perfect set of white teeth. "Enjoy the cannolis." She lifted a finger to her lips. "Oh, and if you're interested, Vincent is single."

Autumn pressed her lips together to stop herself from laughing. "I'm not. But thank you. And good evening."

She couldn't get out of the restaurant fast enough. This town was crazy.

And yet, there was something about it that drew her in.

9

"A few close friends." Autumn grinned at Griff as they walked into Deenie and Wallace Russell's beautiful back yard. She glanced at him from the corner of her eye. "Isn't that what you said?"

Round tables were clustered together on the freshly cut grass, laid with crisp white cloths and stunning pink-and-white floral displays. White paper lanterns hung from the trees, ready to be lit when the sun went down, and pink balloons swayed with the breeze. Soft music vibrated from the speakers fixed in the boughs, mingling with the chatter and laughter of at least fifty people who were standing on the lawn.

"They have a lot of close friends." Griff's eyes crinkled as he grinned back at her. "Most of these guys you either know or know of. There's Ember and Lucas and all our friends over there," he said, pointing at a crowd of twenty and thirty-somethings. She spotted Ember holding Arthur, who was wriggling like crazy trying to grab a balloon. Next to her was Harper, holding baby Alyssa. Mother and baby were wearing matching dresses in a bright yellow polka dot fabric that would be difficult to pull off if you weren't as gorgeous as Harper.

"Okay." It was impossible not to smile back at him. "But don't leave me standing on my own. Unless you're grabbing me a large glass of wine."

He laughed, inclining his head. "Come on. Let's go say hi to Deenie and Wallace." He offered her his arm, and she slid her hand through it. Her fingers curled around his bicep and he felt a jolt of electricity flash through his skin.

Inviting her to the party had seemed like a good idea when they were talking on the pier. He liked Autumn, he really did, and when she'd asked to be friends he'd breathed a sigh of relief. For a couple of days he'd thought he really messed things up between them when he'd kissed her.

Yeah, it had felt good. Better than good. But he knew better than to do things just because they made his skin heat up.

Deenie and Wallace were standing by the door to the kitchen, having a heated discussion over a bottle of champagne. Deenie was the first to look up, her warm face breaking into a big grin when she saw Griff approaching. One of her eyebrows rose when she saw Autumn holding his arm.

"Happy Anniversary," Griff said, leaning forward to kiss Deenie's cheek. She was wearing her silver hair in an intricate updo, coiled at the nape of her neck, with braids curling through it. "This is Autumn Paxton. The new owner of the pier."

"It's a real pleasure to meet you," Deenie said to Autumn, leaning forward to hug her. Autumn hesitated for a moment, before hugging her back. "I would have come and introduced myself before, but we were on a cruise to celebrate our anniversary. This is my husband Wallace. He's a man of few words, so I talk double on his behalf."

Autumn laughed. "It's so nice to meet you both. Happy

anniversary." She gave them the pink gift bag she'd been carrying since they left Griff's truck. "What is it, five years?"

"More like forty," Deenie told her as she opened the bag.

"You must have been a child bride," Autumn said.

"Oh I like her," Deenie said to Griff. "She can stay." She pulled a silver box from the bag and opened it up. "These are beautiful," she said, pulling out two crystal glasses. They were a vibrant red, with gold painted details around the base and stem. "And you knew it was forty years. Our ruby anniversary."

"Griff told me." Autumn smiled. "I have a friend in New York who hand paints crystal. She couriered these over to me."

Deenie's eyes watered. "I love them," she whispered. "Thank you. Now what can I get you to drink?" She slid her arm through Autumn's, pulling her away from Griff. "We have cocktails and wine coolers, and if Wallace can figure out how to use his fingers we'll have some more champagne as well."

"These things are complicated," Wallace said, shaking his head. "You need an advanced degree to open them. What's wrong with screw tops?"

"You want me to do it?" Griff asked.

"Would you?" Wallace glanced over to where Deenie and Autumn had walked. They were standing by the drinks table, deep in conversation. Autumn said something and Deenie laughed out loud, her eyes warm as she touched the top of Autumn's bare arm.

"Sure." He took the bottle from Wallace and unscrewed the cage, then held the cork as he twisted the bottle. It came out with a muted pop, and he passed the bottle back to Wallace who gave him a wink.

"Okay if I tell Deenie I did this?"

"It'll be our secret."

"Excellent." Wallace nodded. "By the way, your girlfriend's very pretty. And Deenie likes her, I can tell."

"She's not my girlfriend," Griff told him, glancing over at Autumn again.

"So you're just dating?"

"Nope."

Wallace's eyes widened. "Is it a booty call? Isn't that what they call it?"

Griff tried not to laugh. "We're just friends. That's all."

"That's a shame." Wallace shrugged. "Well, I best take this over. I don't suppose you can open a couple more, could you? There's a box in the kitchen. Leave the open ones on the island."

"No problem." He'd do anything for Deenie and Wallace.

After opening the bottles, Griff looked around for Autumn. She was still in deep conversation with Deenie, the two of them smiling and talking fast. So he headed for the crowd of his friends on the far side of the yard.

Lucas was the first to see him, shouting out a greeting as he grabbed a beer from a nearby cooler. "Where have you been?"

"I had to make sure everything was okay with the cruise," Griff told him. "It's the second time this week Mike's done me a favor. Then I went to pick up Autumn."

"Lucas told me you were bringing her," Ember said, catching Griff's gaze. "That was really sweet of you."

He shrugged. "She's new in town. It's polite."

"Sure." Was she biting down a smile?

Arthur suddenly noticed him, and clapped his hands together. Then he leaned out of Ember's hold, his arms reaching for Griff. "I think he wants you," Ember told him. "As usual."

"What can I say?" Griff shrugged. "I'm a baby charmer." He scooped Arthur from Ember's hold and lifted him up, blowing a raspberry on his downy cheek. "Hey buddy, what's going on?"

"Ba ba blue."

"Is that right?" Griff asked him, grinning at Arthur's serious expression. "I agree. Forty years is something to celebrate. Though I hope you play the field first before you settle down."

Ember slapped his arm. "Stop it." She grinned playfully. "You're supposed to be his godfather, not his wingman."

"We all know he's gonna be a heartbreaker," Griff pointed out, laughing as Arthur nodded before he let out a huge burp. "That's it, buddy. Start practicing now."

Arthur reached out for Griff's face with his pudgy hands, cupping his broad jaw with tiny fingers. "Giss," he said, then blew a raspberry himself, covering Griff with baby spit.

"Ha!" Ember said, grabbing a cloth and passing it to Griff. "He got you back."

"Careful, bud," Griff told Arthur as he wiped his lips before wiping his own face. "Any more of that and I won't be singing 'Baby Shark' anymore." He looked over Arthur's head toward where Deenie and Autumn were still in deep conversation. She looked so at ease, as though she'd lived here all her life rather than for a few short weeks.

She looked beautiful, too, in a short blue dress and matching shoes that made her legs look a mile long. She leaned forward to whisper something in Deenie's ear and then they both laughed, Autumn's head tipping backward as Deenie patted her arm.

Friends. That's all they were. He could live with that.

"Na no," Arthur said, then he raspberried again.

"Yeah, bud. My thoughts exactly."

"Are you missing New York?" Deenie asked, as she poured Autumn a glass of champagne.

"Not really," Autumn admitted, taking the glass and lifting it to her lips. "My sister says it hasn't stopped raining for days. And if I was there right now, I'd be cooped up in an office with a view of other offices. I think I prefer the sun and beach."

Deenie smiled. "Do you think you'll go back?"

"I guess so. That's where my family is." The thought of it made her feel claustrophobic. It hadn't taken long for her to get used to wearing shorts or sundresses every day. Her skin had already taken on a darker hue, in spite of the sunscreen she lathered herself with constantly. Even the air here felt different. Fresher.

"Well, for as long as you're here, you're always welcome at our house. I'm so glad you came."

"So am I." Autumn smiled into her eyes. "Thank you for being so welcoming."

"It's what we do in Angel Sands. Once you move here, you're part of the community. And even if you do go back to New York, you'll still own the pier. That means something here." Her eyes crinkled at the corners. "I'm glad Griff brought you."

"He's a good guy." Autumn took another sip of champagne.

"He really is." Deenie nodded. "He's like another son for me. All of Lucas's friends are, of course. But Griff's the one who had a horrible childhood. It broke my heart to always see him so alone."

Autumn blinked. "He had a hard childhood?" She glanced at Griff from the corner of her eyes. The man-mountain was holding little Arthur, his expression soft as he stared down at the baby's laughing face. Autumn swallowed hard, feeling her stomach twist at how gentle he looked. He was so at ease holding a baby. As though he was born to do it.

"He didn't have the best upbringing," Deenie said softly, her lips curling into a sad smile. "But that's history now." She looked at him holding Arthur. "He'll make a good father, though he'd never admit to that. Sometimes having bad experiences make us more determined to do things differently in our own lives. Griff's parents were always too busy with each other to pay him much attention."

Autumn thought of her own parents. She could hardly remember her mom, but she knew from photos that she'd loved her and Lydia very much. Then, when her mom died, her dad stepped into the hole she'd left behind.

As a teenager, his helicopter parenting drove her crazy. But it was better than the alternative.

"Am I being a nosey old lady if I ask you whether you and Griff are dating?" Deenie asked.

Autumn pulled her eyes away from Griff. He hadn't noticed her staring, thank god. "No," she said. "We're just friends."

"Oh. That's a shame."

It was on the tip of Autumn's tongue to agree. She swallowed the idea down with a mouthful of champagne. "I'm recently divorced."

Deenie gave her a half-smile. "That doesn't sound insurmountable."

Maybe it wasn't. Autumn frowned, trying to work through the confusion in her mind.

"Don't listen to me," Deenie said, topping up Autumn's glass. "I'm an old romantic at heart. Blame it on all the books I read at work."

It wasn't books that were the problem. It was the way Autumn's stomach did a loop-de-loop every time Griff looked this way. She liked him, but it was crazy. Too soon after her divorce and way too close to her business.

"Ember told me you own a book store," Autumn said, thankful for the change in subject. "Tell me all about it. I can't wait to come and visit."

10

"Are you enjoying yourself?" Griff whispered in Autumn's ear. They'd been at the party for a couple of hours. The evening sun was disappearing behind the rooftops, and the paper lanterns were glowing, along with pillar candles whose flames flickered on every table. Somebody had turned the music up, the deep beats pulsing through the warm twilight air. Ember and Harper had taken their babies inside to sleep, the tots' eyes drooping as everybody blew them a kiss good night.

"I am." She tried not to shiver at the way his warm breath tickled her skin. Turning her head, she looked up at him. He was standing behind her, his eyes fixed on hers, the setting sun making his skin glow.

He was so damn masculine. If she could bottle it, she'd be a millionaire in weeks. It wasn't only the strong lines of his face, or the way he towered over everybody here. It was more than skin and muscles, no matter how glorious they were.

It was in everything he did. He had this way about him that made you feel safe. As though nothing could hurt him.

She had no doubt that he'd throw himself in front of a car to save a stranger.

There were good people in New York, she knew that. But most of the people she met on a daily basis cared more about themselves than anybody else. They were drawn to Manhattan because they wanted to make money, or make something of themselves. And she'd bought into that, too.

Now she wasn't so sure.

The music slowed down, and Deenie and Wallace began to dance on the grass in the space they'd cleared by moving some tables. Ember and Harper walked out of the kitchen door, whispering softly to each other, then grinned as they saw the happy couple dancing in front of them. The next moment, Lucas held his hand out to his wife, and Ember took it, allowing him to spin her across the grass. Pulling her against him, he held her tenderly, leaning down to kiss her hair.

Guests joined them on the grass, until there were more people dancing than not.

"You want to dance?" Griff asked her.

"Yeah, I do." Warmth spread across her skin. "Let me take my shoes off, though. These heels will sink into the dirt." She slid them off her feet, then took Griff's hand and let him lead her across the grass. She felt shorter than ever in her barefeet. The top of her head met his chest as he pulled her close, slipping his arm around her waist, and pressing his palm into the small of her back as he slid the fingers of his other hand into hers.

The music was slow and smooth, as the haunting melody filled the evening air. Autumn leaned her head against Griff's warm pecs, feeling the buttons of his shirt press against her cheek, and the warmth of his smooth skin through the cotton. She took a deep breath, smelling his woody cologne, and let him move her around the grass.

He was a surprisingly good dancer. So sure of himself. She glanced up to see him staring down at her, his eyes dark, his neck undulating as he swallowed. Autumn's mouth felt suddenly dry, as though she hadn't drunk anything for weeks.

"Thank you for inviting me," she murmured. "I'm having a good time."

The corner of his lip quirked up. "I'm glad you came."

So was she. So glad. Only a few weeks ago she'd felt as if life as she knew it was over. But now, there was something new. Something interesting.

Something that made her stomach do tiny flip flops.

The music suddenly turned off. Griff stopped moving but kept her hand in his as he glanced over his shoulder to see what had happened.

"Um, there's a baby crying," Jackson said, looking sheepish as he stood in the kitchen doorway. "Not sure whose though."

"Are you ready to go?" Griff asked her later that evening as the final guests began to say their farewells.

"Yeah. Let me go and thank Deenie and Wallace first," Autumn said, pulling her jacket on. It was almost midnight and the air had turned distinctly cool, causing goose bumps to break out on her bare shoulders.

He slid his palm along the small of her back and steered her over to Lucas's parents. Strange how natural it felt to have him touching her.

Lucas was in the corner, dousing the fire pit that most of them had huddled around for the past couple of hours. Ember and Harper were inside again, along with Harper's fiancé, James, getting their babies ready to take home. Autumn was getting used to everybody's names, thanks to being able to sit around the fire pit and listening to them all talk. She knew that Nate and Ally were engaged, worked together at Déjà Brew and had a daughter, who was out with her friends tonight.

And that Brooke and Aiden were here with Brooke's son Nick, who Aiden had adopted recently. Jackson was here with a girl he'd introduced as Maura, but they'd left early because she'd gotten a headache.

Then there were Caitie and Breck, Harper and James who had baby Alyssa, and of course, her landlords, Ember and Lucas.

And Griff. Her skin tingled at the memory of dancing with him. If she'd been another girl, or this had been another time, maybe something might have happened between them.

Her body certainly seemed to think so. Every time he smiled at her she could feel her heart battering her ribcage.

Most of the glasses had been stacked in the kitchen, and Deenie had waved off everybody's offers of help to clean up, telling them she'd leave them until morning.

She looked up with a smile as they approached.

"We're leaving," Griff told her, leaning forward to give her a hug. "Thanks for letting us come."

"It was a wonderful party," Autumn added when Deenie turned to embrace her. "Congratulations again. Forty years together is something to be proud of."

Griff glanced at her from the corner of his eye. She didn't look upset, but he couldn't help but wonder if she was. Anniversaries must be a reminder of her divorce.

"Are you leaving?" Frank Megassey asked them, hurrying over to where they were standing. His face was bright red, the way it always was when he drank more than one beer. "I was hoping to have a word with Autumn."

Autumn blinked. "With me?"

"Yes. I'm Frank Megassey," he said, reaching his hand

out to her. She shook it, her expression still confused. "I run the Angel Sands Chamber of Commerce. I wanted to introduce myself because we'll probably be seeing a lot of each other."

Autumn's gaze caught Griff's. He was biting down a grin. "We will?" she asked politely.

"Yes. You'll want to come to our meetings as the new pier owner, of course." Frank beamed. "And I also have a little favor to ask you."

She swallowed. "Of course."

"Each year we raise money for a different charity. This year we've chosen the Angel Sands Animal Shelter. And I was wondering if you'd like to hold an event to help us reach our target."

"What kind of event?" Autumn asked him.

"I don't know. Maybe a fun day or a party on the pier. Something that gets the community together. It would be a good chance for you to introduce yourself to the local community and raise money for a good cause at the same time."

Griff coughed, though it sounded suspiciously like a laugh. When she turned to look at him he was staring over at the house, as though he was avoiding her gaze.

"Of course. I'd be happy to help."

"That's great." Frank patted her shoulder. "Do you think you could come up with a plan by next week? We're hoping to have the event next month, so it doesn't clash with our town celebrations in June."

"By next week?" Autumn repeated. "I'm not sure if I can do something that fast. I don't know anybody here, and it'll take me a while to figure everything out."

"That's where we come in," Frank told her. "You come up with a plan and the chamber will help you with the rest." He nodded, as though it was a done deal. "Thank you for being so supportive, Ms. Paxton. And welcome to the town. We're very happy to have you here."

"I'm happy to be here too," she murmured, feeling bulldozed. Had she really just agreed to plan for a charity event in a few weeks?

From the beaming smile on Frank's face – and the amused crinkles at the corners of Griff's eyes – it looked like she'd done exactly that.

The ocean was quiet, waves gently lapping at the shore in a soft rhythm, as Griff walked her to the door of her beach bungalow. "I had a great time," she told him as she slid the key into the lock and pushed the door open.

"I'm glad." The corners of his eyes crinkled as he leaned on the doorjamb, his hands pushed into his jean pockets. "Everybody loved you."

She flicked the light switch. The sunken spotlights flickered for a moment, then plunged into darkness with a loud bang. Frowning, she flicked again, but nothing. "I think I just blew a fuse," she told him. "You go on home, I'll find a spare bulb and the electrical box."

"The electrical box is at the back of the laundry room," he told her. "And there should be spare bulbs in the kitchen. I can change it for you if you'd like?"

"It's okay. I can do it."

"I know you can," he said gently. "But it'll be easier if there's two of us. It's dark in there, and you'll need to stand on a chair to change the bulb. I just want to help."

She caught his eye. "Your help would be much appreciated." She smiled at him. "Here, I'll turn on the flashlight on my phone. That should help us a bit."

Just as he promised, the fuse box was in the laundry room,

the main switch pointing down. Unlike Autumn, he didn't need to pull a chair over to reach it. He flicked it up, and a moment later they were plunged into light.

Then it clicked and everything went dark again.

"Do me a favor," he asked her. "Go into the living room and see which light doesn't come on when I hit the switch again."

She walked into the living room and called out for him to try again. This time, when the lights flickered on she could see the bulb by the front door was dead. Griff used his own phone light to rummage around her kitchen to locate the bulb, then quickly changed it and reset the circuit breaker.

"There." He smiled at her. "Now I can go home without worrying about you breaking your neck on the wooden floor."

She laughed at his expression of mock-horror. "My hero," she murmured. "Thank you."

The flash in his eyes had nothing to do with the lights shining overhead. The lines next to his eyes disappeared, a seriousness coming over him.

Autumn swallowed. *Hard.* He was standing right next to the front door. Another step and he'd be back outside. She couldn't hear the waves anymore, her ears were too full of the blood rushing through them.

"I'm going to head out," he said softly, reaching down to cup her face. She tipped her head up to look at him. Their gazes connected and it set her skin on fire.

His palm was warm against her skin, his fingers rough against her cheek. He ran the pad of his thumb along the line of her chin, and it sent a shiver down her spine.

"I really want to kiss you," he murmured.

"You do?" she breathed. God, she wanted that, too.

"But I'm not going to. Not until you're ready to be kissed."

Disappointment shot through her.

"Good night, Autumn," he said, pressing his lips against her fevered brow. "Sweet dreams."

Then he was gone and all she was left with was the burning memory of his lips on her skin.

"Stop laughing," Autumn told her sister, as Lydia's chuckles echoed over the phone line. "It's not funny."

"Sure it is. Only you would end up running the joint within weeks of arriving in a new town. They must have smelled it on you."

"Smelled what?" Autumn frowned.

"The nice-girl vibes. You should have remembered what I told you. Never make eye contact. Never say yes. That's the way to avoid responsibility."

Autumn chewed her lip. "I must just have that kind of face."

"A sucker face?"

The corner of Autumn's lip quirked up. "Stop it."

"Anyway, your run in with the town busybody isn't what I'm interested in. Tell me more about this Griff guy."

"There's nothing more to tell. He's my tenant, he's become a friend, and he's apparently commitment phobic." Autumn sighed.

"According to his ex-girlfriend, who has an agenda," Lydia pointed out. "And he's hot. I saw his photo on Instagram."

"How?"

"You were tagged in a photo on there. Didn't you see it? A group of you all grinning around a fire pit. I'm guessing Griff is the hulk whose lap you were practically sitting on."

Autumn grinned at her sister's description of him. "The Hulk. I think he'd like that."

"He's gorgeous, Autumn. He looks like he eats lions for

breakfast. Hell, if you're not going to persue that, I might just have to fly in."

"Who said I'm not going to?"

Lydia let out a whistle. "Does that mean you are?"

"It means I'm thinking." And she had been all night. Ever since Griff had pressed his lips to her brow. She'd wanted to run her hands over his body, to feel those muscles that swelled and dipped, to touch his skin that always felt so warm.

"Maybe you should think a little less and do a little more," Lydia suggested.

Maybe Lydia was right. Not that Autumn would ever tell her that.

"What's stopping you from doing what you want?" Lydia continued.

"Well, there's the fact that we kind of work together. And we both know mixing business and pleasure is never a good thing." Autumn picked at a piece of lint on her shorts. "Then there's my divorce. The ink is still wet on it. And everybody says you shouldn't date for at least a year after."

Lydia made a funny sound.

"Not to mention his ex who seems really keen on warning me off. Either she's right and he really is a commitment phobe, or she's crazy and I don't want any part of that either."

"And none of that matters if you keep it between two consenting adults, right?" Lydia asked. "Who cares if he doesn't want a commitment? You don't either. You said it yourself, you shouldn't commit to anything serious so soon after your divorce. And anyway, you're not planning on staying in town for long. What happens between you and him is nobody's business but yours."

"I guess..." Autumn pressed her lips together.

"He likes you, right?"

She thought about the way he looked at her last night. "I think so."

"Stop being so modest. You know he does. Guys don't dance with girls they don't wanna bone."

"You have such a way with words." Autumn shook her head, amused.

"Thanks."

"But you're right. There's a connection there. He looks at me the same way I look at him. And when we touch..." She sighed again. "It feels like magic."

"I'm jealous. It's been a long time since somebody's touched me like that."

"What about that guy in Quebec?"

"Anton? That was years ago."

"Five months."

"Almost half a year." Lydia laughed. "Anyway, we're talking about *your* love life, not mine. Now go and have some fun, and stop thinking about everything that could go wrong."

"Goodbye, Lydia."

"And don't forget to keep me updated. I'm having a dry spell."

Autumn ended the call with a grin and grabbed her sandals, sliding them on her feet. Lydia was her little sister, but it didn't mean she wasn't talking sense.

Maybe it was time to start listening to her.

11

The beach was packed full, even for a Sunday morning. Autumn weaved in between towels and umbrellas, tiptoeing past baby tents and upended surfboards, as she headed toward the pier. In front of the surf zone, she saw Ember sitting on a blanket next to her friend Brooke, whose son Nicholas was playing with baby Arthur. They looked up with a grin as she arrived. Ember shuffled along the blanket, inviting Autumn to take a seat next to her.

"Where is everybody?" Autumn asked. "I'm sure there were more of you here last week."

"Alyssa barely slept a wink, so Harper and James decided to stay home and catch up on some rest," Ember told her, passing Nick a bottle of water. "Ally and Nate are beyond swamped at the coffee shop, and Caitie and Breck are driving to LA for a few days."

"Is Lucas working?" Autumn asked her.

Ember smiled and shook her head. "No, he's in the water with Griff."

Autumn shaded her eyes and looked in the direction Ember had nodded, spotting two distant figures out in the waves. She could tell the difference between the two of them just by the height disparity. Lucas was a tall man, but Griff was a giant. When he climbed on his surfboard and rode the waves it looked like he was defying every gravitational law Newton had discovered.

"I hear Frank Megassey collared you last night," Ember said, grabbing Arthur's hand before he smashed a fistful of sand into his mouth.

"Yeah. He wants me to hold a fundraiser on the pier."

"I'm sorry. I thought he might give you a little longer to settle in." Ember's eyes met Brooke's. "I know Ally tried to warn you."

"It's okay." Autumn smiled at them. "He only pushed up a few plans I had anyway. I've wanted to do something that brings the community to the pier, and shows them how change is a good thing. I'm going to contact a few companies tomorrow to see if we can have some fairground rides put on there. Maybe some music, too. It should be fun."

"If you need any help, just say the word," Ember said. "A couple of years ago, Lucas and I had to help with the Angel Day Fair, so I know what Frank can be like."

"I might take you up on that." Autumn felt her heart warm at the offer. In New York, everybody would have called her crazy and refused to meet her eye if she asked for help. Here, people fell over themselves to do what they could, even though it didn't benefit them.

"I can help, too," Brooke offered. "Although I also have a wedding to organize."

"You've had a wedding to organize for years," Ember said, biting down a smile.

Brooke shook her head. "You're exaggerating. And we will get married. Our lives are so crazy busy at the moment. With Aiden running the resort, and me doing my post graduate training, plus there's Nick to think of," she said, referring to her son. "Trying to sort out the wedding is taking longer than we hoped."

"I keep telling you to get married at the resort." Ember grinned at Brooke. "You sleep with the owner after all."

"I don't want us to get married where he works. Can you imagine it? He'd be in the middle of saying his vows a phone call would come in and he'd have to take it." She shook her head. "Definitely not happening."

"Well, congratulations anyway," Autumn said, looking over at the pier, her eyes narrowing as a thought took root in her mind. "Actually," she said, running her finger over her lip. "That's given me an idea."

"It has?" Brooke tipped her head to the side. "What kind of idea?"

Autumn pulled her lip between her teeth. "Has anybody gotten married on the pier before?"

Ember looked at Brooke, and the two of them shook their head. "I don't think so," Ember said. "It's always been kind of run down."

"I wonder if it could be another way to raise some money," Autumn murmured. "Holding ceremonies there."

"Delmonico's could host the wedding party afterward," Ember said, grinning at Autumn's suggestion. "Or Griff could take everybody out on the boat."

"It would make a great alternative to the resort or the Beach Club," Brooke agreed. "And you could make it look so pretty, too."

Autumn felt the anticipation lick at her belly. She could picture it. The wooden struts and bannisters festooned with garlands of flowers. Strings of lights overhead. And the pretty backdrop of the water – perfect for photographs. She'd start investigating tomorrow.

"Do you think you could have it up and running by next spring?" Brooke asked her.

"Is that when you're planning on getting married?"

Brooke smiled. "Yeah. Aiden wanted to do it this year, but, seriously, there's not enough time." She glanced at Ember. "And not everybody has an event planner for a sister-in-law to pull a rabbit out of the bag."

"I'm almost certain we could be up and running by next year." Autumn looked at the pier again, ideas spinning through her head. She couldn't stop the excitement from bubbling up inside her. She'd spent the last few days trying to figure out how to make a profit from the pier without hiking the rents beyond anything affordable. Using the space for events and weddings could be the exact answer she was looking for. Part of her wanted to run across the sand and up the warm wooden slats of the pier to her office to start working on her plan right away.

But then a movement caught her eye. She turned to see Griff riding a wave, surfing his body into the crest as the board weaved in and out of the spray. He made it look so easy, as though the board was glued to his feet, as he effortlessly surfed to the shallow. When he got there, he jumped off the board and pulled it with him, wading to shore.

"He looks like Aquaman," Brooke murmured. "But bigger."

As soon as he spotted Autumn sitting with his friends, Griff grinned and walked over. "Hey, how's the light bulb?"

"Still working." Autumn smiled up at him. "Thanks for changing it."

Ember looked curiously at her. "Did a bulb blow?"

"Yes, last night. But Griff came to the rescue." She smiled at him again. "Actually, can I talk to you for a minute?"

He blinked. "Yeah, sure." Pitching his board in the sand, he ran his hand through his wet hair, droplets spraying everywhere. "You wanna take a walk?"

She nodded, following him to the shoreline where there

was room to move in a straight line. Blowing out a mouthful of air, she tried to decide what she wanted to say. It'd seemed so easy when she was talking to Lydia earlier.

"So, um, thanks for last night." God, she was lame.

"Any time."

"I was wondering about what you said..." She looked up at him. His bronzed skin was covered in water droplets, clinging to him like limpets. The sun reflected from them, making tiny rainbows appear.

"What I said?"

"About kissing me."

He stopped walking and turned to look at her, his eyes soft. "About wanting to kiss you," he corrected.

She felt a little flutter of excitement. "Yeah," she said, her breath catching. "About that."

The corner of his lip quirked up. "I'm listening."

She could feel her heart race. "I wanted you to kiss me, too." She kicked her toes across the surface of the water. "Just so you know."

That half-smile was still playing on his lips. "I got that impression." He reached out to tuck a stray hair behind her ear, his finger tips trailing across her skin. "But I'm guessing you don't mean here."

She shook her head. "I was thinking you could come over for dinner tonight. I'll cook for you and we can talk." She ran her tongue across her lips, tasting the salt of the ocean. "And maybe kiss again." She looked at him through her lashes.

"Yeah. We can do that." His voice was low. Thick. It sent a shiver through her. "What time do you want me?"

"Does six work?"

"It does for me."

She let out a long breath. "Okay, I'll see you then."

"Yeah, you will." He leaned down and pressed his lips against her brow, his hand cupping the back of her head. The warmth of his mouth was like a shock to her skin. Then he was gone, walking back across the sand as he lifted his board with one hand, waving goodbye to her with the other.

"You okay?" Ember asked her once she'd returned.

"Yeah." Autumn nodded. "I'm good."

Brooke eyed her speculatively, but said nothing. She could feel their unasked questions lingering in the air.

"So tell me about your wedding plans," Autumn said to Brooke. "Maybe we can start to work something out."

Griff ran his fingers through his hair, raking it back from his face before he rapped on Autumn's front door with his knuckles. Funny to think about how much time he'd spent here over the past few years since Lucas had renovated it. Long hours watching sports on his big screen television, even longer cooking out on his grill and drinking ice cold beers as they laughed. But not once had he felt the rush he was feeling now.

And it was all down to *her*.

Autumn opened the door, a huge grin on her face. Her hair was down, light brown waves cascading over her shoulders. She was wearing a dress again, this one with spaghetti straps and a fitted bodice that skimmed her curves before it flared out at the waist. Her skin held a light tan, enough for him to guess she'd sat on the beach for a while after he left this morning. The glow suited her, made her even more attractive, if that was possible.

The caveman in him wanted to lift her up and carry her to her bedroom.

"I brought wine," he said, passing her a bottle as he stooped to kiss her cheek. She was barefoot again, and he liked the way she looked so relaxed. It was as though any vestige of her life in New York had left her, making her as laid back as the Californian sun.

"Sauvignon blanc," she murmured. "My favorite."

"I know. I saw the way you were knocking it back last night." He winked at her.

She shook her head, the grin still lifting her lips, then gestured for him to come inside.

"I'm making steak and potatoes. I hope that's okay."

"Are you kidding? I love steak." He followed her into the kitchen where she opened the bottle and poured them both a glass. She passed one to him and lifted the other. "To new friends," she said, her eyes sliding to his. "And working light bulbs."

He clinked his glass against hers. "I'll drink to that." The wine was cool and crisp against his tongue. He swallowed it down and put his glass on the counter. Next to it was a plate holding the biggest steak he'd seen in a while. It had to be at least twenty ounces.

"Are we sharing that?"

"That one's yours. Mine's here," Autumn told him, pointing at another plate. "I wasn't sure how hungry you'd be, but I figured you probably eat a lot. You have a busy job and you're..." she gestured at his height. "You."

"If you cook it rare, I'll probably eat the whole thing before you lift a fork," he told her. "Can I help with anything in here?"

"You can set the table while I cook the steaks," she said, pointing to the silverware on the side of the counter. "The potatoes are in the oven and the salad's in the refrigerator. I think I have the food covered."

The food tasted amazing. Within fifteen minutes Griff had

finished everything on his plate, laying his silverware down on the white porcelain and leaning back on his chair to rub his stomach.

"How did you learn to cook steaks like that?" he asked her.

"It's all in the cut." She lifted another forkful of steak to her mouth. "And the preparation. I like to tenderize it and let it rest, then add a rub an hour before I cook it."

"Well it was delicious. Thank you."

She smiled. "It's nice to cook for more than one person. I've been living on pasta for a while. There never seems much point in doing all the work when there's nobody to eat with."

She didn't sound sad about it. More matter-of-fact than anything else.

"How long have you been divorced?" he asked her.

"About six weeks."

"That recent?" He tried to hide his surprise.

"We were separated for over a year. We had to be. And the settlement was... contentious." She sighed. "So it feels like a lot longer. Waiting for the paperwork was the hardest part."

He ran the tip of his tongue over his lips. She was a fascinating combination of strong and vulnerable. Maybe they were two sides of the same coin. Whatever it was, it enticed him in a way he hadn't felt in a long time.

Maybe ever.

"I have no idea why you divorced, but your ex was a damn fool."

Autumn laughed. "What if it was my fault?"

"Then it was his fault for not keeping you happy."

"Yeah, well that part was true. And I guess it was both of our faults. Living with somebody and working with them was a recipe for disaster." She thought about the NDA she'd signed. Best not to tell him too much about that.

He raised his eyebrows. "You worked together?"

"Yeah. He bought me out of our company. I used the money to buy the pier." She ran her finger around the rim of her wine glass. "How about you? You ever been married?"

He shook his head. "No. But I never wanted to. Still don't. My parents weren't exactly a great advertisement for marital harmony."

She remembered Deenie telling her something similar at the party. "Are they divorced?" she asked him.

"They should be. But right now they're probably screaming at each other in a bungalow outside of Fort Lauderdale." He caught her eye. "Thankfully I don't have to listen to them tear each other apart anymore."

As though she could sense his discomfort, Autumn pulled her bottom lip between her teeth then released it, her mouth curling into a shy smile.

It was like she was standing on the edge of something. Afraid, but elated. Her eyes were feverish, glancing at him, then looking down at her hands before catching his gaze again. When was he going to kiss her? Her body ached for it. She'd barely thought about anything else all day.

"I'm not looking for anything serious," she told him. "But I really like you, Griff."

"Being un-serious is completely fine with me." He looked serious, though. *Deadly*. And it made her body heat up.

This time she didn't pull her eyes away. They stared at each other for a long moment, the air pulsating between them. Griff curled his fingers, digging his nails into his palms in an effort to stop himself from reaching across to her.

"Why don't you sit on the sofa while I clean up," she suggested. "Then we can talk…or…whatever."

The corner of his lips quirked up. "I'm not sitting down while you wait on me. I'll help you clean," he told her. "Then let's see where the evening takes us."

12

The chinaware was all washed up and put away, the countertops sparkling. Autumn filled their glasses with more of Griff's delicious wine and carried them into the living area.

Though the room was compact, the cream leather sofa was huge, dominating the space. But it looked so much smaller when Griff was on it. She sat down beside him, leaving a gap between them.

"Cheers." They clinked glasses and she took a sip of the cool, crisp wine. She could feel her cheeks warm up as he kept his eyes on hers, his gaze direct and yet soft, too.

"You look scared."

"I feel scared," she told him honestly.

His brows dipped. "Why?"

She put her glass down on the driftwood coffee table and curled her legs beneath her, tipping her head to the side as she considered his question. "Because I feel vulnerable, yet full of some weird anticipation. It's a strange cocktail."

The corner of his lips lifted as he continued to look at her. She felt a shiver snake its way down her spine. God, he was masculine, probably the strongest man she'd ever met. It was like he could melt her with his gaze.

"Come here," he said softly.

She swallowed, then inched across until her thigh brushed against his.

"I mean here," he told her, pointing at the top of his legs. It was her turn to smile as she climbed over him, kneeling on either side of his substantial thighs.

"That's better," he murmured, reaching out to smooth her hair from her face. "We're a little more equal like this."

He leaned forward, his nose sliding against hers. She looked into his warm brown eyes. Being this close she could see little green specks in his irises, like emeralds glistening in stone.

Cupping his face in her hands, her fingertips grazed his cheekbones. The roughness of his beard scraped against her palms as he stared at her questioningly.

"You're very beautiful," he whispered as her thumbs traced the line of his jaw.

"You're pretty hot yourself." She leaned forward until her lips brushed against his cheek.

She could feel his breath against her, warm and fragrant with wine. She leaned closer still, and he ran his hands down her back, cupping her behind as she straddled him.

The first time they kissed she'd felt out of control. This time, she wanted to savor every moment. To experience it in hyper-definition, to remember every eye flicker and caught breath.

This connection between them was fleeting. Time limited. Eventually they'd have to part and the thought already made her heart ache.

He traced his fingertips along her spine and pressed his lips to the base of her throat.

"So damn pretty."

"Thank you," she breathed. He was holding her weight with one hand. It made her so damn delicate. Closing his eyes, he breathed her in, his lips sliding up her throat, her jaw, and to the corner of her mouth. Just one inch more and he'd be there.

Her body clenched at the thought.

"I want to remember this," he murmured, brushing her hair from her face with his free hand. "The way you're looking at me. The way your ass feels against my legs. I wish I could capture this moment."

Her lips curled into a smile. Maybe he was feeling as wistful as she was.

With his hand at the base of her spine, he pulled her closer, her thighs sliding against his until the warmth of her center felt him. Right there. Thick and hard against her.

She let out an involuntary sigh. "Please..."

"Please what?"

"Kiss me already."

Another chuckle. He raked his fingers through her hair, angling her head until it was lifted to his. "Patience..."

Her gaze met his, making her heart jump in her chest. The laughter faded as his eyes darkened and narrowed, as his mouth fell onto hers.

God, his lips were good. Just the right amount of pressure as they moved against hers, his fingers massaging her scalp as his other hand kept her steady. His mouth was warm and strong, his lips opening as his tongue slid between hers, and she rolled her hips, her toes curling at the pleasure.

He broke the kiss, his eyes hooded as he traced his finger down her throat to the tiny dip at the base. Then he skimmed the line of her bodice, swallowing hard, before pushing the spaghetti straps from her shoulders and leaning in to kiss her bare flesh.

"Do you know how much I want you?" he asked her, his

lips brushing against her fevered skin. "How much I've wanted you since I first saw you on the pier with the wind in your hair and those damn inappropriate shoes?"

"I thought you liked my shoes?" She gasped as he sucked at the flesh between her shoulder and throat.

"I do." He rolled his hips and pressed his hardness against her, pleasure shooting from her core to the tips of her curled toes. "A lot."

His lips kissed their way to the soft swell of her breast where it disappeared into her dress. She held her breath as he paused, then reached behind, unfastening the zipper until her dress gaped open at the back.

He traced the line of her cleavage, making her nipples harden beneath her strapless bra, the stretched lace making them tender and achy. Then he pushed her dress down and cupped her breasts in his strong palms, leaning in to suck at her nipple through the fabric

"Oh god." She arched her back, gasping as his lips pulled her in further. "Griff, please..."

It was like there was a direct line from her breasts to her core. Every pull of his lips and scrape of his teeth made her achy and full of need. Until she felt hollow inside.

"Should we go to the bedroom?" she managed to ask him, before he moved to her other breast, sucking and teasing.

He glanced up at her, his eyes dark and needy. "Yeah. We should."

The next moment he was standing up, lifting her with him until her legs were wrapped around his waist and his hands beneath her ass. Without another word, he was striding across the room, pushing open the bedroom door with his foot and carrying her inside.

Gently, he lay her on the bed, and she shimmied out of her dress, loving the way he stared at her ivory lingerie, his throat undulating as he swallowed hard. Then he was leaning down, pulling the pale lace away until her breasts were exposed, the underwire and extra fabric pushing them up high.

When he sucked at her this time, she almost exploded. Her back arched as he slid his tongue against her hard nipples, licking and sucking and driving her crazy. His hand caressed her stomach, his palm warm and rough on her skin, until his fingertips reached the ribboned edge of her panties.

"These are pretty," he told her as he slid his finger along her skin.

She could feel her body pulsate at his touch.

"But you're prettier," he said, pulling them down her thighs and over her knees, lifting her calves to take them the rest of the way off. She arched her back to remove her bra, throwing it to the floor.

With a wicked grin, he moved down the bed, breathing her in, before he slid his soft tongue against her.

"Oh god!" Her eyes widened at the exquisite sensation. "Griff..."

He parted her with his hands as he licked again, and she let out a cry at the pleasure coiling inside of her. She tried to push her legs together, but he was too strong, too intent on giving pleasure.

He knew exactly the rhythm she needed. More than she did herself. Soft, then hard, then soft again, taking her to the edge and making her stay there.

"I'm so close," she gasped, feeling the nerve endings spark inside her.

"I know you are." There was a smile in his voice. He pushed a finger inside her, then two, stroking her in just the right place to make her fall apart, his lips sucking at her clit until all she could see were fireworks behind her eyelids.

"You're even more beautiful when you come," he rasped, when the pleasure finally receded.

She opened her eyes to see him staring at her, that darkness still in his eyes.

"You've got too many clothes on," she whispered.

He grinned. "I can do something about that." He pulled his shirt off, and she drank in the defined lines of his pectorals, the taut ridges of his stomach, and the perfect 'v' that disappeared into his jeans. With his gaze still on her face, he unbuckled his belt and pulled his jeans down, until he was only wearing tight black shorts that revealed everything.

And yeah, the big man was perfectly in proportion.

"I want to see all of you," she whispered. He obliged without a protest, pulling his shorts down to reveal his hard, thick length.

God, he was beautiful. She clambered to her knees, reaching out to touch him. He gasped as her fingers circled around his length. That was beautiful, too. She got closer, enough to swirl her tongue around his tip, then slide her mouth onto him, making him groan loudly.

"Autumn," he said, his voice gravelly. "You need to stop. I don't want to come in your mouth. I want to be inside you."

She pulled her lips from him and caught his gaze. "Condoms, top drawer."

He grinned and pulled the drawer out, raising an eyebrow as he grabbed the 24-pack. "How long did you want me to stay?"

"They were on sale." She swallowed down a laugh. "I love a bargain."

Griff ripped open the packet, sliding it slowly on. Then he lifted her onto his lap, her thighs straddling him the same way she had on the sofa, the tip of him sliding against her wetness.

He bent his head to kiss her, his lips warm and soft, making her feel needier than ever. Her limbs felt languid, almost boneless as he cupped her behind, lifting her up to center himself, before slowly pushing inside her.

"Ohhh..."

"You feel so damn good," he growled. He pulled out, before filling her up again. "Put your hands around my neck, baby."

She did as she was told, hooking her hands together, and he balanced her with one hand. With the other he reached down between them, pressing his thumb against her. She was like the driest of tinder, just waiting for that spark, exploding around him at the faintest of touches. He followed her into oblivion, stilling beneath her as he let out a long, low groan, holding her soft body against his hard muscles until the pulsing inside her stopped.

Autumn was asleep in his arms, her back pressed into his chest, her sweet ass nestled against his thighs. Griff brushed his lips against her ear, and smiled as she murmured something intelligible in her sleep.

God, she was sexy. Not in an obvious way like some women he'd dated. It was in her confidence, her intelligence, and the way she met his eyes every time they spoke to each other.

When he'd gotten up this morning he'd never expected today to end like this, with her naked in his arms. And yet there was something so inevitable about it. As though it was destined to happen from the moment he'd set eyes on her, walking down the pier in those damn sexy shoes.

It would be so easy to lay here all night, to wake her up in the morning for a little more loving, then cook her breakfast before walking to work together.

I'm not looking for anything serious.

That was what she'd said. And she was right. He couldn't offer her anything serious, even if he wanted to. He was a fuck up at relationships, his track record spoke to that. It was better for them both to keep this as fun.

And fun meant getting his things and going home before he got too used to her warm softness against him.

Griff pressed his lips against her temple. "Autumn."

She let out a soft sigh and turned, nestling her head against his chest. He fought against the urge to wrap his arms around her and let himself fall asleep.

"Baby?"

Her eyelids flickered, then slowly opened. Her eyes were heavy with sleep, but as soon as they caught his, her lips curled into a smile. "Hey," she said softly.

"Hey." He smiled back at her. "I'm going to head on home." He gently released her, then rolled over to grab his shorts, pulling them over his thick thighs.

She blinked, the smile slipping. "Of course." She propped herself up on her elbows, the sheet barely covering her chest. "Let me get some clothes on. I'll see you out."

"You stay there. You look cozy." He winked at her. "I'll make sure nobody's watching when I leave."

Her cheeks were pink from sleep. God, she was adorable. "Okay."

"Thanks for a great evening. And for the steak." He pulled his shirt on. "I had a good time."

"I did, too." She licked her bottom lip, her eyes following his every move.

He pulled his jeans on, then his socks and shoes, before he leaned over to press his lips against hers. God, she tasted good. Too good. He wanted to strip everything back off and start all over again.

"I'll see you tomorrow at the pier," she said, a strange expression on her face.

"That you will." Reluctantly, he pulled away. "Sleep tight, beautiful."

"You too. Thank you for..." She gave a little chuckle. "For everything."

It only took a moment for him to reach the front door. Another for him to pull it open and step outside. He closed it gently, checking to make sure it was locked behind him, then he breathed in a lungful of air and headed down the beach toward his condo building.

He didn't want anything serious. And neither did she. So why did it feel so damn hard to walk away from her?

13

Leaning back on the rickety desk chair she'd inherited along with the pier office, Autumn took off her reading glasses, and rubbed her eyes with the heels of her hands. She'd spent most of the morning on her laptop, researching her idea of holding weddings and events on the pier. The afternoon was filled with writing up costs and investigating all the boring things like insurance and permits that made her want to pull her eyelashes out one by one.

And of course her gaze kept flicking up to the window that looked out over the end of the pier. Griff's boat had been gone when she'd arrived at work that morning, making for an early start on a corporate team building event. Her chest felt all fluttery every time she looked to see if the boat was back, and when it wasn't, she felt a strange sense of disappointment wash over her.

She was being stupid. She'd told him she didn't want anything serious, and he'd made it clear he felt the same when he left her last night to sleep in his own bed. It was supposed to be fun, with a little sprinkling of friendship on the side.

Yet here she was, staring at a bit of empty dock like a lovesick teenager.

At five o'clock she walked down the pier to the beach, and headed over to Déjà Brew to order a coffee, just to give herself something else to think about. Ally smiled and waved as soon as she walked through the door, pointing at the medium sized cup. "Your usual?" she asked.

"I'll have a large one," Autumn told her. "I think I need it."

"Late night?" Ally asked, as she filled the filter with coffee then banged it against the machine."

For a moment, Autumn thought about spilling her guts and telling her everything. But what was there to tell? She'd had hot sex with the guy she hadn't been able to get out of her mind, then he went home and she hadn't heard from him since.

It wasn't *exactly* a fairy tale.

"More of a long day at the office," Autumn told her, smiling when Ally passed her the latte. "I need to buy a new chair." She rolled her neck to loosen the muscles, but it did nothing to relieve the aches in the rest of her body. Her thighs felt sore, as though she'd put them through a workout.

"I've got just the thing for that," Ally said, pulling a chocolate covered slice from the glass cabinet on top of the counter. "It's got oats and cherries, which means it's fruit. Great for achy bodies, and practically calorie free." She slid it into a paper bag and passed it to Autumn, along with her latte. "It's on the house."

"Stop it." Autumn laid a ten on the counter. "You're running a business."

"You can pay for the latte, but the cake is on me," Ally told her, pulling some change from the register. "We made too many."

Autumn sipped at her coffee as she made her way back to

the office, the golden sun warming her bare arms. There was a group of kids playing softball on the beach, and she had to duck as a ball came flying in her direction. It passed over her head before landing heavily on the sand.

"Sorry, ma'am!" a boy shouted as he ran to retrieve the ball.

"It's okay." She grinned. "You missed." She pulled the chocolate slice out of the bag and sunk her teeth into it, groaning as the taste radiated in her mouth. Ally was right. It was full of fruit and oats, and dark-as-sin chocolate. It was a shame it wasn't really calorie free.

She was almost at her office before she realized Griff's boat was back. Mike had just set up the metal gangplank, and a horde of passengers wearing company logoed polo shirts and tan pants disembarked, shouting out their thanks before they passed Autumn and walked up the pier. She tried to ignore the way her chest felt all tight at the thought of seeing Griff, and instead, took a deep mouthful of coffee before opening her office door.

"Hey!"

She looked up to see Griff walking down the gangplank, and let the door close again.

"Hey." She composed what she hoped looked like a casual smile on her face. One that didn't give away how much she was thinking about last night. About *him* between her thighs. "How was the ocean today?"

"It was good." He pushed his hands into the pockets of his jeans. For a second, her eyes flickered down to look at his jeans, before she resolutely pulled them back up. "We saw a couple of dolphins, they started following us around. And only half of the guests got seasick. How was your day?" he asked her.

She reached up to rub her aching neck. "Long. I spent most of it pricing ideas for the charity event." She realized she hadn't told him about the wedding plan. "I had a couple of other ideas, too, for the longer term future of the pier. Maybe I could run them past you some time. See how you think they'll go down with the tenants."

His eyes caught hers. "Any time."

"I guess I should get back to work," she said, inclining her head at the door to her office.

"Do you have any plans for tonight?"

She looked up, surprised at his abrupt change of subject. "Nothing apart from a glass of wine and some pasta."

"Let me cook you dinner this time. Repay the favor."

"You're inviting me to your place?"

He shrugged. "It's only fair."

"In that case, I'd be delighted to accept." She couldn't hide her huge grin. It felt like the sun had just gotten a little brighter.

"Good." He nodded. "Oh, and maybe you should bring a bag."

"A bag?" Her brows rose up.

"To carry your pajamas and toothbrush in. I have shower gel, but you might want to bring your own. And you'll probably need some clothes for tomorrow."

She tipped her head to the side. "Are you inviting me for a sleepover?"

"I'm just thinking of all contingencies. I felt like an asshole leaving you last night. So if you want to stay, I'd be delighted to have you. And if you decide you don't want to, you can always carry that bag back home with you. I'll walk you back to make sure you're safe."

A slow smile pulled at the corner of her lips. "You just want to have more sex with me." She knew the feeling. Her thighs felt tight at the thought of him between them.

He grinned back. "You got me."

"Okay then. Send me a message with your address and

what time you want me." She took a sip of her coffee, her eyes meeting his. "And my bag and I will see you there."

"Hey, Griff!" Lorne called out as Griff walked along the boardwalk toward the Fresh 'N' Easy later that afternoon to buy some groceries. "How's it going?"

"Great." Griff grinned. He was in the best of moods. That's what an evening with a beautiful woman could do for you. "How are you?"

"Ah, I'm getting old. I just had a group of teenagers in, messing around with my boards. Lost my temper and told them to get the hell out." Lorne wrinkled his nose. "I swear I'm getting grumpier than ever."

Griff laughed. Lorne was the least grumpy guy he knew. Between the two of them, it was a close tie to who was the most laid back.

"Hey, I saw that your folks were over this way the other week. They doing okay?" Lorne asked him.

Griff blinked. "They haven't visited for a couple of years."

"They haven't?" Lorne frowned, running his palm over his scruff of a beard. "That's strange. Maybe it was an old photo I saw."

"What photo?"

"I'm friends with your mom on Facebook. She posted a photo of them in Silver City. But maybe it was from a while ago."

Silver City was just up the coast. His parents still had some friends there. Griff shrugged and pulled his phone out, bringing up his long-neglected Facebook account. Sure enough, there was the photo Lorne was telling him about. His parents posing with their friends, Gloria and Sam, in a restaurant they'd always loved.

Good friends and good wine. Good times, his mom had captioned it.

He could tell from his mom's hair it was recent. She'd cut it all off a few months ago. It was one of the few photo messages she'd sent him.

Lorne leaned over and looked at the screen. "An old one?"

"Nah. I guess it was a flying visit." Griff quickly closed the app and shoved the phone back in his pocket. "I gotta go. I need to pick up some food."

"Sure. Of course." Lorne gave him a sympathetic smile. "Maybe they'll visit again soon, hey?"

"Maybe. Who knows?" Griff smiled back at him. "We're all busy people around here."

"Tell me about it." Lorne seemed glad of the change in conversation. "I'm dreading the season ramping up. As I said, I'm getting too old for this game."

"Aren't we all?" Griff said, winking. "I'll catch you later, my friend."

"Dinner should be ready in a half hour." Griff passed Autumn a glass of wine, and she walked over to the huge floor-to-ceiling windows that overlooked the Pacific, flipping her dark hair over her shoulder as she took in the view.

"Your apartment is beautiful," she said, turning around to smile at him. "But the view is even better."

"Thanks. I kind of like it myself." He grabbed his glass and walked over to join her, staring at the expanse of water. The dark blue waves were tipped with orange and pink from the setting sun. "It's the first thing I look at in the morning, so I can determine how good or bad the conditions are for the boat trip that day." He tipped his head to look down at her. "And surfing, of course."

"Have you always surfed?"

"Ever since I can remember." He ran his hand through his thick hair, pushing it away from his brow. "I was a young kid when I started. I'd go out with Lucas, Breck, and Jackson on Saturday mornings. Jack's dad taught us. He was a pro when he was younger. Long retired now."

"Can you imagine yourself living away from the water?"

He frowned. "No, not really. It's part of me. Not just the location for my job or my leisure activity. It's like my lungs or something. Essential for life."

She swallowed a mouthful of wine, then leaned against him, the top of her head touching the hard curve of his chest. "Sometimes you remind me of a water god," she told him softly. "Neptune or Poseidon. I bet if you were cut open you'd bleed saltwater."

He laughed. "I'd prefer if you didn't check out that theory." He slid his arm around her shoulder, his rough fingertips feathering her bare shoulder. "God, I'm glad you came tonight. I've been thinking about you all day."

She smiled up at him. "I've been thinking about you, too. And the way you've made my muscles ache."

"Did I hurt you?" He frowned. He thought he'd been gentle. Being a big guy, he'd learned not to put his weight on a woman, to be careful unless she asked for it a little rougher.

"No. I'm just a little out of practice. Used a few muscles I haven't needed for a while."

The thought warmed him. "Maybe we both were." He traced a line from her shoulder to her throat, then tangled his fingers into her soft hair.

"Not you," she whispered. "You're at the peak of your game."

He leaned his head down, angling hers until they were a whisper away from each other. "I haven't come like that in a long time," he told her softly. "Maybe never. You do things to me, Autumn. Things I can't stop thinking about." He brushed his lips against hers, the simple contact sending a siren call to his groin. He'd been hard since he touched her skin, but now he was aching. She turned until she was facing him, her back to the window, her front pressed against his, and she wrapped her arms around his neck to deepen the kiss.

In her bare feet she was a foot shorter than him, and he had to bend his back and his neck to get the right angle. Sliding his hands down her sides, he lifted her against him, pressing her against the window pane to steady her, as she wrapped her thighs around his hips.

"Sorry," he murmured against her lips. "It's just easier."

"Don't be sorry," she told him as their lips moved together. "It's sexy as hell to have a guy who can lift me." She rolled her hips against him, the sensation making him harder than ever. He pressed his mouth against hers, his tongue plundering, his hands digging into her sweet behind. He turned to carry her to his room, where they'd have a little more privacy.

The shrill *bleep* of the oven timer made him stop in his tracks. "Damn, it's the pot pies."

"You made pies?" she grinned, her legs still wrapped around his waist. "Put me down right now and check them. I don't want them to get burned."

"I'm the one who's burning," he muttered, releasing his hold on her as she slid down to the floor. He was still painfully hard and had to adjust himself before he walked over to the kitchen and washed his hands before turning off the timer. Then he opened the oven, watching as the steam escaped from the door, smelling the savory aroma of chicken and pastry.

"It looks like it needs another ten minutes," he called out.

"Then come back here," she said, grinning at him. "I've got an idea of what we can do while we wait."

"Where did you learn to cook pot pies?" Autumn asked, leaning her elbow on the mattress and propping her chin on her palm. The sheet was loosely gathered around her, and underneath it she was naked.

They both were, thanks to the way they'd torn each others clothes off after dinner, leaving a trail of devastation from the living room into the bedroom.

"Deenie taught me. I was the first of all our friends to have my own place. The day after I moved in she came over and insisted on showing me three things to cook. An omelet, chili, and chicken pot pie. She was afraid I'd starve to death otherwise."

"She taught you well." Autumn rubbed her swollen stomach. "It was delicious."

He grinned. "Well thank you. I aim to please."

Yeah, he did, and her body was still tingling thanks to him.

"You need to stop looking at me like that," he told her softly. "Before I do something about it."

"What kind of thing?"

"The kind of thing that will make your muscles ache even more than they already do. I don't want you limping on the pier tomorrow."

She laughed, reaching out to thread her fingers through his thick hair. "I didn't realize what a big ego you had."

"Is that what we're calling it?" He wiggled his eyebrows, making her laugh all over again. "Okay, I'll admit it, you've worn me out. Distract me, tell me about your plans for the pier."

He looked genuinely interested, and it warmed her. Maybe there was something to this friends with benefits thing after all. Yes, the sex was amazing, but so was eating together, and shooting the breeze. She was enjoying spending time with him.

"I want to make the pier a location for weddings and other events like that." She leaned in, resting her chin on her palm. "I spent this morning contacting people at the county and the insurance company, and this afternoon talking to suppliers who can help. The short story is, there's nothing to stop me advertising the pier as a wedding location. I can start as soon as I want." She pulled her lip between her teeth. "There are a few kinks to iron out, of course. Like access to your boat on wedding days, and for Delmonico's patrons. But I think we can work that out."

His eyes were soft as they met hers. "I'm sure we can," he said. "And I think it's an amazing idea."

Her face lit up. "You do?"

"Yeah. It's the perfect location. Right now, the only places you can get married are either at the Beach Club or the resort. Or the sand itself if you get the right license. The pier would be beautiful, especially as the sun goes down. It's at its most picturesque then."

"I thought you might object," she told him. "Not everybody likes change."

"I'm a business owner," he pointed out. "I know how important it is to get the most out of your assets."

"I've been thinking about Delmonico's, too," she told him. "I could either create a separate entrance for their restaurant, or they could be part of the package. The restaurant would be perfect for the reception afterward."

He raised an eyebrow. "You've thought of everything."

"The boat would make an amazing location for a rehearsal dinner, too," she mused, tracing the swell of his bicep with her finger. "If you ever wanted to do dinner cruises."

He laughed. "Are we back on that?"

"It's just a suggestion."

"It's a good one, actually. Let me think about it."

"Okay."

"Now come here," he said gruffly. "You have some more assets I'd like to exploit."

"What happened to me getting sore and you being tired?" She tipped her head to the side, amused and turned on by the heat in his eyes.

"I figure I'll go easy on you this time," he said, pulling her toward him until she was straddling his lap. "Or maybe you'll go gentle with me."

She leaned forward to capture his lips with her own. "I wouldn't count on it."

14

"If you keep cooking for me like this, I'm going to think you've got an ulterior motive." Autumn leaned on the kitchen counter, watching Griff crack an egg into the pan, then move it around with a spatula. Ham was sizzling beneath the other burner, the smell making her mouth water. She couldn't take her eyes off him. He was wearing a pair of soft jersey jogging pants and nothing else. The waistband was low on his hips, revealing the sweet ridges of his six pack and that 'v' she traced with her fingers last night.

"I think we both need some food after last night." He raised an eyebrow at her. "And we have a long day of work ahead of us. I figure we should start the day right."

"I usually just grab an apple or banana, then buy a coffee from Déjà Brew."

"You need to eat protein, too," he told her. "That's what'll stop you from feeling hungry before lunch."

"Is that right?" She grinned at him. "In that case, I'll have to come here for breakfast every morning."

He winked. "Works for me." Grabbing two plates from the cupboard next to the stove, he slid the eggs onto them, followed by grilled ham and tomatoes, plus the bread he'd toasted and buttered. She followed him over to the table, still smiling when he put the plate in front of her.

"I think you're the first guy that's ever cooked for me."

Griff's brows knitted together. "I thought you were divorced."

"I am."

"And your ex never cooked?"

She shook her head. "He was very skilled at picking up take out, though."

"How about you? Did you cook a lot when you were in New York?"

"Not really. We were both working crazy hours building up the business. A lot of our meetings took place over dinner."

He speared a piece of ham with his fork. "Do you miss New York?"

"Not yet." She shrugged, biting into the crisp toast. "Maybe I will in a few weeks, but right now I'm liking it here."

"I'm liking that you like it here." His eyes caught hers.

A flash of warmth washed through her. "What time are you taking the boat out today?"

"I'm not. Today's an admin day." He lifted his coffee cup. "Usually I hate them, but it's starting out pretty good."

"I love admin."

"That's not possible."

She laughed at his outraged expression. "It's true. I like being organized. I get a thrill when I tick something off my to-do-list."

"Maybe you can do mine. I'll go surfing instead." He winked at her.

"I could help. What do you need to do?"

He tipped his head to the side, looking at her through

thick lashes. "It's boring stuff. I need to get some numbers together to refinance the boat. I need to raise a bit of cash to make some repairs."

"Oh, I love numbers." Her eyes lit up. "And spreadsheets. Do you have spreadsheets?"

He laughed at the excited expression on her face. "Yeah. Really big ones. But it's okay, I can do it this morning. Then I'll treat myself with a surf this afternoon."

"Maybe I'll come and watch you do that instead. You look hot in board shorts."

"You should come with me. I'll teach you."

"To surf?" Her eyes widened. "Oh no. You don't want to see that."

"Yeah I really do." He leaned across to tuck a lock of hair behind her ear. "I want to see you on a board. Come on, I'll make it fun. I promise."

"I've never surfed."

"I'm a patient teacher." His smile widened. "And we both know you're strong enough. I've seen the muscles in your legs. I'll even let you play with my numbers if you'd like."

She laughed and shook her head, watching as his eyes danced with amusement. "Okay, but I've got the feeling you're getting the better end of the deal."

"It's a win-win." He sipped his coffee. "Come on, let's get some work done, then I'll meet you at the beach."

He swallowed hard as she pulled her t-shirt over her head, then unbuttoned her cut-offs and climbed out of them, and tried really hard not to ogle her. Autumn Paxton could rock a swimsuit better than any woman he'd seen.

He was fighting a losing battle.

Taking a long, deep breath, he told his body to behave

itself. He was thirty-one-years-old, long past the age when it was acceptable to get a hard-on at the beach.

She pulled her hair back, fixing it into a messy bun with a brown hair tie, then inclined her head to look up at him. "I don't have a wetsuit," she said, glancing down at her blue swimsuit, cut high at the hips and low at the back. "Is this okay?"

This time he wasn't going to look. "Try this top, courtesy of Lorne's surf shop." He passed her a waterproof, long sleeved surf top, with a zipper from the neck to the mid section. "I think the guy might have a little crush on you. When I told him I needed surf gear for you, he offered it up." He grinned and looked out at the sparkling blue ocean. "The water's not too cold at this time of day, and we won't be hitting the strong waves, but you don't want to hurt your chest when it's against the board." He pulled his own surf top on over his head, tugging at the hem until it reached his long board shorts. "We'll be starting your lesson on the beach, anyway."

"We will?" she asked, pulling the top over her head and re-fixing her hair. And no, he wasn't looking at the way it lifted her chest high. Not him.

He cleared his throat. "Yeah. I'm going to teach you how to stand on a board."

She caught his eye and started to laugh. "I've been standing since I was about six months old. I think I have it covered."

"Try it on the board in the water without practicing and you won't be laughing," he told her, raising an eyebrow. Put your board on the sand and lie stomach down on it."

"You're very bossy," she told him. "I kind of like it."

"It would be a lot easier if you didn't answer back every time." He grinned and shook his head.

She gave a mock-pout. "That wouldn't be much fun." She

pointed at a black cord, attached to a thick cuff. "Is that to put around my ankle?"

"Yep. But you don't need it on now. We'll attach it when we get to the water. Now stop talking and get down on the board, woman."

She blew him a kiss. "As you command, sir."

He rolled his eyes.

She did as he told her, putting the board down on the warm sand, then lying flat until her stomach and chest were pressed against the waxed surface.

Griff knelt next to her, taking her feet in his hands and placing them at the end of the board. "You'll start off paddling through the water like this," he said, adjusting her toes until they were flexed against the board. "But you need to be ready to jump up when you see a wave." He grabbed his own board and laid down next to her. "See where I have my hands?" he asked, placing his palms on the board and lifting his chest up from the surface. "You want to push up with your toes tucked at the end." He flexed his biceps, centering himself as he lifted his entire body up from the board, balancing for a moment on his palms and toes. Then he tucked his leg beneath him, placing the sole of his foot firmly on the board, before bringing the other one further forward, in the space between his braced hands. "Make sure your feet are far enough apart to keep you stable."

"Like this?" She mimicked his movements, arching her back as she pushed herself up from the board and set her feet forward in a one-two movement. God, she looked good.

"Yeah. Just like that. This time, let go and use your thighs to stand up. Keep your knees bent."

Ten minutes later they were in the water. Griff had left his own board on the sand, and was holding Autumn's steady as she climbed on and sat down on it the way he showed her.

"A lot of surfing is about sitting down and judging the

waves," he told her. "That's something you'll learn over time. You don't want to hit it too early or too late, or take a wave somebody else is heading for. For now we'll practice here in the shallows until you get used to balancing in the water."

"Okay. Can I try it now?" Her eyes glinted with excitement.

"Sure."

The first three times, she ended up plunging underwater, coming back to the surface and spluttering as she coughed the water from her mouth. The fourth time, though, she managed to balance for five full seconds before going under.

"I forgot to say you'll get really wet. All the time. Even if you hit a wave right you can end up going under." He grinned. "It's a good thing you look sexy when you're soaking." He lifted her back up onto the board, his strong hands circling her waist. "Try to look ahead when you stand instead of at your feet. Trust your body to know what it's doing."

"Like this?" She lifted her head, keeping her eyes set on the water ahead as she pressed her hands on the board and bent her legs, scooting them forward until she was balanced.

He grinned. "Perfect. Now lets go a little deeper. See if you can get used to the waves." She was a natural, and it made him want her more. She didn't care about getting wet, or spending more time underwater than a dolphin. She was too determined for that. She was flexible, too, and lithe.

Thank god the water was more than waist deep.

"I think you're ready to catch a wave," he murmured, when she'd mastered paddling and turning on her stomach. "You're looking to hit it just before it breaks. If you're too early you won't be able to ride it. Too late and the foam will take you under."

"How can I tell that it's the right time?"

"Look for a swell coming forward." He grabbed hold of her board and turned it around until she was facing the horizon. "See that one?" he asked, whispering in her ear. "It looks like it might come good."

"So when the wave gets here I start to paddle with it?"

"Yep, and when you feel your board connecting at the right speed, you stand and let the wave do the rest."

She nodded, her face serious. "Wish me luck."

He stood back, crossing his arms over his broad chest as Autumn checked over her shoulder to see how close the wave was. She began to slowly paddle, her long strokes increasing in speed when the swell was a few yards behind her, but she wasn't fast enough for the wave, and it lifted her before crashing onward, leaving Autumn floating in the flat.

"Don't worry," Griff called out to her. "I see another good one coming. You spot it?"

She turned her head and nodded, looking back at him with determination. "Okay, I got it."

"Start paddling *now*," he told her, keeping his eye on the approaching swell. "You've got about five seconds until it reaches you."

Autumn pushed her hands through the water in long, fast strokes, her board moving parallel to the shore.

"It's here," he called out. "Stand and try to ride it."

She slid her feet forward, hands pressed against the flat of the board, then pushed herself to a wobbly stand. For a long moment she surfed along the crest, but then she lurched to the right as the wave began to peak, her body pushed under by the force. Griff swam toward the spot he'd last seen her, frowning when her board surfaced before she did.

"Autumn?" He pulled at the board. It was too light to be attached to her still. Damn! He dove under the water, moving his head to seek her out. His heart began to beat again when he saw her breaking the surface.

She was coughing and spluttering, shaking her head. He

swam toward her, gathering her in his arms, smoothing the wet hair from her face.

"You okay?" he asked, frowning as he scanned her for injuries.

"I swallowed water," she told him between coughs. "And snorted it, too."

Relief made him want to laugh, but he managed to bite down the urge.

"Did you see that I caught it for a second?" she asked, tipping her head up to meet his gaze.

He grinned. "More than a second. It was at least three."

She wiped her mouth with the back of her hand. "It felt good, right until my mouth filled up with salt water."

"You want to go back to the beach?" he asked her. "Try again another day?"

"No. I want to try again now. I want to stand for at least five seconds."

He cupped her face, his hot gaze meeting hers. "You're amazing, do you know that? You never let anything defeat you."

Her lips curled up. "I have a good teacher."

"Yeah, well this teacher wants to kiss you." He watched as she glanced to the side. "It's okay. I can wait until we're away from prying eyes."

"When we're away from prying eyes, I can guarantee we'll be doing more than kissing."

"That's why you're my kind of girl."

15

"Did you ask Dad to talk to Josh about something?" Lydia asked over the Bluetooth speaker as Autumn pulled her car into the parking lot of the Angel Sands Beach Club.

"No. Why would I?" She parked in a space a few cars down from the entrance. "I don't have anything to say to him."

"Oh." It wasn't like Lydia to stop at one word.

"Why do you ask?" Autumn grabbed her purse and checked her make-up in the mirror. "Has he said something to you?"

"I saw Josh coming out of Dad's office yesterday," Lydia told her. "I thought it must be something to do with your divorce."

"The divorce is final. Everything is done. I never have to see him again." And neither should her dad. Autumn frowned. Just the thought of him talking to her ex made her stomach contract, especially when she'd asked him not to. "What do you think they were talking about?"

"I've no idea."

"Did they look friendly?"

"I don't know. I was turning the corner and saw Josh walk out of Dad's office door and into the hallway. I hid so he couldn't see me. And when I saw Dad, he didn't mention anything about it. Should I have asked him?"

Autumn sighed. "No. Don't worry about it. It was probably nothing." It had better be nothing. She gritted her teeth.

"Maybe he was asking Dad for a loan."

"Ugh. I hope not. Listen, I gotta go. I'm about to head into a meeting."

"Ooh, what kind of meeting? Is it with a guy?"

"There will be about fifty guys there. It's a Chamber of Commerce meeting. I have to give a presentation about my plans for the charity day on the pier."

"The one next month?"

"Yeah."

"Oh! I have the most fantastic idea. I'll come out to see you. I can help you with whatever you need." Lydia's voice rose with excitement. "Hey, and maybe I'll get to meet that guy you keep pretending you don't like."

"I didn't say I don't like him." Autumn shook her head with a smile. It was impossible not to be cheered by Lydia's enthusiasm. "And it would be great to see you if you can make it. But I need to go before they drag me out of the car, okay?"

Lydia laughed. "Okay. Send me all the details and I'll book a flight. I can't wait to see you. It's been forever."

"It's been a few weeks," she pointed out.

"I know. But it's usually me who flies off into the sunset while you stay in New York. I don't like it when we reverse roles."

Autumn shook her head. "Goodbye, Lydia."

What the hell was Josh doing with her father? She pressed her lips together and climbed out of her car, grabbing her laptop before she walked across the lot to the Beach Club where the Chamber of Commerce was due to meet. They shouldn't need to talk to each other ever again. Yes, they had mutual acquaintances, since Josh was a commercial realtor and her dad was a real estate lawyer, but there were hundreds of those in Manhattan.

The only conclusion was... her father was doing *exactly* what she'd asked him not to.

She could hear the babble of conversation before she made it to the ballroom. Shaking her head clear of thoughts – her father and Josh could wait for another day – she pushed the door open and stepped inside, trying to ignore the way everybody turned to stare at her.

"I've managed to secure the decorations for free, and the fairground rides will be set up at a reduced price. The kind owners of Déjà Brew have kindly agreed to do the catering as their contribution to the charity." Autumn's gaze roamed across the attendees until she saw Ally grinning out at her. She grinned back. "All we need are volunteers to help set up and assist throughout the day, so if you think you can help, please either come and talk to me after tonight's meeting, or send me an email – the address is on my card, and you should all have one." She looked around again. "Does anybody have any questions."

A slender arm at the front shot up. "What about the restaurant?" Carla Delmonico asked. "I don't think it's fair that we have to compete with free refreshments. We'll lose money."

"The refreshments are drinks, cakes, and ice cream," Autumn told her. "I don't anticipate any competition between those and the restaurant. If anything, the extra influx of people will give you more customers. It should be a win-win for all of us."

"Delmonico's is exclusive," Carla muttered. "Maybe we don't want *those* kind of customers."

Autumn ignored her, painting a smile on her face. "Any other questions?"

A woman on the far side of the room stood. "Is it true you're going to host weddings on the pier in the future?"

Autumn blinked. Word sure got around fast. She hadn't even talked to the Delmonico's about her wedding plans yet. "I'm looking into all options for increasing income from the pier. Running events is one of them."

"I heard you spoke to the permit department. I know someone who works there," the woman added.

"You're going to do this sort of thing regularly?" Carla asked, her brows pinching together. "When were you going to tell us about it?"

"I'll be talking through all the options with the tenants on the pier as soon as I have a plan," Autumn said, trying to keep her voice patient. "But right now the charity event is my main concern. And I can guarantee it won't adversely affect your business."

Another hand shot up, this time at the back. She couldn't see who it was. "Um, yes, the person at the back?"

Griff stood, his lips curling into a smile as his eyes met hers. "As a tenant of the pier, I just wanted to say how refreshing it is to see the owner so involved in the community. Myself and my crew will be at your disposal to help with the event." He leaned on the back wall. "We love a party."

Carla rolled her eyes.

"Well that's wonderful. It's good to see some community spirit," Frank Megassey said, walking across the stage to join Autumn. "And thank you very much for all your work on the charity event, Autumn. I for one am very much looking forward to it." He gave a little laugh when he saw Carla's scowl. "And of course I'll be eating at Delmonico's afterward. Now, let's bring this meeting to an end. Please go help yourselves to coffee and baked goods in the corner, and if you have any questions about the pier, come and talk to Autumn or me."

There was a scraping of chairs as people stood, then a murmur of conversation that increased as friends greeted each other. Autumn felt a hand on her back, and turned to see Ally grinning at her. "Here, take this," she said, passing her a plate of chocolate cake. "You look like you need it. I'd have brought wine, but Frank would have had a fit."

Autumn grinned at her. "I've had worse responses. Try telling a whole building of bankers that their executive bathrooms will be out of operation for a week. Until then, I'd never seen a man in an Armani suit cry."

From the corner of her eye, she could see Carla talking furiously to Griff. "I think I might have caused some problems there."

Ally followed her gaze. "Carla always has a problem with Griff." Her voice dropped. "Has she said anything to you about him?"

"She told me to steer clear and that he's a womanizer." Autumn shrugged.

"I guess she hasn't found out about you guys then?"

Autumn blinked. "What about us?"

Ally's smile melted from her mouth. "Oh shit. I just assumed you two had a thing going on. I saw you at the beach the other day. You looked way too close to only be friends or workmates, or whatever you are."

"We *are* just friends," Autumn told her.

"It's really not my business. I'm sorry for mentioning it."

"With a few fringe benefits." Autumn winked and Ally laughed, relief washing over her face.

"Still none of my business, but for what it's worth, Griff is a good guy. Ignore what Carla has to say about him."

"He is. But it's nothing serious. Carla can think what she likes."

"Does that mean you'll come out with us for his birthday?" Ally asked, her shoulders relaxing.

"When is it?" Autumn asked. Griff hadn't mentioned it to her. They'd been way too busy to talk dates of birth.

"On Saturday. Lucas and the guys are trying to persuade him to go to a club in White City. He was kind of reluctant. I guess now I know why."

"But it's his birthday!" Autumn said. "He has to celebrate. Let me make a plan."

Ally nodded happily. "Sure."

"What's the name of the club in White City?" she asked. "I'll call them. Make some arrangements."

"I guess that's one of the fringe benefits you were talking about," Ally said, still grinning. "Sex and birthday parties. Griff's a lucky guy."

16

"So what's this all about?" Griff asked, as they climbed out of the black limo that had driven them to White City. It was almost nine at night, and a soft breeze tickled at Autumn's bare shoulders and played with her hair, even though the air still held a hint of the daytime warmth.

She looked up at him with a smile. He was wearing a dark blue shirt, unbuttoned at the neck, and charcoal pants that skimmed his hips and clung to his muscled thighs, making her mouth water.

"You've been hiding things from me," she told him, raising an eyebrow.

"No I haven't." He grinned and shook his head. "I told you I'm an open book."

She tipped her head to the side, and raised an eyebrow. "So why didn't you tell me it was your birthday?"

Realization washed over his face. "I don't celebrate my birthday."

"That's what Ally and Ember told me. But tonight you do." She slid her arm into his. "Come on. Let's go inside."

The hostess led them to a booth in the VIP area, and

Griff's face lit up when he saw all his friends waiting for him. Ember and Lucas were talking with Ally and Nate, while Brooke and Caitie were laughing as Aiden and Breck talked about the Silver Sands Resort, where Autumn had stayed when she first arrived in town. Next to them, Harper and James were looking at her phone, grinning at a photograph of their little girl the babysitter had sent them.

"I don't know whether to kiss you or kill you," Griff murmured to Autumn as everybody turned to look at him. The next minute he was surrounded by all his friends, their loud voices wishing him a happy birthday as they assaulted him with hugs.

A waiter carried over a tray full of champagne, along with bottles of beer for those who didn't enjoy the sparkling wine. Griff's eyes met hers as he clinked his bottle against Lucas's, and the warmth in his eyes took her breath away.

"Okay, we need to dance," Ember said, grabbing Autumn's hand and inclining her head at the dance floor. She called the other girls over, and they agreed excitedly.

"What about Griff and the guys?" Autumn asked.

"They're too busy talking about the game tomorrow," Ember said, rolling her eyes. "They'll come and join us when they notice we're gone." She tugged at Autumn's hand, and all six of them made their way down the steps to the dance floor, joining the mass of bodies undulating to the beat.

Ally was the first to let go. She shimmied her hips, raising her hands into the air as her long blonde hair flowed out behind her. She looked amazing in a tight silver dress, the metallic fabric clinging to her athletic curves. All the guys on the dance floor were looking at her, although she was way too busy dancing to notice.

Autumn tipped her head back, letting the music wash over her as she let her own hips and body sway. When was the last time she danced in a club like this, with friends, and without a care in the world? She should do it more often.

For the first time in a long while she felt happy. Really and truly content. Maybe it was the new start, or maybe it was being in Angel Sands. It was almost impossible to be unhappy with the warm sun and deep blue ocean surrounding you.

Or maybe there was another reason. Her lips curled into a smile as she glanced over her shoulder and saw Griff looking at her from the VIP area, as he talked with Lucas. Maybe it was about finding a friend who made her feel excited to wake up every morning. One who made facing life so much easier.

Whatever it was, she liked it.

"One more dance," Ember said when the song finished. "And then we should go and give Griff his birthday presents."

"Yeah, and get another glass of champagne." Harper grinned at their laughter at her suggestion. "Hey, it's the first time James and I have been to a club since the baby was born." She wrinkled her nose. "In fact, I think it's the first time we've ever been somewhere like this. I want to make the most of it."

Harper had filled Autumn in on the unusual way she and James had gotten together. They'd met at the opening of the Silver Sands Resort, and spent one amazing night together. She'd never expected to see him again until she realized she was pregnant and had to track him down. Until their baby was born, they'd been so busy getting used to being expecting parents that they hadn't had time to date the way people usually did.

"Sounds good to me," Caitie said. "I've been working way too many hours this month. I need all the champagne to calm my nerves."

"It's Autumn who needs the champagne," Brooke pointed out. "She's organizing a charity event for Frank as well as trying to make some changes at the pier, and we all know certain people will try to make it difficult for her. And on top of that, she organized Griff's birthday party."

"I like planning stuff." Autumn shrugged. "I'm weird that way."

Brooke caught her eye. "Well Griff's a lucky guy to have you as a friend."

"Yeah he is." Ally winked. "Really lucky."

"So, you're just friends, then," Lucas said to Griff as the waiter passed them two more beers.

"Yeah, right." Jackson rolled his eyes. "Because friends are always organizing parties for each other."

"To be fair, Caitie organized our wedding," Lucas pointed out.

"Yeah, but she's your sister so it doesn't count. Autumn clearly has the hots for Griff, and by the way he's staring down at her, he feels the same way."

"I'm right here, guys," Griff murmured. "And whatever's going on between me and Autumn is none of your business." He took another mouthful of beer and turned to look at his friends. "And by the way, I think those guys are making the moves on your wife and sister." He inclined his head to the floor and watched as Lucas's brow furrowed.

Two men were dancing behind Ember and Caitie, looking down at them as though trying to catch a glimpse of their cleavages. Lucas was usually as mild mannered and laid back as Griff, but he was already tapping Breck on the shoulder and pointing at the dancefloor. Breck frowned as he followed Lucas's direction. "Should we sort this out?" he asked him, his jaw tight as one of the men slid his arms around Caitie's waist.

"Sure we should." The two of them walked across the VIP area and to the stairs.

"Completely whipped," Jackson said, shaking his head. "Good job I have you, bro, and you're not at all interested in Autumn."

Griff opened his mouth to tell Jackson to shut up, but then two more men were walking over, heading directly to the spot where Autumn and Harper were dancing. His jaw tightened and he glanced over his shoulder. "We should go down too," he told Jackson. "In case the guys need our help."

Jackson grinned. "Sure, man. Whatever you say."

By the time they reached the girls, they'd already given the strangers the brush off, and Ember looped her arms around Lucas's neck and was smiling up at him as she asked him to dance with her. Lucas placed his hands on her hips and began to sway with her, leaning down to press his lips against her forehead.

Griff looked at Autumn, who was still swaying to the beat, oblivious to the interested stares she was attracting from guys all over the dance floor. "You okay?" he asked her.

"I'm great." She grinned at him, her eyes sparkling as their gazes met. "And you?"

"I'm good." His body relaxed as soon as he caught her stare. It didn't matter who was looking at her, she was looking at *him*. "Enjoying my party. Thanks for arranging it."

"Any time." She pulled her lip between her teeth. "You want to dance?" she asked him, stepping to the right to make a space for him.

"With you?"

"Yeah. Isn't that what friends do?"

He raised an eyebrow. "I'm good for that if you are."

She grabbed his hand and pulled him toward her, her eyes sparkling beneath the flashing disco lights. Even in her skyscraper heels, the top of her head only grazed his chin as he held her hands, moving them both to the sensual bass.

"You're a good dancer," she murmured.

"Probably uses the same muscles as surfing." God, she smelled good. He wanted to bury his face in her hair and inhale deeply.

The next song was slower, enough for him to pull her in close and have her arms wrapped around his neck. He could feel every inch of her pressing against him, the sensation making him grit his teeth.

"You're very handsome," she whispered. "But you know that." Her eyes were a little fuzzy from the champagne.

"Thank you." He winked at her.

"Seeing you in those pants does things to me." Her voice was still low, enough for the beat to swallow her words up. But he still heard them.

"Yeah?"

"Yeah." She sighed. "Everybody keeps asking me what's going on between us."

"What did you tell them?" His eyes met hers.

"That we're friends."

"We are," he agreed, tucking a lock of hair behind her ear. "Good friends."

"Friends with amazing benefits." That drink had definitely gone to her head.

"Amazing?" he repeated, amusement dancing in his eyes.

"Really, really amazing."

He cleared his throat. "You probably want to stop grinding your body against me soon, or those amazing benefits might happen in front of everybody."

She bit down a laugh. "Sorry. I forgot where we were."

He slid his hands down her back, resting them in the dip above her ass. "It's okay. I kind of enjoyed it."

"Is it wrong that I want you to kiss me right now?" Her eyes were dark as she stared up at him.

"In here?" he asked, his throat feeling tight. He wanted to kiss her like crazy. To spin her around and press her against the wall and move his body against hers until neither of them could think straight.

"Yeah, here." She nodded. "Now."

"In front of our friends? What will they say?"

"I don't care what they say. I don't care what anybody thinks. I want you to kiss me right now, Griffin Lambert."

God, she was beautiful. With her head tipped up, her lips parted, and her eyes wide and needy as they stared at him. He cupped her cheek with his hand, his lips twitching as she turned her head to kiss his palm, the sensation affecting him more than it should.

He stared at her intently, his gaze not leaving hers as he grazed his nose against hers, inhaling her skin like it was an illicit substance. Then his lips were brushing against hers, his hand sliding to the back of her head to angle her face, his tongue running along her swollen bottom lip.

She was intoxicating. One kiss could never be enough. She was a cool drink after a long day, slating his thirst yet making him want more. She pressed her body against his, her fingers raking through his thick hair.

It was only when they parted that he realized all their friends were looking at them. He froze for a moment, half-expecting Autumn to panic or hide. But then Ally started laughing, and Autumn grinned at him, desire still flashing in her gaze.

"Well thank god for that," Ally said, giving Autumn a high five. "I was starting to choke on the UST. Can we go give Griff his birthday gifts now?"

✾ 17 ✾

It was almost two in the morning by the time they grabbed their jackets and Griff's birthday gifts and headed for the car waiting for them at the sidewalk. Breck, Caitie, and Jackson climbed in with them, Autumn having offered them a ride home since they lived near Griff's apartment. The driver pulled smoothly away, making a U-turn to join the road out of town.

"God, my feet ache," Caitie said, taking off her high-heeled silver sandals and wiggling her bare toes. "Babe, can you give me a massage?"

Breck sighed and took her feet into his hands, rubbing his thumb over the soles.

Jackson grinned at the two of them, then turned to look at Griff. "Babe, maybe you can massage my feet, too."

"Get out of here." Griff shook his head.

"It's kind of your fault my feet hurt," Jackson pointed out. "I was dancing at *your* birthday party."

"I'll buy you a foot spa," Griff muttered, then rolled his eyes at Autumn. "Let's drop him off first, okay?"

They pulled up outside Jackson's sprawling house half an

hour later. Griff had to climb out first to avoid his friend clambering over him. He didn't want another request for a foot rub.

"Hope you had a good birthday, man," Jackson said, giving Griff a hug.

Griff hugged him back. "It was good. Thanks for coming."

"Autumn's the one to thank. She arranged everything. Called us all up and told us when to get to the club. She's great."

Griff's voice was rough. "Yeah, she is."

"So are you two an item now?" Jackson asked, glancing over Griff's shoulder at the car. Autumn and Caitie were laughing about something, and Breck was checking his phone, while the driver waited patiently for Griff to climb back in.

"We're just friends."

"A little more than that. I saw that kiss."

"Yeah, well it's casual. The way she wants it."

"And you? What do you want?"

Griff's smile was tight. "I want whatever she does." He slapped Jackson on the back. "Now go inside, drink a glass of water, and get some sleep."

"G'night, man."

They dropped Breck and Caitie off next, and as the car pulled out of the lot, the driver turned around to ask, "Where next?"

Griff gave the man his address and leaned back, stretching his arm across the leather seat. Autumn nestled into him, her head fitting perfectly into the crook of his arm.

He could see his face faintly reflected in the passenger window. Who was that guy looking so contentedly back at him? His skin felt hot, his chest full of emotions he couldn't quantify. Then Autumn caught his eye and smiled, and he realized what a lucky bastard he was.

She was beautiful and funny and everything a woman should be.

Even better, she wanted him.

"You okay?" she breathed, snuggling even closer to him. She lifted his hand and pressed her lips to his palm, sending a shiver straight through him.

"Yeah." His voice was thick. "I'm good."

For so long he'd thought relationships were like cages. Bars that confined his parents until they snapped and spat at each other like wild animals, yet could never part. They just ignored everything – and everyone – around them.

Including him.

But being with Autumn didn't feel like that at all. It wasn't a cage, but a soft cocoon instead. Something he wanted to run to rather than avoid. He'd spent so long being afraid of intimacy that it was a shock to realize how pleasurable it could be.

She turned in his arms, her eyes bright as she smiled up at him. God, he wanted her. He wanted her kisses, her gazes, her soft words... everything. He craved them like a fix. He didn't care what he had to do to get it.

"Are you sure you're okay with me coming back to yours?" she asked him.

"Yep. I want to wake up with you in my bed." He gave her a crooked grin. "It's my birthday."

"The day after, technically."

He pressed his lips to her brow. "Whatever. You're coming home with me."

Autumn blew out a mouthful of air, her head falling back on the pillow, her skin covered in a sheen of perspiration. They'd barely made it through the doors of his apartment before they were tearing off each other's clothes, the sexual tension from the club spilling into his living room.

Griff rolled onto his side and smiled down at her. "You want anything? A glass of water, some juice." He traced the line of her upper lip with the tip of his finger. "A sandwich?"

"A sandwich?" She lifted an eyebrow.

"Sex is hungry work. Plus I haven't eaten since seven. I could eat a sandwich."

Her stomach gurgled as though it was listening. "A sandwich sounds pretty good," she confessed. "Even if it's going to kill my body clock."

"Tomorrow's Sunday. Or today is. You can sleep in."

"Okay. Give me your shirt." She scrambled to her knees.

"Why?"

"Because I didn't bring pajamas and I'm not making a sandwich naked."

Heat flashed in his eyes. "That's a shame. And for what it's worth, I'm making the sandwiches. You can watch."

"You don't think I can make a sandwich?" She cocked her head to the left.

"Babe, my ninety-year old grandma can make a sandwich. I just want to make one for you. I'm not the kind of guy who expects to be fed by his woman. I'd rather feed her."

She grinned. "Okay, let me go freshen up and I'll see you in the kitchen."

Pulling her arms through his oversized sleeves, she wrapped his shirt around her and padded into his bathroom. It was sleek, with bright white ceramic wear and shiny grey wall tiles. She leaned on the basin and looked into the mirror, barely recognizing the woman staring back at her.

It was Autumn... but different. Younger, less careworn. As though the distance between Manhattan and Angel Sands had worn off the roughness and made her new.

She felt different, too. Less afraid of failing, of letting people down... of earning her dad's disapproval.

For so long she'd thought that being herself wasn't enough. She'd twisted herself into knots to please people. To be the perfect daughter, wife, real estate manager.

And in it all, she'd forgotten who she really was.

Buying the pier was the first thing she'd done to please herself and nobody else. The second was falling for Griff.

And it felt so, so good to be this Autumn. The one who felt strong in the office and a little bit slutty in the bedroom. But always safe in his arms.

For the first time in her life, she could see an alternate ending to the one her dad had always planned on. Was she strong enough to take it?

The early-morning half-light was spilling into Griff's open plan living area as she walked to the kitchen and sat on a stool at his breakfast bar. He grabbed two glasses and filled them with orange juice, passing one to her and chugging the other back. Then he pulled out a loaf of sourdough bread, along with some deli meats, pickles, and salad, toasting the bread on one side before loading it up into a tall sandwich Scooby Doo would be proud of.

"You don't do things halfway," Autumn said, smiling at the way he carefully cut each sandwich, before sliding them onto a plate and garnishing them with chips.

"I like food. The first taste is always with the eyes."

"Did Deenie teach you that, too?"

He grinned. "That one I learned for myself. Now eat." He sat down next to her, refilling their glasses with juice. "You'll need the energy for tomorrow."

"What's happening tomorrow?" she asked, lifting the

sandwich to her lips. She had no idea how she was going to fit it in her mouth.

"After the morning sex?"

She laughed. "Just the morning?"

"Yep. We're going to the beach after that. I figure you need another surf lesson."

"Getting touched all over by a hot instructor? Count me in." She bit into the sandwich, a pickle escaping from the end and falling onto her plate. A sensation of flavors exploded on her tongue. Spicy pastrami mixed with sweet, juicy tomatoes and creamy mayonnaise, making her sigh out loud as she swallowed it down. "God, that's good."

"Thanks." He picked up the stray pickle and lifted it to her mouth, feeding it to her. "I'm hoping you'll make a lot of mistakes. I kind of like touching you myself."

"People will talk," she said, finishing off the first half of her sandwich. Her stomach growled with appreciation.

"Does that worry you?" he asked, his eyes soft as they caught hers.

She ran a tongue along her lip, considering his question. "I guess it doesn't, or I wouldn't have danced with you tonight. Or kissed you." She bit down a smile. "All your friends are so kind and non-judgmental. They genuinely care about your happiness, and I guess they care about mine, too."

"They do. And they like you a lot. They think we're crazy for making this a casual thing."

"Oh." She blinked. "And what do you think?"

He wiped his hands on a napkin and reached out to cup her cheek. "I think you're the best thing that's happened to me in a long while. And I'll take whatever you want to give."

Her chest tightened. "What if I want more?" she asked, her voice low, remembering her thoughts as she stared at herself in the bathroom mirror.

"Then I'll grab it with greedy hands. I know it's still early between us, and you've been through a lot." He leaned forward to brush his lips against hers. "But I'd like to take you out for dinner without worrying about people talking. I'd like to kiss you in your office when I've come back from a long day on the water. I want people to look at you and know that you're taken. *By me.* And I know that makes me sound like a caveman, so I'm gonna shut up." He shook his head, grinning.

His words made her skin tingle like crazy. "You want me to tattoo your name on my ass?"

He laughed. "I don't want anybody looking at your ass except me."

She traced her finger around the rim of her glass. "And when I go back to New York? What happens then?"

"We'll worry about that later."

He made it sound so easy. And maybe it was. Maybe she was anticipating problems where there weren't any to be seen. Yeah, people – well, Carla – might talk, but within a few days they'd be old news.

Could she push down her worries? Just let the tide take her where it wanted, and then swim home afterward?

Maybe she could. At the very least, she wanted to try.

"Okay. Let's go surfing tomorrow." She smiled. "Well, today."

"And if I want to kiss you because you look all cute spluttering up water?"

She grinned and shook her head. "Then have at it. Saltwater and all."

He winked. "That sounds good to me. Now let's get back to bed and get some sleep. We're gonna need all the rest we can get."

"I really need to sleep at my place tonight," Autumn told him as they carried their surf boards back up the beach. "I have laundry to do and I want to take a long, hot shower to get the sand out of my hair." She wrinkled her nose at the tightness of her skin. That's what spending more time submerged in the ocean than surfing on top of it gave you. Her hair felt like straw on a hot summer's day, all stiff and sticking everywhere.

"You could always do laundry at my place." Griff took the board from her and rinsed it beneath the beach shower, then placed his own head under, sending spray all over his tanned skin. Droplets clung to his hair like they were planning to make a home there, making him sparkle in the sunlight.

"Yeah, and I also need sleep." She stretched her arms over her head to work out the kinks in her muscles. "I don't get a whole lot of that at your place."

"Blame my hormones." He grinned at her. "Parts of me wake up at six a.m. sharp every day."

"And those parts seem to really like waking up my parts," she said, smiling back at him. His good mood was infectious. He'd kept her laughing all day.

"Okay. Stay home if you insist. But if you hear someone knocking on your window just before dawn you'll know it's me getting lonely." He ran his hand through his hair, slicking it back from his face.

"You don't strike me as the type of guy who gets lonely."

"I didn't think I was the sort of guy who could get used to waking up next to the same woman every day. But it turns out I am."

She put her palm on his warm, damp chest, splaying out her fingers. "And I'm glad you are," she said, her voice low. His heart beat strong against her hand, making her breath catch in her throat. When she looked up, he was staring down at her with those dark, needy eyes. It sent a thrill straight through her.

"You know what we said about public displays of affection?" he asked her.

"They're okay, right?" She brushed her thumb against his tight nipple, making him gasp.

"I think I feel one coming on now." He leaned down to brush his lips against hers, his hand cupping the back of her head. She flicked his nipple again and he groaned. "You need to stop doing that," he murmured against her mouth. "Or I'll take you home and tie you to my bed so you can't leave."

"Don't make promises you can't keep." She kissed him back, rolling onto the balls of her feet and looping her arms around his neck.

"It was a threat, not a promise."

"Tomayto-tomahto." She smiled against his lips.

A sharp trill came from a phone. She pulled away from him with a sigh. "Saved by the bell."

"You or me?"

"I'm not sure yet." She reached down to pull her phone from her purse, her brows pinching together when she saw it was her father calling. "It's my dad. I need to take this."

"Sure. I'll put the boards in the truck."

She flashed him a grateful look then swiped her finger across the screen, steeling herself for the conversation ahead. "Dad, hi."

"Autumn." His voice was clipped. "How is California?"

"Hot." She looked over at Griff who was lifting the boards into the flatbed. He hadn't put a shirt on yet, and she could see every muscle in his back rippling. "And busy. I haven't had a moment to myself."

"When are you putting the pier back on the market?"

He didn't waste any time, did he? Autumn sighed, tracing circles in the sand with her pointed toes.

"I'm not putting it on the market. I'm going to do some upgrades and make it profitable first."

"I looked at the financials. It's going to take a long time to make that monstrosity profitable," her dad said gruffly. "You'd make more money by selling it at a loss and reinvesting."

She frowned. "How did you see the financials?"

"I know people, Autumn."

She felt like a child again, being chided for telling untruths. "Well I don't want to sell it. I have plans."

"So Lydia tells me. Something about a charity day and weddings." Her dad sighed. "Aren't you bored of being in California? Don't you want to come home where you belong?"

No, she really didn't. The thought of it made her stomach twist. "I'll come home when I'm ready." She sat on the wall that separated the beach from the boardwalk, and looked out at the ocean. It was a perfect blue, dotted with heads bobbing up and down, and the white of surfboards as they caught the waves. The beach itself was just as busy, full of families and teenagers. At the water's edge, somebody had set up a volleyball net, and there was a ferocious game taking place, the ball whizzing over the net at a fast speed.

"Lydia mentioned something about a man you'd made friends with." Her father cleared her throat. "Who is he?"

Thanks, sis. Autumn sighed. She knew it wasn't Lydia's fault. Her sister couldn't keep a secret to save her life. "I don't know what you're talking about," she lied. There was *no way* she was going to tell her father about Griff. He'd be calling a private investigator in a heartbeat, and running a full background check before the sun went down.

"You don't?"

"No. There is no guy here. I'm just working hard on the pier, that's all." She glanced over at the truck. There was no sign of Griff. "Speaking of guys, why have you been talking to Josh?"

"I haven't."

"Yes you have. Lydia said she saw him in your office."

Her dad chuckled. "Well we both know Lydia has her head in the clouds."

That was it! The laugh. The one that he always did when he lied. Ugh, it was aggravating.

"Well that's good, because I see no reason for you to be talking to my *ex*-husband."

"I have a call on my other line," her dad said abruptly. "I'll speak to you next week. Maybe you could send through the details of the charity day to Annabelle for me. I'd like to make a donation."

"That's very kind of you."

"Oh and Autumn?"

"Yes?"

"Think about what I said. You need to come home to where you belong."

"Bye, Daddy." She ended the call and shoved her phone back in her bag, grabbing her t-shirt and shorts to pull on over her swimsuit. When she turned around, Griff was standing right next to her, twirling his truck keys around his finger.

"You shocked me." She put her hand to her chest.

"Sorry." He grinned sheepishly. "You want to grab some ice cream before I take you home? I'll need the sugar to get through the night without you."

"Ice cream sounds great." She slid her arm through his. "And I'm pretty sure you'll be fine tonight."

18

"These are amazing," Autumn looked up at Frank Megassey from the black and white photographs spread out on her desk. He'd brought a whole album of them over for their meeting. They showed the history of the pier in photographic detail, stretching from the day it opened in 1899, all the way to present day.

She was fascinated by the sepia images of women wearing long dresses, holding classy umbrellas over their heads as they strolled on the wooden structure. Men wearing bow ties and straw boaters played at stands to try to win prizes for their sweethearts. And at the end there was a fleet of fishing boats, their daily catch captured on shiny paper, buckets filled with fish for the local community to eat.

There was no Delmonico's in the first photographs. No whale-watching boat, either. But the pier was full of life, nevertheless. A central part of the Angel Sands' society.

"I have a lot of old photographs of the town," Frank told her. "My wife tells me I should build a museum to show them all off."

"You should." She smiled at him. "People are fascinated by

things like this." She ran the pad of her thumb along her bottom lip. "Do you think I could borrow some for the charity day?"

Frank blinked. "Sure. What will you use them for?"

"I don't know yet. Maybe I'll blow them up and frame them. Or have some actors in clothes like these," she said, pointing to the Victorian ladies smiling into the camera. "I just like them."

"Then they're yours. They belong with the pier, anyway. And I could talk to the Angel Sands Amateur Dramatic Society about volunteering their time." He gave her a big smile. "I'm the president. I'm sure they'll help us out."

She had a feeling he had a finger in a whole lot of pies.

"I'll give them back afterward," Autumn told him. "It's a loan, not a gift."

He shook his head. "Not at all. I want you to have them. It's nice to see how much you appreciate them."

"I've always been fascinated by old photographs," she admitted. "They tell such amazing stories. I like to imagine what the people in them were thinking, what they were planning to do after the photograph was taken." She laughed and shook her head. "You probably think I'm crazy."

"No. I know exactly what you mean. That's why I like them, too." He smiled at her as he stood from the rickety guest chair in her office. "Well, I shall leave you to it. No doubt you have a lot of work to do."

"Thank you for stopping by." She walked him to the door.

"It was good to talk through the plans for the day. Let me know if you need anything else." He lifted a hand to say goodbye, then walked out of the door and down the pier. Autumn closed the door behind him and walked back to her desk, looking at the photographs once more.

The door behind her clicked, and she looked up to see Carla walk into the office, her long, dark hair swept up into a bun, her pretty face enhanced with a sweep of blush and a slick of red lipstick.

"I thought you were Frank for a minute," Autumn said, trying to ignore the tugging at her gut.

"I knocked, but you didn't answer."

Autumn turned and leaned her back against the desk. "Is everything okay?"

"Yes." She nodded, crossing her arms over her chest. "I just wanted to tell you that my dad will be donating a percentage of earning to the animal shelter on the charity day. He wants to do his part."

"That's very kind of him." Her chest loosened. "I really appreciate that."

"He loves animals." Carla shrugged. "And the restaurant is completely booked up for the day. We should make a good profit."

"I'm glad to hear that." Autumn gave her a genuine smile. "I hoped it would. I think together we can make this place work well."

"Okay. Well I should get back to the restaurant." Carla pressed her lips together, lingering at the door.

"Sure, thanks for coming over. I really appreciate it."

Carla tapped her fingers on the door handle, then turned back to Autumn. "Is it true what I hear about you and Griff?"

Autumn's stomach dropped. "It depends on what you've been hearing."

"Are you dating?" Carla's brow furrowed as she asked. For a moment, Autumn felt bad for her.

"We are," she said softly. "But it's a fairly new thing."

"You remember what I said about him, right?"

"I do." Autumn nodded. "But you don't have to worry about me. I'm a big girl."

"That's what I thought." Carla smiled sadly. "But I still ended up with a broken heart."

God, this was awkward. And a good reminder of why it was so stupid to date where you worked, even if it was way too late for her and Griff. He pulled her in every time she looked at him. Made her heart skip like a kid whenever he was close.

No wonder Carla was upset. If Autumn were in her position, she would be, too.

"I'm sorry," Autumn said softly.

"It's okay. And I should go. Dad will be wondering where I am." Carla's smile was tight. "I guess I'll see you around."

"Sure."

Autumn watched as Carla walked out of her office, then stared at the closed wooden door, her eyes tracing the knots and lines in the grain.

Her relationship – or whatever it was – with Griff was starting to feel like a bubble. One she had to carefully guard from the people wanting to burst it.

Her father. Carla. Maybe even Josh. Everyone seemed to want to break her fragile happiness.

She was determined not to let them.

Mike was finishing sweeping the deck when Griff's phone rang. He pulled his cell from his jeans pocket and blinked when he saw the caller.

"Dad?" he said, lifting the phone to his ear. "Is everything okay?"

For a minute, just one small minute, he thought his dad might be calling to wish him a belated happy birthday.

"Yeah, I'm good," his dad said gruffly. "We're having some work done on the bathroom, and your mom's sent me to the hardware store. Just trying to work out what kind of damn cabinet she won't hate."

Griff swallowed down a laugh. He could only imagine her response if his dad got the wrong one.

"Anyway," his dad continued. "I only have a couple of minutes, but I wanted to ask a favor."

"What kind of favor?"

"It's Sam. His boat's a mess and he needs to take it over to the marina. I'm hoping you can help him."

Sam was one of his dad's old friends. The same one they visited in Silver Sands not long ago.

"Ah, yeah, sure. When does he want to go?"

"Tonight. It'll only take a couple of hours. You can do it, can't you?"

Griff glanced at his watch. The marina was about three hours up the coast, add into that the time it'll take them to drive back again and that was his evening gone.

"Yeah, sure, I can help. I'll give him a call."

"That's great. I gotta go. Your mom sends her love."

Griff opened his mouth to say goodbye, but his dad had already hung up. It was the first time they'd spoken in months and he hadn't even bothered to say it.

After all this time, Griff was used to that.

"What's with the long face?" Ally asked as Autumn leaned on the Déjà Brew counter and watched her expertly work the coffee machine.

"Ah nothing. Just feeling overworked."

Ally passed her the steaming mug, and Autumn took it gratefully.

"I know how that feels. I've been working since five. Two of our staff are off with that bug going around. And Nate's in Seattle for some meetings, which means I'm pretty much working for four." She tipped her head to the side. "I know!

We should have a girl's night to decompress. Maybe we can head to the mall first for a little bit of retail therapy, then go to the Mexican restaurant nearby." She grinned. "I'll call Ember and the girls. What do you say?"

Autumn grinned. She couldn't remember the last time she'd been on a girls' night out. "That sounds good. I need some new shoes."

"I heard you had a shoe thing." Ally leaned on the counter. "How many do you have?"

"Here or in New York?"

Ally's smile widened. "I need a total."

Autumn took a sip of coffee as she made the mental calculation. "Um, maybe a hundred?"

"Seriously?" Ally's mouth dropped open. "I have about twenty and Nate already complains about them taking up too much space in the closet."

"I guess that's the beauty of being divorced." Autumn shrugged, her eyes dancing. "Or maybe the reason for it."

Ally chuckled. "In that case, we *definitely* have to go shoe shopping. I know a couple of great places. The mall's open until nine, and the restaurant is open until midnight. It's meant to be."

"You had me at shoe shopping," Autumn told her as her phone beeped with a message. A glance at the screen told her it was from Griff.

"Great. I'll pick you up once I close up at seven. Don't wear anything too glamorous. It'll put me to shame." Ally beamed.

"See you later." Autumn lifted her free hand, carrying her coffee with the other.

When she got outside, she unlocked her phone and read the message.

. . .

I missed you last night. My bed's too big without you. – G

She shook her head, a smile on her face, and quickly tapped a reply.

Your bed is big, but so are you. I'm pretty sure you survived okay without me. - A

Almost immediately, another message flashed up.

I have to work late tonight. A friend's taking his boat down the coast for repairs and asked me to crew for him. But I still want to see you. Will you hate me if I turn up at your place after midnight? – G

Like a booty call? – A

Pretty much. ;) - G

In that case, you're on. See you at midnight, Cinderella. – A

"These shoes are amazing," Ally said, lifting them to the light and turning them around. "But where the heck will you wear them around here? One step on the beach and they'd pin you to the ground. And if the tide came in you'd have to call the Coast Guard out."

Autumn laughed as Ally handed them back to her, carefully placing them into the dust bag and back into the box. She was sitting with Brooke, Caitie, and Ally around a table at Pancho's Taqueria, sipping at ice-cold margaritas and nibbling on tortilla chips while they decided what food to order.

"I have no idea where I'll wear them," she said, lifting her glass and taking a sip. "But they were too pretty to pass up."

They'd shopped at the mall for almost three hours, and though the time had passed quickly, Autumn's feet were aching from walking on the tiled floors. She'd slipped her sensible two-inch heels off and was circling her bare feet under the table. Maybe Griff could give them a rub tonight.

"You don't need to wear them anywhere. Just put them on for Griff and he'll fall at your feet. You ever notice what a thing most guys have for high heels?"

"Aiden loves them," Brooke admitted, lifting a tortilla chip between her lips. "He's always asking me to wear them, but they're so damn uncomfortable."

"I like the extra height they give me," Autumn told her. "And I've been wearing them since I was a teenager. It's second nature now. It's different here, but in New York power dressing is still a thing. Your clothes are the first thing everybody notices."

She glanced down at the pile of shopping bags beside her chair. Two pairs of shoes, some cosmetics she was desperately in need of, and a black, white, and pink striped bag that contained the skimpiest lingerie she'd ever seen. It was pretty, though. Silky black lace, weaved with pink ribbon across the hem of the panties and the center of the plunging bra. She was planning to greet Griff wearing that and the shoes tonight.

It was fun to go shopping. For the months after her separation she'd felt too low to indulge. She didn't really want to do anything, apart from work, and that was taken away from her pretty early in the process.

Trying on clothes and shoes had made her feel pretty. Alive. She couldn't wait for Griff to see them.

"When are you planning on going back to New York?" Caitie asked her. She was sitting across the table from Autumn, next to Brooke. Harper and Ember couldn't make it – Alyssa had a cold so Harper was staying home with her, and Lucas was working the night shift, leaving Ember without anybody to look after Arthur on short notice.

"I don't know," Autumn admitted. "At first I thought I'd only be here a little while. Long enough to get the pier up to speed. But I like it here, even if you guys don't wear high heels." She grinned at them all.

"I'd wear high heels if you agreed to stay," Brooke offered. "It's nice to see Griff happy."

"It really is." Caitie nodded. "He's like a different guy. Have you noticed he's always smiling now?"

"Let's make a toast." Ally lifted her glass. "To new friends who make our old friends happy."

"I'll drink to that." Brooke grinned. They clinked their glasses together, and Autumn swallowed another mouthful of her margarita, looking over the rim of her glass at her newfound friends.

It felt as though she finally belonged somewhere, after years of searching for a place to call home. Maybe she'd been looking in all the wrong places.

And trying to please all the wrong people.

Her life in New York had felt like a constant battle. To be the best at work, to make her father happy, to be a better wife for Josh whenever he criticized her. Sometimes it felt as though she had so many plates spinning, if she took a moment to breathe they would crash to the ground. It was exhausting. She hadn't realized how much, until she'd walked off the airplane and driven into Angel Sands.

Yeah, she still had challenges to face. The pier was still losing money, and it would take a hell of a lot of work to make it profitable. And then there was her relationship with Griff. It brought her so much pleasure – in more ways than one – but the scars from her divorce were still raw. She didn't want to be hurt again.

But those things all felt surmountable. They were little foothills compared to the mountains of problems she'd left behind in New York.

She loved being here. It really was beginning to feel like home.

And a lot of that was thanks to the big guy who'd be in her bed right after midnight.

19

A loud bang on the front door jolted Autumn out of her dream. She blinked her eyes open, looking around the darkened room. She was wearing the lingerie she'd bought and nothing else, having put the pretty bra and panties on after the shower she took when she got home from her night out with the girls. She planned to give Griff a sexy surprise.

Another bang on the door knocked some sense into her brain. That *had* to be Griff. Had she really fallen asleep while she was waiting for him? Those margaritas were stronger than she thought.

She grabbed her robe and wrapped it around herself, then slid her feet into those gorgeous shoes she knew were going to make Griff's eyes pop out. But before she made it to the living room, she heard a shout.

"Griff, are you in there?"

Why the hell would Griff be talking to himself? She shook her head to try and clear away the muddiness of her sleep. Thank god she had enough sense to tie her robe up tightly and kick off those shoes, because when she opened the door, Lucas was standing on the top step, wearing an

Angel Sands Fire Department t-shirt and dark blue utility pants.

"Hi. What's going on?" Autumn asked, her voice croaky and deep.

"Is Griff with you?" Lucas looked over her shoulder. She noticed a tic in his jaw.

"No." Autumn frowned. "He's supposed to get here a little after midnight."

Lucas's face paled. "It's three a.m."

Three a.m.? She looked over her shoulder to the clock on the driftwood side table, but couldn't make out the hands.

"I fell asleep." She frowned. Had he changed his mind? "Come in. Let me check my phone."

She pulled her robe tightly around her as Lucas followed her inside, all too aware of how little she was wearing underneath. Not that Lucas would look – he was too in love with Ember to even notice another woman – but she was embarrassed at being caught wearing so little.

Her phone was next to her bed, and she quickly unlocked it with her thumb. There were no messages at all, just three big numbers telling her it was exactly 3:21 a.m. More than three hours after he'd promised to be here.

"He hasn't left any messages," she told Lucas as she walked back into the living room. She pressed the phone symbol next to his contact details. "I'll try calling him."

"I've been trying for the last hour. I went to his place and let myself in with the spare key. He's not there."

"You went to his place to look for him?" she asked, frowning. "Why?"

"We got a call from the Coast Guard. They found a boat half submerged about five miles off the coast. It belongs to one of Griff's dad's old friends, and I wanted to let him know before anybody else does."

"Was there anybody on it?" Autumn asked, her voice tight.

Lucas shook his head. "They said it was empty."

She swallowed hard, rolling her lips between her teeth. "Griff said he was crewing for an old friend tonight. Helping him take a boat up the coast."

"Did he say who it was?" Lucas asked urgently.

She shook her head. Her throat felt so tight it was hard to talk. "He just said an old friend. You don't think..."

"It was Sam?" Lucas blew out a mouthful of air. "It seems too much of a coincidence not to be. Let me talk to the Coast Guard, okay. Tell them there are two people missing."

Missing. She covered her mouth as Lucas talked with a low voice into his crackling radio. His usual easy-going demeanor was completely absent, replaced by tight lips and narrow eyes, his back stiff as he held the handset to his lips.

"Okay, I'll meet you there." He clipped the radio back on his belt and blew out a mouthful of air. "They found Griff's sweater in the water about a mile away from the wreck. I'm heading down to meet them. They'll need an EMT crew if they find him or Sam."

"If," she repeated the word, tasting the bitterness on her tongue.

Lucas ran his palm over his buzz cut. "I meant *when*," he said, his voice tight. There was a dimple in his cheek from where he was grinding his teeth together. "I'll call you when we hear anything, but try to get some sleep. Hopefully everything will be cleared up by morning."

"I'm coming with you," she told him. "Just give me a second to get changed."

His eyes flickered over her silky robe and bare thighs. "Okay."

She turned on her bare heel and ran to the bedroom, narrowly avoiding tripping over the new shoes she'd planned to wear for Griff. Only one side of the bed was messy, a new occurrence for her. After her separation, she'd made it a point to sleep starfish in the middle of her king size mattress. When had she started sleeping on the left again?

Ugh. She didn't have time to think about that. Shucking off her robe, she grabbed a pair of yoga pants and a tight hooded sweater, pulling them over the stupid lingerie that wasn't going to see any action tonight. Then she twisted her hair into a messy bun and slipped her feet into a pair of sneakers.

Lucas was by the door when she emerged from the bedroom, talking fast into his cellphone. "No, sweetheart, you stay at home. Arthur needs you, and there's nothing you can do here." He glanced up at Autumn. "Yeah, she's here." Another pause. "Okay." He held the phone out to her. "It's Ember. Can you walk and talk?"

"Yep." She took the phone from his gentle grasp and lifted it to her ear. "Hi, Ember. You're up late." She followed Lucas out of the house, slamming the door closed behind her.

"Arthur was awake so I thought I'd check in with Lucas," Ember said, her voice trembling. "Oh god, Autumn, I can't believe what's happening with Griff. Are you okay?"

"Yeah," she lied. "I know he's going to be fine. This is Griff we're talking about." She tried to laugh, but it came out strangled. "No ocean would mess with him."

"Are you sure I shouldn't come and meet you? Or you can come and wait here with me while they search. You shouldn't be alone."

"That's so kind of you," Autumn said, as Lucas opened the passenger door and she climbed inside. "But I want to be there when they find him, you know?"

"I know. When this is all over I'll tell you about the time Lucas disappeared for days fighting forest fires. I had to be there when he came back. My heart couldn't take it if I wasn't."

Her heart. That's what the strange aching in Autumn's chest was. It felt like the muscle had expanded to fill her ribcage, pushing on her lungs until she could barely keep a breath.

Arthur let out a wail. "He's teething again," Ember said, making a cooing sound. "I should go, but call me as soon as you know anything, okay?"

"Of course."

"And tell Lucas to be safe. He's usually so calm, but he didn't sound it a minute ago."

Autumn glanced to her left. He was holding the steering wheel so tight his knuckles were blanched, and that tic was still pulsing at the edge of his jaw. "I promise," she said before they ended the call.

The streets were empty as they headed out of Angel Sands, Lucas driving his truck past the Silver Sands Resort toward the rockier coastline where Griff's sweater had been found. She twisted her fingers together and stared out of the window, trying not to notice how dark and foreboding the ocean looked.

It was just her imagination. It *always* looked that way at night. But she couldn't help but shudder at the thought of Griff being out there somewhere.

"He's a strong swimmer," Lucas murmured as he parked his car on the grassy lot that led down to Cutter's Cove. It was like he was reading her mind.

"Yeah. And he knows the water like the back of his hand."

"He'll be fine." Lucas climbed out, Autumn scrambling after him across the rocks toward a group of people standing at the beach. Somebody had set up a row of spot lights, enough for her to see the faces of the people standing there.

Jackson and Breck looked up at them as they walked

across the sand. Lucas left her standing with them while he went to talk to a man wearing a blue uniform, his cap pulled down over his brow.

"You okay?" Jackson asked Autumn as she watched Lucas walk away.

She shook her head.

"Me either. When Lucas called I couldn't stay at home and wait, you know? I needed to be here, see if I could help."

She nodded, knowing exactly how they felt. Her jaw was tight, her teeth gritted together as she felt her body shiver. It was so cold out here tonight.

Lucas walked back, his face grim. "The Coast Guard is still patrolling the water. They're gonna send a chopper out at first light."

Jackson shook his head. "I feel so fucking lame waiting here. We should be out there, looking for him."

"No you shouldn't. You'll just give the Coast Guard more people to search for." Lucas checked his watch. "It's only a couple of hours until the sun comes up. If we don't find him before, we'll form a search party then."

"He was out with his old man's friend, right?" Breck asked. "Sam Hawkins?"

"Yeah." Lucas's eyes were on the dark water. "That's right." One of the lieutenants from the fire department called his name, and Lucas walked over to talk to him.

"What the hell were they thinking, sailing a wreck like his boat at night?" Breck asked. "Anybody who looks at it could tell it's an accident waiting to happen."

"I heard Sam lost it in a poker game," Jackson said, his eyes narrow. "He probably wanted to stash it before the winner got ahold of it."

"Griff said they were taking it to the boatyard for repairs," Autumn said. They all turned to look at her.

"You spoke to him?" Jackson asked. Three deep lines were

furrowed in his brow.

"He texted me yesterday to say he was crewing for a friend." Her lips tasted salty from the spray in the air. "He was supposed to be home by midnight."

"So he was definitely on it," Breck said, his voice low. "I was hoping he'd just fallen asleep somewhere."

"His sweater was in the water," Jackson said. "Do we need any more proof than that?"

Autumn turned her head so they couldn't see her blinking back the tears. Was he out there in the darkness, his muscles battling to keep his body afloat? He *had* to be. The alternative didn't bear thinking about.

"You okay?" Jackson asked, rubbing her shoulder. "You're shivering."

"I just had something in my eye," Autumn said, lifting her hand to wipe away the tear escaping down her cheek.

"Yeah, I had that problem earlier," Jackson said, his voice thick. "Must be a lot of sand in the air."

A car door slammed and Aiden Black walked along the beach, lifting his hand to greet them. He was wearing a fitted blue suit, with no tie, his white shirt unbuttoned at the collar. "I came straight from the airport," he told them, his dark hair lifting in the breeze. "Are there any updates?"

The director of the Silver Sands Resort, and Brooke's husband-to-be, Autumn knew Aiden and Griff had become friends over the past couple of years.

Breck shook his head. "Just what we messaged. They found his sweater in the water just up there." He pointed along the rocky coast. "No sign of Griff or Sam, though. The coasties are still looking, and the fire department, too." He glanced over at the group Lucas had joined.

"I've got three helicopters waiting for first light," Aiden told them. "And I've called in every staff member I can get. We'll find them."

He sounded so sure as Autumn looked around at the somber faces surrounding her. Every one of them was here for Griff. If her heart didn't ache so much, it would have warmed at the thought.

Autumn curled her arms around herself, breathing in the salt air. The sun hadn't risen, but a halo of hazy light peeped over the craggy peaks of the mountains to the east, giving her hope that the daylight would be here soon. How long had Griff been in the water? Seven hours? Eight? Could he survive that long?

She felt more than useless, standing there, waiting for something to happen. For somebody to do something that would get the man she cared about safely home. She wanted him to be in her bed, his large body surrounding hers, his early-morning bristles scraping her skin as he kissed her.

Autumn looked up to see Lucas approaching their group, his face grim.

Jackson caught his gaze. "Has something happened?" he asked.

"We just got word from the Coast Guard. Two men were found down the shoreline. From their descriptions, it sounds like Griff and Sam."

"From their descriptions?" Breck asked, his brows knitting together. "What does that mean? Are they okay?"

The heart that had swollen to twice its size felt like it was trying to force its way out of Autumn's chest.

"I don't know," Lucas said, his voice full of angry confusion. "They're in an ambulance on the way to the hospital. I'm heading there now if you want to come."

"Which hospital?" Aiden asked.

"Silver City."

Aiden nodded. "Okay, I'll take my car," he said to Lucas. "I can fit Breck, Jackson, and Autumn in. We'll meet you there."

20

"Are you okay?" Aiden asked as he pushed his foot down on the gas, his wheels spinning on the grass as the car lurched forward. Like Lucas on the drive to the cove, his jaw was tight, his eyes narrow as he steered the car toward the coastal road that led to the highway and the hospital twenty minutes away.

"Me?" Autumn asked, looking around to check who he was talking to.

"Yeah, you." His lip quirked up. "You haven't said a word since I got here."

"I don't know what to say," she admitted. *Or how to say it.* "I don't even know if I should be here. If he'd want me to come to the hospital."

"He'll want you," Jackson said from the backseat. "I can guarantee that. If you weren't here we'd never hear the end of it. So stop worrying."

The sun was beginning to rise above the mountains, pale orange rays flooding the land between the foothills and the ocean. Aiden blinked as the road curved toward it, pulling down the visor to shield his eyes.

"He'll be okay, right?" Breck said to nobody in particular. "He's a strong guy. Nothing can hurt him."

"He was okay when we surfed the scree," Jackson said, and Breck let out a short laugh. "And when we dived off the cliffs for a dare."

"We were kids then," Breck murmured. "Invincible. Or we thought we were."

"Yeah, but we also ended up in the hospital both times."

"Remember the way Deenie screamed at us?" Breck asked. "She scared the hell out of me."

Jack shook his head. "And now she's almost your mother-in-law. How's that working out for you?"

Autumn turned to stare out of the window, letting their conversation wash over her like a cool balm. They weren't panicking, and neither should she. He'd be okay. He had to be. She couldn't live with it if he wasn't.

She couldn't live without him. The thought hit her like a wrecking ball.

She was still thinking about it when Aiden pulled up in the hospital parking lot, and the four of them hurried over to the main entrance, the glass doors opening silently to let them inside. One of Lucas's fire fighters was waiting for them in the lobby, and he walked across the grey tiled floor when he saw them.

"They're on the third floor," he told them. "Lucas just went up. Take the elevator over there."

The sound of their footsteps echoed through the mostly-empty waiting area, none of them saying a word as Breck pressed the button to call the elevator. The silence accompanied them into the elevator, the only sound their shallow breaths as the car slowly accelerated to the third floor, then made a loud ding as the doors opened, ready for them to step out.

"He's there," Jackson said, his voice loud and full of relief as he turned left down the hallway. "He's okay. He's all right."

Autumn looked over his shoulder, her mouth dry. Then she saw Griff standing by the wall, wearing green scrubs, his hair wet, his face and bare arms covered in bruises and cuts. He was talking to Lucas, who was nodding and answering his questions. But then Jackson ran over and threw his arms around him, hugging him tight.

"Damn it, man. You scared the hell out of us. I thought you were dead."

Griff hugged him back. "You can't get rid of me that easily."

Then Breck was there, too, hugging them both and laughing. "You okay? Where did all those cuts come from."

"I got a little battered swimming to shore. I had to drag Sam with me."

"Is *he* okay?"

"They're looking him over as we speak. They're going to admit him to keep an eye on him. He swallowed a lot of water, so they need to check on his lungs."

"I need to make some phone calls," Aiden said in a low voice to Autumn. "Call off the helicopters. I'll be right back."

She nodded, standing in the middle of the hallway, her hands curled into balls as she watched Griff standing with his friends.

He slowly turned his head, his eyes widening as he took her in. "Why didn't you assholes tell me my girl was here?" he muttered.

"I figured you could still see," Jackson told him.

Griff walked over to her, reaching out to stroke her cheek as though he couldn't quite believe she was there.

"Hi," he said softly, his thumb tracing her jaw.

"Hi." Her voice trembled.

Close up she could see a bruise forming on his right

cheek, along with two lacerations that had been closed up with sutures. There were deep scratches on his arms, too. Livid red ones that made her wince. "Are you okay?" she whispered.

"I am now." He tipped her head up with his thumb, his eyes soft as he gazed down at her. "Thank you for coming."

"I was scared to death," she admitted. "What happened to you?"

"The boat hit a rock as we headed out. We thought it was containable, and they'd be able to repair it at the yard when we got it there. But the wood pretty much crumpled under the pressure. We had no choice but to abandon ship. Problem was, we were two miles off shore."

"Didn't you have life jackets?"

Griff pressed his lips together. "They should have been on board. They weren't."

"I heard you say you had to swim Sam back to shore with you."

"Yeah." He ran a hand through his wet hair, dragging it away from his brow. There were dark shadows beneath his eyes. "He started to struggle about a half mile in. The current is strong out there. By the time I turned back, he'd gone completely under. I had to dive to find him."

"You saved his life," she said. "And nearly lost yours."

"There was no chance of that. I can swim two miles easily."

"At night? Carrying another body?"

He gave her a half smile. "Yeah, well that made things a little more complicated."

"What did the doctors say about you? Shouldn't you be monitored, too?"

"They offered. But I just want to go home as soon as I know Sam's okay."

She opened her mouth to protest, then closed it again.

He'd been through more than enough. He didn't need her begging him to listen to the doctors. "Okay. But you're coming home with me. That way I can keep an eye on you, even if the doctors can't."

"Is that some kind of code for a booty call?" he asked, giving her a crooked smile.

She bit down a laugh, her muscles relaxing for the first time in hours. "If that's how you want to take it."

"I do." He nodded, his expression serious. "Just as soon as I've had some sleep."

"Okay then." She blew out a mouthful of air. He was all right. No, better than all right. He was alive and smiling at her like nothing had ever happened.

Right now, she'd take that.

It was another hour before they made it home. Lucas gave them a ride to the beach cottage, lifting his hand in a wave as he pulled away to head back to the fire station. Griff was still wearing the scrubs he'd been given, his clothes too far gone to bother bringing home, and his feet were stuffed into undersized white slippers, the kind you saw in expensive hotels.

Autumn unlocked the door and stepped to the side so Griff could follow her in. The early morning light flooded in through the doorway, illuminating the white washed wooden floor and pale walls. Griff closed the door behind him and Autumn looked at him with raised brows.

"What do you need?" she asked, kicking her sneakers off and feeling the warm wood on her bare feet. "Food? A shower? Or do you want to go straight to sleep?"

He slid his hands around her waist and buried his lips in her hair. "I just want to hold you for a minute."

"Okay." She let him pull her body close against his, feeling the hardness of his muscles through the thin fabric of the scrubs. He smelled different, of somebody else's body wash, but underlying it was the deep scent of him.

She could have lost him. Lost *this*. The thought of it made her legs tremble. She lifted her head up and saw the darkness in his eyes, and knew last night had been so much worse than he made it out to be.

Griff slid his hands beneath her hoodie, his palms splaying on the soft skin of her back. "God, you're warm," he murmured. "You feel so damn good."

"It must have been cold in the water."

"It was, but I didn't notice until we reached the shore." He swallowed hard. "The adrenaline took over."

"Were you scared?" She reached up to cup his jaw. He leaned into her palm, his lashes sweeping down as he closed his eyes.

"There was a point where I wasn't sure we were gonna make it." He let out a mouthful of air, the warmth sweeping over her fingers. "There was a voice in my head telling me to stop trying to save Sam. To let him go and save myself." His own voice cracked as the words came out. "I thought about it."

"But it didn't happen," she soothed. "You're both okay."

He opened his eyes and the darkness was still there. "Yeah, but what kind of man does that make me?"

"The best kind. It's easy to be brave when you're not scared. But when you are and you do something anyway? That makes you a hero."

He gave a little half laugh, though there was no humor in it. "You're biased."

"Yeah. Well somebody should be."

"I called my dad," Griff told her. She blinked at the abrupt change in subject.

"When?"

"Tonight at the hospital. Called him to tell him about Sam and me being in the hospital. Sam's been his best friend since they were kids. I figured he'd want to know he was in a bad way. Especially seeing as I was helping Sam at his request."

Autumn ran the tip of her tongue over her bottom lip. "You did the right thing."

Another mirthless laugh. "Yeah, well not according to him. He asked why I couldn't have waited until he was awake to call him, then told me to send him a message later." He shook his head. "He hung up on me without even asking how I was."

Autumn winced, her heart aching for him. "I'm so sorry."

"I don't know why I bothered. Neither of them came to see me in the hospital when I was a kid and got hurt. Why the hell would they care about me as an adult?"

"You bothered because *you* care," she told him, cupping his rough cheeks and tilting his head down until his brow was touching hers. "Because every kid deserves parents who love them. And they should love you, Griff. Not just because it's natural, but because you're a good man. A strong man." She slid her nose against his, then softly kissed him. "You're loveable."

She felt lost. As though there was no way of making his sadness go away. But then he kissed her again, his mouth hot and needy, and she felt herself melt against him as his tongue ran along the seam of her lip.

She snaked her hands around his neck, steadying herself as his own hands roamed over her back, her side, her stomach. Then he pushed her hoodie up more, letting out a strangled groan as his fingers traced the fabric of her bra. "What's this?" he asked, touching the satin ribbon.

"It's new," she whispered against his lips. "I bought it last night and was wearing it for you."

His eyes brightened. "You bought it for me?"

"Yeah. I had it all planned out." She shook her head. It felt like years ago that she went shopping with the girls, not last night. "I was going to be laying on the bed, wearing the lingerie and some new shoes. But then Lucas arrived and I grabbed the first clothes I could find and went with him to the beach."

"Did he see this?" he asked, dipping his finger into one of the cups, tracing the swell of her breast.

"No." She let out a sigh as he grazed her nipple. "I was covered up."

"Good. Now go into your room and lay on the bed the way you planned."

"You need rest," she protested, but when she saw the expression on his face she closed her lips. God, he looked hot. His gaze was intent, eyes narrowed as he looked at her. A pulse of desire shot through her body.

He needed this. She knew that much. And maybe she did, too. There was only so many things that words could say. Their bodies would do the rest.

21

Griff rolled over on the mattress, pain shooting through his back muscles and making him groan. Bright sunlight was spilling in through the cracks in the curtains of Autumn's bedroom, and he blinked his eyes open, lifting his head to look around.

The space next to him was empty, though the pretty panties he'd all but ripped off her last night – or more specifically this morning – were still there, the vivid pink ribbon a contrast to the pale whiteness of the sheets. His lips curled at the memory of her standing there, her eyes never leaving his as he told her in a deep, needy voice, what she had to do. He'd never seen her look so beautiful. Or so vulnerable. She'd made him feel about ten feet tall.

His stomach rumbled like an approaching storm. When was the last time he'd eaten? It growled again, as though it was answering him.

About twenty hours ago, you asshole.

He grabbed the drawstring pants they'd given him at the hospital, pulling them over his bruised legs. Catching sight of himself in her dresser mirror, he raked his fingers through his hair to neaten it up, then gave up. It was a fool's battle.

Autumn was sitting cross legged on the sofa, her laptop balanced on her thighs, a pair of glasses resting on the bridge of her nose. Her hair was pulled back into a high ponytail, and in those cut-off shorts and tank top she looked more like a college girl than a business woman.

"Hey." She smiled brightly when she saw him. "I didn't hear you get up."

"I'm silent like a ninja," he joked, and she rewarded him with a laugh. "Can I use your phone to call the hospital? I want to see how Sam's doing."

"I just called. He's doing good. They're hoping to release him tomorrow. I said you'd probably visit him later."

His eyes crinkled as he looked at her. "Thank you."

"Any time." She closed her laptop and put it on the table, uncrossing her legs to stand.

"Don't stop working on my account. I just came out in search of something to eat."

"Other than me?" She grinned at him.

"Don't tempt me." Who was he kidding? She was *always* tempting him. His body felt shattered, and yet he could still feel himself stir at the sight of her as she uncurled her legs and stood, her ponytail swinging.

"I'll grab myself a sandwich if that's okay with you. Then I'll head home to get some real clothes."

She glanced at his green-cotton clad legs. "I kind of like those scrubs. They fulfill all my doctor fantasies."

He shook his head at her wicked grin. "In that case, I'll keep them."

She walked into the kitchen area, brushing past him. He couldn't stop himself from squeezing her ass. "Hey, stop mauling the cook," she told him, grinning as she opened the refrigerator. "What do you want on your sandwich?"

"I can make it."

She turned, tipping her head to the side. "I know you can. But I'd like to make it for you. Go sit down, you must be aching like crazy. How are the cuts?"

He ran his finger down the one on his face. "Not hurting."

"That's good. Now shoo," she said, waving her hands in the direction of the sofa. "Let me feed my man."

"You're bossy."

"I'm learning from the master." She blew a kiss at him as he sunk into the sofa's squashy cushions, then pulled the bread from the cupboard, deftly making two pastrami sandwiches. She carried them over, along with two glasses of ice water, before sitting next to him, her thigh skimming his.

"Thank you," he said softly, as she passed him a plate.

"It's just a sandwich."

"I wasn't talking about the sandwich. I was talking about last night. You coming to the hospital, then taking me home. It means a lot." He brushed his lips against her cheek.

"It meant a lot to me that you let me." She gave him a shy smile. "I know Lucas wanted you to come home with him. And Jackson, too."

"I can't imagine Jackson looking after anybody." Griff raised an eyebrow. "There's probably nothing more than a six pack of beer and a moldy lemon in his fridge. I prefer the pastrami." He took a bite of the sandwich, letting out a low moan. "God, this is good." He swallowed and his stomach gurgled in appreciation.

"How's your work going?" he asked her after drinking some water.

"It's okay. I'm trying to get everything finalized for the charity day on the pier. And my sister keeps bugging me on instant messenger, asking how you are."

"What's your sister's name?" he asked.

"Lydia. She's a few years younger than me."

"Does she look like you?"

"I think I've got a picture of her somewhere. Hang on." Autumn grabbed her phone and scrolled through it, biting her lip as she concentrated on the screen. "There you go. That's us at my dad's summer party in the Hamptons."

"The Hamptons, huh?" He raised an eyebrow, then took her phone, looking at the two women grinning on the screen. Autumn was wearing a pale blue dress, her shoulders bare, and her hair cascading in curls down her back. Her sister was smaller, more athletic, with skin a darker shade and her hair blonder and longer. But the resemblance between them was unmistakable, from the same pale blue eyes to the wide, toothy grin. "She's pretty, but not as pretty as you."

"I'm glad to hear you say that."

"What does she do?"

"Lydia? Oh god." Autumn laughed. "She's Lydia. That's pretty much her full time job."

"She's different than you, huh?"

"Yeah. I was the good girl. The one who worked hard and got all top grades and went on to grad school. She was the force of nature."

"Sounds exhausting."

Autumn laughed again. "You'll be able to see for yourself next week. She's coming to visit. She's staying until the charity day. I figure she'll be able to persuade everybody to donate big amounts. She has that way about her." She put her plate on the coffee table, her sandwich only half eaten.

"Can I have that?" He nodded at her sandwich.

"Help yourself." Autumn watched as he bit into the sandwich. "Oh, and by the way, Lydia wants to meet you."

He swallowed the chunk down. "She does?"

"Yeah. I'm sorry, I should have kept my mouth shut about you."

It touched him that she hadn't. "I want to meet her, too.

Maybe we can take her out." He looked around her tiny cottage. "Where's she going to stay?"

"I guess she'll take the sofa. Or she can bunk up with me. She's slept in worse places."

"You should both come stay with me. I have a guest room with it's own bathroom."

"Really?" She leaned forward to kiss him. "That would be wonderful. Thank you. Underneath all those muscles you're kind of sweet."

"Don't tell anybody," he whispered. "It's our secret."

She pinched her fingers and drew a zip across her lips.

Shaking his head, he grinned and picked up their plates, carrying them over to the kitchen. Autumn was a tidy chef, so it only took him a couple of minutes to fill the dishwasher and wipe the counter, until it was spotlessly clean.

"Okay. I'd best head home." He stretched his arms up, his shoulder muscles groaning in relief.

"Yeah. Stop cluttering my cottage with all that bare skin." She winked. "Some of us have work to do around here."

He walked over to the sofa and kissed the top of her head, pulling at her ponytail until she squealed.

"I'll speak to you later."

"Are you walking home like that?" she asked, her eyes scanning his bare chest, the thin pants and his unshod feet.

"I figure it's better than going home naked." He quirked an eyebrow.

"You look like you're doing the walk of shame," she pointed out.

"I kind of am," he said, grinning at her look of horror. "I'll tell you what, I'll put the top on. That way nobody will know what you did to me last night."

"Remember what I said about keeping them for my doctor fantasies," she told him. "Oh, and Griff?"

"Yeah?"

"What time will you be back?"

"Back where?"

"Back here? You're staying tonight, right?"

He curled his hand around her neck and brushed his lips against hers. "Yeah, I am," he said, his mouth curling up. "And I'll bring dinner with me."

"Griffin Lambert, come here and let me look at you," Deenie said, pulling his head down as she scanned her eyes over the cuts on his face. "Ugh. That ocean really battered you about. Do they hurt?"

"They're fine," he said, gently pulling away from her hold, biting down a smile at her using his full name. She only did that when she was cross or scared. "I look worse than I feel.

"I hear you saved Sam's life," Frank Megassey said, shaking Griff's hand. "That was a brave thing to do, son."

Ally pushed his large Americano across the counter. "This one's on us, hero." She winked.

Griff rolled his eyes. He'd only walked into Déjà Brew to grab a caffeine fix on his way to the pier, where Mike had been keeping the Ocean Explorer going for the day. But Lorne had seen him walk in, and told half the shop owners on the boardwalk and Main Street, because now Griff was surrounded by their concerned faces.

"I knocked on your door this morning," Deenie said, as Griff took a mouthful of coffee. The bitter liquid washed over his tongue. "I wanted to check on you on my way to work, but you didn't answer."

"I wasn't there." He glanced at the door from the corner of his eye. Three strides and he could be out of there. Shame his muscles ached too much to make a run for it.

"Oh." Deenie's lips formed a perfect circle. "Were you with Autumn?"

"You can't ask him that," Ally said, leaning across the counter. "What kind of gentleman would admit to it?"

Deenie clamped her hand over her mouth. "Sorry." Her voice was muffled. "I only wondered if she looked after you."

"Yeah, she looked after me." His voice was low. The memory of her washed over him. Those kisses, her touch, the way they couldn't pull their gazes away. It made his chest feel tight.

"She's a lovely young woman," Frank Megassey said. "And she's doing a lot of work for the charity day. I know she's from New York, but I hope she sticks around."

Yeah, well so did Griff. The thought of her leaving felt like a slap in the face.

He lifted his coffee cup again, and noticed Ally staring at him, her brows drawn together. "What's up?" he asked her.

She shrugged. "Nothing."

"Oh come on. You can't look at me like that and then say nothing."

Ally licked her dry lips. "I'm just glad you're okay, that's all. When I heard you were out there..." Her voice faded as she shook her head. "I was scared."

"We all were." Deenie nodded. "Wallace had to hold me back from going down to the beach. He said I'd be a liability." She wiped the corner of her eye. "Promise me you won't do anything like that again. I don't think my heart can take it."

They were all staring at him, waiting for him to respond.

"I promise I won't save anybody's life again," he replied, deadpan. Ally looked away, stifling her laugh.

"Now stop that," Deenie said, swatting his arm. "You know what I mean."

"I do." Griff nodded, his face serious. "And I'm not planning on taking any broken down boats into the ocean again.

It was a favor for a friend. I knew the boat was unseaworthy as soon as I stepped on it, but I figured we'd get it to the marina before anything happened."

"Sam should never have asked you to go." Deenie folded her arms over her chest. "When he's better, I'm going to have words with him."

"He's an old friend." Griff shrugged.

"Of your dad's." Deenie sighed. "Not yours. You don't owe him anything."

"It's over now," he told her. "I'm here and I'm okay."

"I'm so glad you are." Her voice cracked as she hugged him tight. "And you should call your parents. Let them know you're okay."

"I already did," he said gruffly.

"Oh." Deenie's eyes softened. "What did they say?"

He attempted a smile. "I think I disturbed their sleep." It was crazy. A thirty-something guy shouldn't hurt when his parents treated him like shit;. It shouldn't matter at all. And yet his heart ached at the memory of that phone call. Another rejection to add to the already-long list.

Frank clucked his tongue as though he didn't know what to say. Then Deenie hugged Griff again, her arms barely reaching around his waist.

"They love you," she said softly. "Even if they don't show it. Who could stop themselves?" She smiled up at him. "You're adorable."

It was a strange echo of Autumn's words from that morning. Yet it didn't soothe the pain completely. It was always there, like a low-level sound. A constant hum that reminded him he wasn't wanted by those who should love him the most.

"I should go," he told them. "Mike is waiting for me."

"Of course." Deenie nodded. "Would you like to come over tonight? Or I can bring some food to you if you prefer."

"Can I have a rain check?" He gave her a gentle smile. "I have plans."

"I bet you do," Ally said, laughing.

He lifted his eyebrows at her, and gave Deenie a hug, then shook Frank's and Lorne's hands. Walking outside, he let the warm California sun wash over him, heating up his bare arms and face.

A wry smile lifted his lips. Maybe Autumn was right. He was loveable. His friends' concern certainly seemed to confirm that.

But right now, the only opinion he cared about was hers. What did *she* think of him?

Because after last night, he was pretty sure he was falling in love with Autumn Paxton.

22

"I have an offer for you," her dad said, as she switched her phone onto speaker. Autumn leaned back in her chair, staring out of her office window at the sapphire blue ocean.

"What kind of offer?" She frowned, tracing her finger around a knot in the wood of her desk.

"A monetary one, of course. We've found a buyer for you, and you'll actually make money on it. Isn't that great?"

"*We*?" Autumn repeated, her body tensing. "Who's been helping you?"

"A friend. He located a buyer in California. He already owns three piers up and down the coast. I sent over the details and he stopped by to take a look."

"When?" She pressed her lips together. "Why didn't you tell me?"

"Because I didn't know if he'd be interested. But he is."

She didn't like the thought of a stranger looking the pier over without her there. It felt invasive, like somebody rifling through her underwear drawer. "I told you before I'm not interested in selling. Not yet."

"I know that. But that's because you wanted to make it

profitable first so you could get a better sale. But the buyer doesn't need you to do that. In fact, it would be a waste. They have plans of their own, including ripping a portion of it apart and rebuilding it. Your efforts would be a waste of time."

"They want to rebuild?" she repeated, ignoring the pulse thrumming in her neck. "What about the businesses here? That would affect their trade."

"They'd be given notice. His plans for the pier don't include them. He wants to build a casino there. It's been lucrative for him in his other locations. Isn't that a great idea?"

She sighed. A few months ago she would have agreed. From a pure business perspective, changing the use of the pier would be a savvy decision. Maybe one she might have made herself, if she hadn't spent so much time here in Angel Sands.

"I don't think a casino would work here," she told him. "Angel Sands isn't that kind of town."

"Well *he* says it can. He thinks he can work out a deal with the resort there. It'll be ideal for us, and that's what counts." His voice lowered. "I need you to think about it, okay?"

"I like the pier as it is." Her voice was firm.

"Autumn, sweetheart. You'll want to come home soon. It'll be impossible to manage the pier from New York. And you said yourself it's going to take years to make it profitable. You're a real estate developer and agent. A businesswoman. I know you've been through a lot lately, but it's time to get back on the horse. Come home. Let me help you."

"I can't," she whispered. The thought of getting on a plane to go back to her old life made her feel sick. "I'm staying here."

"Is it something to do with the man Lydia was telling me about?"

She let out a mouthful of air. "Yes it is."

"The whaleboat captain?" Her dad laughed. "Come on, sweetheart. You had a vacation fling. It happens. And maybe you needed it. But that isn't real life. Real life is here in Manhattan. It's making deals and feeling the rush as you walk into an expensive restaurant knowing you're the top dog. It's winning, not settling for some humdrum life in a California backwater town."

Maybe she should have been surprised he knew all this information about Griff. But he was a lawyer, he dealt in information. It had always been his currency.

"I'm not settling for anything," she told him.

"He's a rebound, Autumn. Josh hurt you, I know that. And maybe this is what you needed to get over it. But this sailor guy? He's not the one for you, sweetheart. He won't challenge you. He won't make you be the best businesswoman you can be. And I know you, whatever you do you always want to be the best. He won't be able to keep up with you. And then he'll resent you, the same way men always do when their wives are more successful than they are."

"Maybe success isn't always measured in dollars," she told him. "Maybe it's about loving somebody and being loved by them. Isn't being happy more important than being successful?"

"I don't think so, no. And you wouldn't either, if you had no money." His tone was short.

"I'm going to make the pier work. I'll do whatever it takes."

He sighed. "Let me at least arrange a meeting with the buyer. Let him tell you what he has to say. And if you decide to not go ahead, then I'll stop asking. Okay?"

"I don't know." She shook her head, looking out of the dusty window to the pier beyond. "I'll just be wasting his time."

"Let him be the judge of that. Just do this for me, sweetheart." His voice softened. "This way I'll know that I've done everything I can. And if you make a decision with all of the choices in front of you, we'll both know you've made the right one."

"Okay." She sighed. "I'll talk to him. Give him my details and we'll set something up." Once the charity day was over, she'd call him, invite him over, then find a reason not to sell. It was simple, really.

She wanted to stay here. Of that she was certain.

"Thank you. That's all I ask. And Autumn?"

"Yes?"

"I love you, sweetheart. I miss having you here."

She parted her lips, a ghost of a smile curling at the edges. He was aggravating as hell, but he was still her dad. "I love you, too."

Autumn looked up to the sky, closing her eyes as the sun warmed her face. It was the first time she'd been back to LAX since she'd arrived all those weeks ago. She felt like a different person. Lighter, even though all the walking and surfing had put some additional muscle on her lean body. And so much more relaxed than the uptight recent-divorcee who'd wheeled her luggage out into the Californian sunshine.

As she stepped into the crowded atrium, Griff's arm slung casually around her shoulders, there was a huge smile on her face.

She was buzzing at the thought of seeing Lydia. Of introducing her to Griff and showing her around Angel Sands.

"Her flight arrived a little early," Griff said, glancing up at the arrival screens. "Unless she has a lot of luggage, she should be here pretty fast."

"Lydia always travels light. She hates waiting for anything, including the luggage carousel."

The glass doors beneath the arrivals sign slid open and a group of travelers walked through, pulling cabin-sized suitcases. Autumn spotted Lydia almost immediately. She was dressed for the sun, a pretty flowered Bardot top exposing her smooth shoulders where her blonde hair cascaded over them. Her denim skirt had metal buttons down the front, the hem ending halfway down her slender thighs. Her eyes scanned the crowd until they landed on Autumn and Griff, and a huge grin split her face. Abandoning her suitcase in the middle of the crowd, she squealed and ran to them, throwing herself into Autumn's arms.

Autumn couldn't help but laugh, though it came out a little strangled thanks to being winded by her sister's onslaught. A man wheeled her suitcase over and passed it to Griff, before walking away, shaking his head.

"Oh my god, you look so different," Lydia said when she finally released Autumn from her grasp. "Your hair, it's down." She ran her fingers through Autumn's light brown tresses. "And you're wearing shorts. *Actual shorts.* I hardly recognize you."

"It's so good to see you, too," Autumn said with a grin. "And this is Griff."

He held out his hand to Lydia, but she enveloped him in a bear hug. "Oh god, I want to climb you like a tree," she told him, tipping her head up, her smile radiant. "Come here." She pulled his head until her lips pressed against his. "I'm so happy to finally meet you."

He hid any shock well. Autumn reminded herself to congratulate him later. Lydia was enough to surprise anybody.

"Are you okay now?" Lydia asked him. "Autumn told me about your accident." She traced one of the cuts on his face. "Does it hurt?"

"Only if somebody touches it." He grinned.

"Oops." Lydia quickly pulled her hand away. "Sorry."

"Let's head to the car," Autumn said. "Unless you need the bathroom?"

Lydia shook her head. "Nope. There was a cute flight attendant in my section, so I made it a point to go pee every five minutes." She pulled a piece of paper from her pocket, showing them a phone number. "We're meeting up when I'm back in New York."

Griff grabbed her bag as Lydia slid her arm through Autumn's, and they followed him to the parking lot. "Oh my god, sun!" Lydia said as they emerged from the building. "It was raining in New York. You should have seen all the looks I got wearing this at the airport. Who's the loser now?"

Autumn could see Griff's shoulders shaking with laughter.

"How's New York?" Autumn asked her.

"Same as when you left it. Boring. Stuffy. Cold." Lydia wrinkled her nose. "I've stayed there for too long. I'm planning on flying to Hawaii when I leave here."

"What about your date with the flight attendant?" Griff asked.

She shrugged. "I'll contact him the next time I'm back."

And he'd come running. Autumn was certain of it. Her sister was different, that was for sure, and that allure seemed to hook men like bait hooked a fish. They wanted to tame her, but she'd never be tamed.

Didn't stop them from trying.

When they reached the truck, Griff slid Lydia's case into the flatbed and opened the passenger door. Lydia clambered onto the backseat, her bare legs squashed as she tried to get comfortable.

"You want me to sit in the back instead?" Autumn asked her.

"Nope. You sit next to your man." Lydia grinned. "I can interrogate him from back here."

Griff raised an eyebrow as he started the engine. "I'm an open book."

Lydia clapped her hands together. "Oh good. I can't wait to ask you *all* the questions."

Autumn bit down a smile and let the sun warm her face through the windshield, the same way her sister and Griff were warming her on the inside. She was surrounded by people she loved and it felt so right.

"This view of the ocean is *wow*," Lydia said, pressing her nose against the glass doors that led to Griff's balcony. "I'd sleep out here every night so I could hear the waves. So much better than listening to traffic."

Griff poured a glass of wine for Autumn and her sister, then grabbed a beer for himself. "Autumn's view is better. Her cottage opens onto the beach. You can hear the Pacific from her bed."

Lydia turned her head to give him a cheeky grin. "I bet that's not all you can hear."

Autumn shook her head. "Lydia."

"What?" She shrugged. "I'm just telling it how it is." Griff passed them the wine, winking at Autumn as she rolled her eyes at him.

"Sorry," she mouthed.

He leaned forward to press his lips against her brow. Her love for her sister shone out of her. It was in her smile, her amused exasperation, and most of all in her eyes. "She's right, babe," he told her with a grin.

"See. I knew it. I only had to take one look at him to

know he's good in bed. And after your ex, that's a good thing. Am I right?"

"We should think about dinner," Autumn said, ignoring her sister. "Do you want to get take out?"

"No, I want to go out and explore. We should go to that place on the pier."

"Delmonico's?" Autumn's eyes met Griff's again. "I don't know..."

"It's okay." Griff told her. "We can go there. It'll be fine." He knew she was thinking about Carla and her reaction to them. But Carla would have to get used to it. He wasn't planning on hiding his relationship with Autumn, not anymore. Wasn't sure he could if he tried.

Not that he wanted to try.

An hour later, the three of them walked through the painted blue glass doors into the Italian restaurant, where most of the red-and-white checked covered tables were occupied, couples, friends and families leaning forward to talk to each other, the hum of their conversation filling the air.

"Griff. And beautiful Autumn." Pietro held his arms out as he walked to the desk. "Welcome. A table for three?"

"I'm Lydia, Autumn's sister." Lydia reached forward to shake Pietro's hand. "I love this place already. I bet you have the best baked ziti."

Pietro smiled. "Yes, we do. And it's a pleasure to meet you. I didn't realize Autumn had a sister."

"I'm visiting for a few days, and this is the first place I had to try. I've heard so much about your food. Autumn tells me your cannolis are to die for." She leaned forward. "I don't suppose you have a table for us on the terrace, do you? I really want to dine overlooking the Pacific. I've never seen the ocean before."

Autumn's mouth dropped open at her sister's blatant lie. Griff tried to swallow down a laugh. Pietro didn't notice, though, he was too busy smiling at Lydia and calling the waiters over to free up a table. Within a couple of minutes, they were seated around a square table with warm, fragrant bread in a wicker basket that was making Griff's mouth water.

"So this is the pier," Lydia said, looking around, then smiling at Autumn. "I can't believe you own this."

"Some days neither can I," Autumn admitted.

"So tell me about the charity day this weekend," Lydia said as the waiter filled their glasses with a cool Sauvignon Blanc.

Autumn tore off a hunk of bread and dipped it in the herby olive oil, closing her eyes as she savored the taste on her tongue. "We're raising money for the local animal shelter," she told her sister. "One of my friends, Brooke, volunteers there. It's for a really good cause. We've got old fashioned fair rides and food vendors and a series of bands playing at the end of the pier, but more than anything it's about the community. I want this pier to be the center of Angel Sands, like it was when it was built. Somewhere people come to sit and look out at the water, or to walk along with a sweetheart when the sun is just about to go down. I want the kids to feel welcome here, because god knows there aren't enough places around here for them to hang around." She shook her head. "Maybe I'm reaching too far."

Griff was smiling at her, his eyes soft and warm.

"I've never heard you talk about somewhere like that," Lydia said, grinning. "Whenever you bought in Manhattan it was all about yields and profitability. You didn't mention money once when you talked about the pier."

She hadn't? Autumn ran a finger along her lip. "Money will help, too," she said.

Griff leaned over and pressed his lips against Autumn's.

"It sounds fantastic. And exactly what this place needs. Frank Megassey's gonna have a fit. In the best way."

She wrinkled her nose. "Let's hope so."

He slid his hand around to the back of her head, his fingers tangling in her long hair as he kissed her deeper. God, it felt good. Better than all the bread in Delmonico's. When he broke away, she felt dazed.

"Hey, who's that woman looking at you guys like she wants to throw you in the ocean?" Lydia asked, sipping at her wine.

"Which woman?" Autumn turned to look over her shoulder. When she saw Carla standing at the window, she felt her stomach drop. Poor Carla. She'd feel the same if she saw Griff kissing somebody else.

He wasn't the kind of guy you got over easily.

Before she could tell her sister who it was, Carla was walking out of the restaurant and over toward their table, her face dark and serious.

Dear lord. It looked like things were about to get a whole lot trickier around here.

23

"Griff," Carla said, standing on the terrace next to their table. "Can I have a word with you, please?"

His skin prickled at her question, and his eyes immediately caught Autumn's. She gave him a quick a nod, as though she didn't mind.

"Ah, yeah, sure." He turned back to Autumn and Lydia. "I'll be back in a minute, okay?"

"Works for me." Autumn shot her sister a reassuring smile. "If your food arrives, I'll ask them to keep it warm."

Lydia was watching with a rapt expression, as though she was enjoying the drama a little too much. As soon as Griff followed Carla around the back of the restaurant, he heard Lydia whisper loudly to Autumn, "who's that?"

"I'll tell you later," Autumn replied, clearing her throat.

There was nobody at the back of the restaurant. Just him, Carla, and all the trash cans, along with stacks of furniture waiting for repair. With a sigh, he turned to look at her. Her mouth was pressed together tightly, and her eyes shone a little too hard.

"You okay?" he asked, his voice low. She might've hated his guts but he wasn't an asshole. He could tell she was upset.

"Not really, no." She shook her head. "I can't believe you brought her here, to my dad's restaurant, to flaunt it all in front of me. How could you kiss her while I was watching?"

"I'm sorry. I didn't think." He shot her a sympathetic look. "What happened between us was a while ago, Carla. And you were the one who called an end to it. I kind of assumed we were over this."

"I was." She shook her head. "No, I thought I was." She lifted her gaze to his, her eyes glinting. "But you told me we couldn't work because *you* weren't into commitment. That you only wanted something casual. That it wasn't about me."

"It wasn't."

"So why is it not casual with her? Why are you ready to commit with her when you said you never would be?" Her bottom lip trembled.

It was the same question he'd been asking himself for the past couple of weeks. What was it about Autumn that made him want to change all his perfectly ordered rules? To open up the armor he'd carefully constructed around his heart and let himself be vulnerable?

"She's different," he said softly. "That's why."

Carla's face fell. "You said you couldn't commit to *anybody*."

"I didn't believe I could."

She took in a ragged breath, then blew it out again. "So why couldn't you be with me?" Her voice broke, and it made him break a little. Because they'd been friends once, before he'd messed everything up between them. And even if they hadn't, he wasn't inhuman. He didn't want to see anybody suffer.

Especially not because of him.

"I told you before. It's not you, it's me." He looked down

at the wooden planks beneath his feet, fixating on a raised knot. "I was really careful to be honest with you all along. I didn't lie to you. I didn't make any promises I couldn't keep." He looked up. "And I never meant to break your heart."

She stifled a sob. "But you did. I really thought you were a good man, Griff. An honorable one. And maybe I thought I could change you."

"I'm sorry." It was all he could say, because she was right. He'd tried to be good and honorable. Never to hurt anybody the way he'd been hurt all his life. But he'd done it anyway, without meaning to, and it made him feel like crap.

"It's not going to work between you two," Carla said, lifting her chin up. "You must know that. She's out of your league. I can tell that just by looking at her. She's rich, she's classy." Carla laughed. "And I have no idea what she sees in you."

Any vulnerability she'd had was gone, replaced by the hissing anger he'd become used to. The Carla she'd been ever since they'd ended things. The crazy thing was, he preferred it this way. He could deal with furious Carla.

But tearful Carla was another matter altogether.

"I have no idea either," he admitted. "But I'm just telling myself I'm a lucky sonofabitch."

"Luck always runs out," she spat.

"I guess we'll see about that." He rolled his stiff neck and looked out at the ocean. "Is that everything you wanted to talk about?"

"Yeah. I have nothing else to say." She crossed her arms over her ample chest.

He flashed her the briefest of smiles. "Okay. Take care of yourself."

"I will. And you can go fuck yourself."

His lips twitched, but he managed to stop himself from laughing. God, she was certifiable. Her abrupt change of mood made it much easier to walk away from her, even though he still felt like a piece of shit.

Relationships weren't for the faint hearted. He knew that much.

But once in a lifetime you found the one person it was worth risking everything for. And for him, Autumn was that person.

He just hoped he was her person, too.

"So Griff is hot," Lydia said, fanning her face as she sat down on the corner of Autumn's old mahogany desk. "And big. Jesus, he's like Aquaman. But a bit less wet."

"I'm sure he'll be happy to hear that." Autumn shook her head as she pulled an old photograph out from beneath Lydia's butt. It was one she'd scanned to be blown up onto the huge canvasses that would line the pier on the charity day. It showed a beautiful woman wearing a long, pale dress, an elaborate bustle pushing the fabric out from her hips, emphasizing her tiny waist. She was holding a lace-edged parasol, the stem resting on her shoulder as she lifted her head up to the sky, her eyes closed.

Of all the photographs Frank Megassey had loaned her, this was Autumn's favorite. She wasn't completely sure why. Maybe it was the rapt expression on the woman's face, or the beautiful clothes she was wearing. Whatever it was, it made Autumn feel warm inside. Content, even.

"So who was that woman who looked at him like he'd just killed her cat?" Lydia asked casually. "Cara, was it?"

"Carla," Autumn corrected her. "Her dad owns the restaurant. And she and Griff had a thing a while back."

Lydia leaned forward, flipping her blonde hair over her

shoulder. "They did? When? Is that why she looked like she wanted to swallow him whole?"

"A year or so ago, I think. But it wasn't serious, according to his friends."

"Whoa. He must be *really* good in bed for her to still look upset about losing him." Lydia leaned even closer. "Is he?"

"I'll never tell." Autumn tried – and failed – to hide her smirk.

"You don't need to tell me. I can read it on your face. I knew it!" Lydia clapped her hands together. "The big guys always know what to do with their bodies. It's like they understand their power or something, and know how to use it wisely. Did I tell you about the guy I met in New Zealand? He was bigger than Griff, if that's even possible. And when I say big, I mean in *every way*."

Autumn clamped her hands on her ears. "Stop! I don't want to hear about my baby sister having sex."

Lydia laughed and peeled Autumn's hands away. "Okay, I won't mention him again. Or the multiple orgasms he could give a person just by looking at them."

Autumn's mouth dropped open. "Seriously?"

"Almost. But that's not what I want to talk about, anyway. From the way he's been looking at you all day, I think Griff has a few ideas of his own. The guy adores you."

"Shut up."

"I mean it. The way he looks at you is sizzling. He's got this whole protective thing that's impossible to see if you're not looking closely. If somebody is walking toward the two of you, he speeds up just enough to put himself in front of you. I swear he'd take a bullet for you if he could."

Autumn's eyes widened. Lydia had to be seeing things.

"And I've seen the way you look at him, too, so don't tell me I'm imagining stuff," her sister continued, lowering her voice. "He's gotten under your skin, hasn't he?"

Glancing out of the dusty window, Autumn could see the pale blue painted building that housed Delmonico's. Behind it was where Griff had talked to Carla, and she'd be a liar if she said it hadn't bothered her a bit.

"Yeah, he has a bit," she admitted.

"I knew it." Lydia hugged her, the impulsive action taking Autumn by surprise. "I'm so happy for you. I knew all that bullshit about no strings was just lies. You two are perfect for each other."

"They weren't lies," Autumn said softly. "I really believed them. I didn't think I was ready for a relationship so soon after getting divorced."

"Pah. Your divorce was inevitable. Anybody could see Josh was the wrong guy for you. I always thought he and dad were more suited than you two were."

"Josh and Dad?" Autumn laughed. "What are you talking about?"

"Oh, I'm not saying in a romantic relationship. But Dad was always subtly trying to push you and Josh together. And I swear he was more upset than you were when the two of you split. Like you ruined their bromance."

"You think?" Autumn wrinkled her nose.

"Yep. And it scuppered all his plans. You've always been the daughter he can show off. You made him look like a winner. His daughter with a business degree and a successful marriage to a man who's making waves in Manhattan real estate. Did you ever notice that your wedding photo was on his office wall next to all his certificates and commendations?"

"I never thought about it like that."

"Of course you didn't. He's like one of those guys in those historical romances, giving his daughter's hand to the man who'll bring the most prestige to the family. No wonder he was devastated when you told him it was over."

Autumn's breath caught in her throat. Was Lydia right?

She thought about the night she met Josh, at a garden party in the Hamptons. He'd walked over to her with a glass of champagne and told her she was the only beautiful woman at the party. And she'd fallen for him, hook, line, and sinker. But now she could also remember him telling her he'd been talking to her father, and asking about his business.

"When I told him Josh and I were divorcing, Dad begged me to give it another year," Autumn admitted. "Said that I wasn't a quitter, that I just needed more time to get used to things."

"He doesn't like not being in control." Lydia walked over to the window that faced the bright blue ocean, pressing her nose against it. "I think this is the first time in your life you've done something that makes him angry." She looked over her shoulder at Autumn. "And it looks good on you."

"He wants me to sell the pier."

Lydia sighed. "Of course he does. He wants you back home and dating a suitable guy. Imagine how pissed he'll be when he meets Griff."

Autumn's stomach fell at the thought of it. Angel Sands felt like a million miles away from New York, not just the couple thousand that separated the East Coast from West. She liked it that way. Liked who she was here, and the people who took care of her. Sometimes it felt like they'd get eaten alive in Manhattan.

"Oh god, you're in love with him!"

Autumn blinked. "What?"

"That expression on your face. All soft and faraway. You love the pants off Griff." Lydia's eyes widened. "What did he say when you told him?"

"I haven't." Autumn shook her head.

"Why not?"

"Because it's too soon. And I'm not sure he believes in love."

"Doesn't matter whether he believes it or not, it exists." Lydia turned until her back was against the window and folded her arms across her chest, the way she had when they were kids and she was being stubborn as hell. Not much had changed. "And he feels the same way about you. I know he does."

"Do you think so?"

"Absolutely. You have to tell him. And before I leave town. I can't get on a plane all worried that you're going to mess things up."

"Thanks for the vote of confidence." Autumn chuckled.

"So, you're going to stay here in Angel Sands? Keep the pier? Settle down with the man mountain?"

"I haven't thought that far ahead."

"But you've told dad you're not selling the pier, right?"

"Kind of." Autumn shrugged.

"What does that mean?"

"It means he's sending a guy over to meet with me and discuss the sale. I tried to say no, but he wouldn't have any of it." And she was so tired of fighting against him. "But I'm not going to sell. I'll listen politely and explain that it's not for sale, and then at least I can tell Dad I heard him out."

"What a waste of time." Lydia sighed. "One of these days you'll learn to say no to Dad, the same way I have."

"It was okay for you. I took the heat off you."

Lydia's eyes softened. "I know you did. And I'm grateful for it, I really am. But it pisses me off to see him try to make you do the things you don't want to. He's thousands of miles away, what's so scary about him?"

"Nothing. I'm not scared. I just don't want to let him down."

Lydia walked toward her, taking Autumn's hands in hers. "You haven't let anybody down. Not ever. You're the best big sister in the world. I know you used to cover for me when I snuck out at night. And I heard you stand up for me when I refused to go to college and wanted to travel the world." She squeezed Autumn's palms. "I just wish you could stand up for yourself, too."

"I will." Autumn felt sure of it. "Just let me get this charity day over with, then I'll let dad know I'm not selling the pier. I'll even tell him I'm serious about Griff."

"You should probably tell Griff that, too." Lydia winked.

Autumn laughed. "Whatever you say." She reached forward to hug her sister tight, breathing in the aroma of strawberry shampoo in Lydia's flowing hair as it tickled her nose.

There was nothing to be afraid of. Not anymore. Angel Sands meant safety, and Griff meant happiness. The thought of it made her smile.

24

Autumn woke to the sensation of warm lips sliding down her back, pressing a kiss to the sensitive skin at the base of her spine. It made her toes curl with delight, and her breath catch in her throat. The sun was streaming through the floor-to-ceiling windows, the bleached color telling her it was early in the morning, before the yellower rays had stretched their arms to wake up.

She was laying on her front. Looking over her shoulder, her eyes met Griff's as he ran his fingers over her ass, his suntanned skin almost eclipsing the white of her flesh.

"Good morning." He grinned lazily at her.

"Morning." She closed her eyes as he ran his fingers down the back of her thighs, his thumbs pressing into her skin. "You're the best alarm clock I've ever had."

He chuckled. "I aim to please." He slid his hands around until his palms were brushing her inner thighs, the tips of his fingers tickling the crease where her legs ended and her torso began. She felt herself clench at his gentle touch, then again when his thumbs feathered against the warmest part of her. She arched her back, her breasts and stomach pressed against the mattress. Griff kissed her ass, scraping his teeth against the smooth globes.

"You have the most beautiful ass," he told her, kissing her warm skin before he slid his lips down, curling his hands around her thighs to pull them apart.

"I'll take that as a compliment."

"You should." He feathered his lips against the inside of her thigh, then pushed her legs up, until her knees were bent, her ass raised, her face still on the mattress. "And this," he said, kissing her right where she needed him. "Is even prettier."

"We shouldn't," she whispered as he brushed the very tip of his tongue against her. "Lydia is across the hall."

"Then you'll have to be quiet." There was a grin in his voice.

"I'm not sure I... oh..." She pressed her face against the pillow to stifle her groan as he dragged his finger along her crease, that teasing tongue still flicking at her as he pushed first one, then a second inside. Her legs were shaking, and he used his free hand to steady her thighs as he continued his teasing onslaught on her body.

She gripped the edges of the pillow, pressing her lips closed as pleasure began to spark like electricity inside her. "Griff," she called out, her voice muffled.

"It's okay," he murmured, not letting up on the rhythm. "I've got you."

With her trembling body still kneeling on the bed, she felt Griff pull at her thighs until they were wider, then the hardness of his own legs as they pressed against her.

Something else was hard, too. Like steel cased in velvet. She covered her mouth with her hand as he pushed inside her, pleasure flickering and coiling as he slowly slid in and out. His hands reached around to grab her hips so he could move her the way he wanted.

He was overwhelming in every way. Leaning forward until his hard abdomen pressed against her spine, he pressed his lips to her neck, sucking and nipping at her skin, setting every part of her on fire.

The sparks danced, touched, then exploded inside of her, a kaleidoscope of colors igniting behind her closed eyes. Griff slid his hand between her face and the pillow, still grinding against her as he gently cupped her chin and turned her head to brush his lips against hers.

She was breathless, still riding the pleasure his body had brought her. He kissed her hard, her body rocking on the bed, the grinding of his hips making the pleasure dance and hiss all over her. Then he was coming, his body freezing as his fingers held her body tight against him, the lowest of moans escaping his lips as he spilled inside her.

And when it was over, he rolled to his back, lifting her until her body was curled into his, his hands brushing the hair from her face as he showered her with kisses.

"If you wake me up like that every morning, I'm never going to want to leave your apartment," she whispered into his chest.

"That was the plan." He pressed his lips against her hair. "I'm glad it's working."

"This place looks amazing," Lydia said as she walked onto the pier. Autumn had been there all morning – after she'd somehow managed to peel herself away from Griff's body and staggered into the shower. Her body still tingled at the memory of his touch.

"I can't believe you've gotten so much done in a couple of hours." Lydia grinned with delight as she looked around.

Autumn looked at her watch. It was twelve-thirty. "More

like five hours," she said dryly. "I've been here since seven-thirty this morning. Some of us have to get up with the sun."

"Was that what that noise was?" Lydia grinned. "I wondered."

"Shut up."

Lydia held up her hands. "I'm just saying I've never heard you be so vocal about getting up." Her eyes danced. "That's what having a good man does for you."

"Do you want me to show you around or would you prefer if I threw you in the ocean?" Autumn asked, her mouth quirked with humor. "Just say the word."

"Ah, I'll save swimming with the sharks for later. Talking of sharks, where's the pleasure king?"

"Helping set up the stage." Autumn nodded at the end of the pier, where a stage and rig rose up from the wooden planks, electrical leads trailing from the speakers and lighting equipment as the electricians deftly wired everything up. Behind, she could see the *Ocean Explorer*, lights wrapped around the railings, ready to be illuminated as darkness fell.

The pier was exactly as she'd pictured it all those weeks ago when she'd started making plans with Frank. A white flower garland was woven over the rails and around the buildings, and over-sized black and white canvases were fixed in front of them, depicting scenes from the pier throughout the ages. From the early days when bustled women and sharply dressed men walked along the planks just to be seen, to the days when a fleet of fishing boats launched from the end of the gangway, bringing back cratefuls of seafood to the town every evening.

One canvas showed the construction of Delmonico's, Carla's proud great-grandad standing in front of the half-built restaurant, his arms crossed proudly in front of his chest, his sleeves rolled up, and his straw boater perched over his dark hair.

Another showed a huge crowd lined up for the first sailing of the *Ocean Explorer*. A small boy stood by the captain, a huge grin on his face.

"Oh my god, is that Griff?" Lydia asked as she leaned in to take a closer look.

"Yeah. Though he tried to deny it when I showed him."

Lydia laughed. "There's no denying that dark hair, or that smile. I can't believe he was ever that small." She gave Autumn a sideways glance. "He's very cute. Maybe your kids will look like that."

Autumn shook her head at Lydia's jibe. "Come and look at the rides," she said, pulling at her sister's hand. "They're a lot of fun."

They'd only managed to fit a few fairground rides onto the pier, thanks to the space restrictions and safety requirements. But she'd chosen them carefully, smiling that she'd found an old fashioned fairground company to supply them.

Her favorite was the red and white helter skelter, which stood proudly at the center, rising like a lighthouse as it overlooked the ocean. A bright red slide circled around it, spiraling to the bottom where a large cushioned landing area would catch the slipperiest of children.

Then there was the carousel, piped music already echoing out of the speakers as the owner gave it a test run. The horses were beautifully painted, each one with a different expression, hair flowing from their manes as they rose up and down in circles.

For the more brave-at-heart there was a wooden rollercoaster. At the top, the owner reassured her, the riders would feel like they were about to be launched into the ocean, only to dip and careen downward toward the pier, making them scream and laugh as they enjoyed the view.

"I love it all," Lydia declared, clapping her hands. "And all these actors look fabulous."

People dressed in old fashioned clothes were weaving in and out of the rides. The women wore their hair in intricate updos, and carried pale umbrellas to protect their skin from the sun. The men wore bow ties and straw boaters, which they lifted up to greet Autumn and Lydia as they passed by.

"They're from the local amateur dramatic society," Autumn said, smiling as she saw Frank Megassey perfectly dressed in Edwardian attire. "They're donating their time for free."

"Good day to you, young miss," Frank boomed out, taking Autumn's hand and lifting it to his lips. "What fine weather we have for such a wonderful event. Pray tell, is there anything you need assistance with?"

Autumn swallowed her amusement at his old fashioned language. "No, I think we have it all covered. We're due to open in a half an hour. Maybe you can help cut the ribbon then?"

"It would be my pleasure, ma'am." Frank doffed his hat to them, then walked jauntily up the pier, swinging the white-painted cane he was holding in his right hand.

"Is he English?" Lydia whispered into Autumn's ear.

"No. I've no idea why he's talking like that. Maybe he thinks it makes him more authentic."

"He's like a weird cross between Charlie Chaplin and Dick Van Dyke."

"You should tell him that," Autumn said, shielding her eyes as she looked around. "He'll take it as a compliment."

"Sure. Hey, Frank, wait up!" Lydia shot her sister a grin then ran off, reaching Frank within moments, leaving Autumn alone by the Helter Skelter. She took in a deep breath, tasting the salt in the air as it rose up from the ocean. Halfway down, Déjà Brew had set up their booth, selling coffee and funnel cakes, along with sweet sticky popcorn that reminded Autumn of being a child again.

Somehow, she'd actually brought this whole day together. Weeks of making phone calls, writing contracts, begging and borrowing items to add those finishing touches. And it was all worth it. She couldn't remember the last time she felt so content. So happy with everything that surrounded her. It was a wonderful feeling.

"I brought you coffee," Ally said, sliding a cup into Autumn's hands. "I thought you might need it."

Autumn took a sip, letting the liquid warm her from the inside out. "God, that's good."

"I have funnel cake, too." Ally grinned and passed her a bag. "You deserve a treat after all you've done. I've never seen the pier looking so good. Have you seen all the people down there waiting for it to open? There are hundreds of them."

"Thank god." Autumn felt her lungs expand. "I was worried nobody would turn up."

"It's all anybody's been talking about in the coffee shop. I can't believe you managed to get such amazing bands to play for free. And these fairground rides are fantastic. They make me feel like I'm a kid again. I can't wait to ride them later." Ally glanced at Autumn from the corner of her eye. "Speaking of riding, how are things with you and Griff?"

Autumn choked on her coffee, narrowly avoiding getting it on her pale blue summer dress. "Um..."

"Oh god, I'm sorry." Ally grabbed her cup and gave her a napkin, which Autumn used to wipe the coffee bubbles from her nose. "I was just kidding. Kinda. Though I notice he keeps looking over at you."

Autumn's eyes were immediately drawn to the stage, where Griff was finishing setting up the last speaker. Sure enough, his eyes caught hers, and she felt a jolt of electricity rush through her.

"Things are good," she murmured, swallowing hard when

he gave her one of *those* smiles. The one that promised all sorts of bad things as soon as they were alone together.

"It's so nice to see him happy. And to see you smiling, too. I remember when you walked into my coffee shop the first time. You looked a bit dazed and confused. I wasn't sure you'd stay for long."

"I *was* dazed," Autumn admitted. "I felt like I was out of control, and life was just dragging me where it wanted."

"And now?"

"And now I've decided to let life do what it will, and enjoy the ride." She winked at Ally, who laughed out loud.

"Well I hope you stay. It's nice to have you around."

"It's nice to be here. And you've all been so welcoming and supportive. You have such a lovely community here."

"Made all the better by you working hard on the pier. It's been neglected for so long. It's wonderful to see it coming back to its former glory." Ally hugged her. "I'd better go back to the kiosk, but let's talk later. Maybe we can have a glass of champagne when it's all over."

"Champagne sounds good." It really did. For the first time in forever, she felt like she had something to celebrate.

25

The first Paxton's Pier charity day opened at one p.m. sharp, with Frank Megassey making a speech on behalf of the Angel Sands Animal Shelter, followed by Autumn welcoming everybody and telling them how excited she was to be there.

Griff hung back with his friends, but his eyes didn't leave her face once as she spoke. "This pier isn't just about the ironworks or the wooden slats," she said, leaning toward the mic so everybody could hear her. "It's about Angel Sands' history. Our community. And more than anything, it's about the future. I can't wait to welcome you back here again and again, so you can explore all the wonderful things the pier has to offer. And now, without further ado, please come in and enjoy the day. And don't forget to spend lots of money. It's all for a wonderful cause."

"She's good," Jackson said, leaning against the rail with a beer in his hand. Along with Lucas and Breck, he'd been helping Griff set up the stage and the audio system. "You're batting way above your average there, my friend."

"Don't I know it," Griff murmured.

"Yeah, we all end up there eventually," Lucas said, flashing his friend a smile. "It keeps us on our toes, knowing we're the lucky ones. Makes us treat them like the goddesses they are."

"If you say so." Jackson took another mouthful of beer. "But I'm thinking that Griff needs to watch out. She's not just gorgeous, but she's rich enough to buy this pier. And you only have to look around to see what a great business woman she is. Did you hear that old man Delmonico has agreed to donate a percentage of his profits to charity today? That's unheard of."

"I think I hear a little jealousy in there," Breck joined in, giving Jackson a grin. "Didn't you have your eye on her when she first arrived in town?"

"Yeah, but I backed down when Griff made it clear he was interested. Even if it took him forever to admit it."

"So what's the plan?" Lucas asked. "Is she going to stay in town? When she first arrived, she was talking about hiring a manager once she'd made all the changes she wanted."

"I don't know," Griff admitted.

"What do you mean you don't know?" Jackson frowned. "Have you not talked about it? You guys are serious, right? Every time I see you, you're either with her or going to meet her. This is more than the fling you talked about."

Griff watched as Frank cut the ribbon at the end of the pier, and the crowd surged forward. The four of them stood back against the rail to let the excited children and their parents push past, their backs pressed against the iron until they got a little space again.

"We're serious," Griff said. "But we haven't ironed out all the details yet."

"Wait. You're not going to New York with her, are you?" Jackson asked, frowning.

"We haven't talked about that either." He could see Autumn talking to Frank, Lydia standing next to her. Lydia turned around and spotted Griff, and waved madly at him, her face bright.

"Who's that?" Jackson asked.

"Autumn's sister." He glanced at his friend from the corner of his eye. "And before you ask, the answer's no."

Lucas laughed at Jackson's outraged expression.

"I didn't say anything," he protested.

"But you thought it." Griff looked at him through narrowed eyes. "And if I'm batting above my average with Autumn, her sister is out of your stratosphere. So no, I'm not introducing you or putting in a good word for you, or doing anything that might encourage whatever crazy notions are going through your head."

"I only asked who she was." Jackson shook his head. "Man, you're protective for a guy who doesn't even know what his future plans with his girlfriend are."

"It's *your* future plans I'm worried about." The thought of Jackson anywhere near Lydia made Griff shiver. Not because Lydia couldn't handle herself, because god knew she'd probably eat Jackson for breakfast. No, it was something else. Something that made him question his own thoughts.

Jackson was a player, and he didn't want him near Autumn's sister.

Wasn't that something, coming from the guy who never wanted strings attached? The man who didn't mean to break hearts, but did it anyway – you only had to ask Carla Delmonico if you wanted to know more.

Yet here he was, worried about Lydia, because hurting her would mean hurting Autumn. And the thought of causing her any pain made his hands curl into fists.

His jaw ticked as he remembered the way she'd looked this morning, her breath tight, her body supple, as he'd pressed himself into her. Every time they made love, he felt like he was falling a little deeper. It was scary as hell, yet exhilarating.

He'd never felt anything like it. Some of that was because he'd been too afraid to open himself up. But the majority of it was because of *her*. She touched him in places he'd never let anybody see before, not since they'd been so badly bruised by his parents.

And now here he was, protecting her sister from a guy just like him. It was ironic.

"Come on, let's go join the girls and enjoy the day," Lucas said, inclining his head toward the stage, where Ember, Arthur, and all their friends were watching the band set up. "And Griff's right. Leave Autumn's sister alone, Jack. She's completely out of your league."

An hour later and the charity day was in full swing. Music from the band mingled with the excited squeals from the rollercoaster, and the air was full of loud chatter as old friends met, and new acquaintances were made.

Autumn was talking to Ember and Lydia about the old photos she'd had blown up when she felt an arm slide around her waist. She looked up to see Griff smiling down at her. He pressed his lips against her brow.

"You okay?" he asked her.

She grinned, the apples of her cheeks plumping. "I'm good. Thank you for all your hard work on the stage. Everybody's loving the band."

"Ah, I got Lucas and Breck to do most of it. And Jackson just bitched about breaking a nail."

Ember coughed out a laugh, hiding her face in Arthur's fluffy hair.

"Who's Jackson?" Lydia asked.

"Nobody you need to know." Griff lowered his mouth to whisper in Autumn's ear. "He's already asked whether your sister is single. You might want to warn her."

"She'd eat Jackson for breakfast." Autumn shook her head.

Griff looked stunned. "I had that exact same thought."

"That's because you two are nauseatingly in tune with each other," Lydia told them. "And seriously, who's Jackson and why do I want to eat him?"

Ember laughed again. "I'm going to let you two dig your way out of this one. And for what it's worth, Jack's a good guy. He just needs someone to tame him a little."

"He's wild?" Lydia asked, leaning in close to tickle Arthur's pudgy cheeks. "Why do I like the sound of him already."

"He's not wild. He runs his own business. But he's not great with women." Griff sighed, deciding to change the subject. "Anybody want a drink?"

"I'd love one." Lydia grinned. "Is it too early for champ..." Her voice trailed off, and she swallowed hard as she stared over Autumn's shoulder. "Um, it's okay. I'm not thirsty." Her faced paled as she pulled her gaze to Autumn's.

"What's wrong?" Autumn asked her. "You never turn down champagne."

"Did you invite Dad?" Lydia asked, her brows pinched together.

"No. Why would I?" Autumn smiled at the suggestion. "He wouldn't have come if I did."

"You might want to turn around." Lydia's voice was low. "Oh shit, is that Josh with him?"

"Who's Josh?" Griff asked.

It was as if Autumn's neck muscles had gone into spasm, as she stopped mid turn. Little goose bumps broke out across her skin. Without thinking, she stepped out of Griff's embrace. His arm fell back to his side, and he looked down, as though he was surprised to see it there.

"Josh is my ex-husband," Autumn said, before she finally managed to turn and look at the coming onslaught.

Autumn was as stiff as a board beside him. Griff leaned closer to check if she was actually breathing. Natural instinct made his arm want to curl back around her and pull her close, but he somehow resisted the urge.

He got the feeling it wouldn't have been welcome.

"Why the hell are they here?" Lydia asked. "And who's that man with them?"

"I have no idea." Autumn's voice was croaky. She glanced at her sister and then back at the three men walking toward them, as though she had no idea what to do next.

Griff wasn't sure whether he should disappear or walk forward to shake her dad's hand. Autumn was giving him no clues, so he licked his lips, watching as they approached.

"I should..." Autumn's hand fluttered to her neck, "go talk to them." Her wide eyes caught his. "I'll catch you later, okay?"

No, it really didn't feel okay. He felt invaded, like these men dressed in dark suits and sharp ties were here to stake a claim. His fists curled with the need to defend what was his.

God, he really was a caveman. Autumn was her own person and she didn't need defending.

Yeah, well tell his body that.

Ember licked her lips, shifting Arthur in her arms. "Maybe we should go find Lucas?" she said to Griff, curling her lips in what looked like a smile. "Come on."

"Are you okay?" he asked Autumn before she could walk away or Ember could pull him away. He wasn't sure what he wanted the answer to be. Yes, he wanted her to be okay, but he also wanted her to want him to stay.

Christ, what a mess his head was.

"Yeah," she said, not looking at him. "I just need to find out why they're here."

"You want me to stay here with you?"

Her eyes widened at his question. "No," she said quickly. "I don't think you should... Ember's right, you should go."

Her suggestion felt like a slap on the face.

"Autumn!" her father boomed. "We've been looking all over for you. What's going on?" He looked around, a bemused expression on his face. "Why didn't you answer your phone? I've been calling you all morning." His eyes alighted on Lydia. "And you, too."

Lydia shrugged. "I left my phone back at Griff's place. And Autumn's been a bit busy. She organized this whole event single handedly."

"Not quite." Autumn shook her head.

"Who's Griff?" Josh asked.

"I am." Griff's jaw was tight as his gaze met her ex-husband's.

"And you're dating Lydia?" He laughed. "Oh man, I don't know whether to hug you or stage an intervention."

"We're not dating." Lydia frowned. "I've only been here a few days."

"Doesn't usually stop you," Josh murmured.

Lydia shot him a dirty look. "I just remembered why I'm glad you're Autumn's ex. And for the record, it's not me Griff's dating, it's Autumn. If you can call hot sex at all hours of the day dating."

26

"Okay, I really think we should get out of here." Ember hitched Arthur into the crook of her right arm and slid her left into Griff's as they watched Autumn take her father, her ex-husband, and the other man into her office. Before she closed the door, Autumn shot Griff a look that he couldn't quite translate.

Whatever it was, he didn't like it. He gritted his teeth at the thought of her in that room with the father who always tried to railroad her, and the husband who'd hurt her. Gently pulling his arm from Ember's, he turned to walk over to the office.

"Griff, don't." Lydia put her hand on his substantial chest, her eyebrows rising up as though she was surprised at the muscles there. "Ember's right, you should go. Be cool and let Autumn handle this."

"I'm not going anywhere until they leave. Who was that other guy with them?"

"I don't know," Lydia admitted. "I've never seen him before."

"Then I guess there's only one way to find out." He

started walking toward the office, his strides so long that Lydia had to break into a fast jog to keep up with him.

"Seriously, Griff, let Autumn manage this. She'll be mortified if you go in there all guns blazing."

"But what if she needs some support?" He slowed down to look at Lydia. Her cheeks were pink, her mouth open as she panted.

"I'll tell you what," Lydia said, sliding between Griff and the office door. "Let me go in. I'll find out who that man is and what the hell Josh is doing here. Autumn's had enough of guys thinking they know best for her. Let her sort this out herself."

"I don't like it."

"I get that. I don't like it much either." Lydia gave him a worried smile. "Just give me a few minutes, okay?"

He looked through the grimy windows of the office. The sun was shining too bright for him to make out anything more than the shadows of the people inside. All he could see was himself, his jaw set straight, his arms hanging at his side, and his hands forming two formidable fists.

Lydia opened the door, and he tried to see past her, but she pulled it closed too fast. But he heard the raised voices, and they made him grit his teeth.

"What's going on?" Carla asked, coming to a stop beside him. "I heard yelling."

"Nothing," Griff said through his clenched jaw. "Go back to the restaurant."

"Why are you hanging around here staring at the office like you want to kill somebody?" Carla tried to peer around him.

"No reason." He wanted to swat her off like a fly.

"Are you okay?" she asked him, laying a hand on his arm. The edge of concern in her voice made him feel like an asshole. "Is there a problem with Autumn?"

"No." Would she just leave already? He could feel the fire burning inside him, heating up the fear and anger laying right below the surface.

The office door opened, and Lydia stepped out, pulling her bottom lip between her teeth the same way he'd seen Autumn do a hundred times. She looked at Carla with a wary expression, then sighed and walked toward them. "Okay, we should go," Lydia said, inclining her head to the passage between the office and the restaurant.

"Is Autumn okay?" Griff turned his back on Carla.

"Um..."

"Have you found out who the other guy is?" he asked, nodding his head at the door.

"His name's Carlsson. He's a property developer from L.A."

"What's a property developer doing here?" Carla frowned.

"I'm sorry, who are you?" Lydia asked her, though Griff was perfectly aware that she knew exactly who Carla was.

Carla squared her shoulders. "You know who I am. My dad owns this restaurant. So who's the property developer? Why is he here? Are they talking about changes to the pier?"

The door opened again, and the three of them looked at it expectantly. But instead of Autumn walking out, it was Josh. He gave Lydia a huge grin. To Griff's satisfaction, she gave him a scowl in return.

"You want me to point you to the airport?" she asked him.

"Hi, I'm Carla Delmonico." Carla pushed past Griff and Lydia to offer Josh her hand. "A friend of Autumn's. I don't think we've been introduced."

Josh's eyes lit up. "Hey Carla, it's good to meet you."

"And you are?" Carla prompted.

Griff looked at Lydia, and she lifted her shoulders back at him. It was like watching a train wreck. If two exes meet, does the universe implode?

"I'm Josh Garner. Autumn's husband."

"*Ex*-husband," Lydia corrected him, and Josh turned to look at her.

"Sorry," he said, that inane grin never wavering. "It's been such a short time, I forget about that."

"I didn't know Autumn was married." Carla's gaze slid to Griff. "Did you know?" she asked him. He hated the way her expression was full of compassion.

"Yeah," he said roughly. "I know all about the divorce."

"You must be Gruff. The whaleboat captain. Autumn's dad has told me all about you."

"It's Griffin," He shook the man's hand, trying not to smile as his grip made Josh wince.

"Of course it is. Though Gruff rhymes with rough, which kind of suits you, right?"

"Sorry, can we get back to the property developer that Autumn's talking to?" Carla said. "I didn't know she had plans to develop this place."

"Oh, she doesn't," Josh said casually. "She wants to sell it to him."

It felt like a punch in Griff's gut. "She's selling the pier?" he asked, frowning as he tried to take it in.

"His offer's too good to refuse," Josh carried on. "I should know, I'm the one who found him. She's one lucky son of a gun to find someone willing to pay that much money. Especially since she was completely hammered when she clicked the buy button."

"She was?" Carla's mouth dropped open. "As in drunk?"

"To her eyeballs." Josh grinned. "Didn't she tell you the story? She woke up to the listing on her browser. Couldn't even remember sending an offer in, but she did. If it had been me, I'd have rescinded right away, but you know Autumn." He shook his head, chuckling. "She has this sense of duty and felt she had to do her best for the place."

The way Josh was talking about Autumn, as though she was still his wife, made Griff's teeth grind together.

"How do you know all of this?" Lydia asked Josh, her face even redder than when she'd run after Griff.

"Well from you, of course," Josh said, shaking his head as if she'd just told the funniest joke. "Via your dad. He said you told him it was all a drunken mistake."

"I didn't say that," Lydia muttered. "Not in those words, anyway. You're twisting them." She turned her head, her eyes catching Griff's. "It wasn't a mistake. It never has been. She wanted to come here."

"She wanted to hurt her dad. And probably me, too. God knows I hurt her enough." For the first time, the smile slid from Josh's lips. "I'm just hoping I can make it up to her and get her to come home with her head held high." He shrugged. "I can't help but feel this is all my fault."

"So that's why you're here? To make up for being such an asshole?" Lydia's laugh was short. "When did you die and become Mother Teresa?"

"Isn't Mother Teresa dead?" Carla asked, frowning.

Griff's nails dug into the hard skin on his palms. Not that he felt it, not really. He was too damn confused for all that.

Autumn bought this place as a mistake? Though he'd never asked her outright why she'd purchased the pier and come to Angel Sands, it still felt like a lie. The kind of story she should have told him while they were curled up in bed together, their voices heavy with sated desire.

So why didn't she tell him? He could understand her being a little embarrassed about it, but they'd been naked together so many times, for god's sake. They were way beyond being embarrassed about things they'd done.

He swallowed hard, remembering something she'd said to him after the first time they'd kissed at the top of the cliff.

I'm making bad decisions left, right, and center at the moment.

She'd been talking about buying the pier, he was certain of it now. But not just about the pier. More than one decision. At least two.

The second one was kissing him.

You were a mistake. You always have been. The voice in his head sounded exactly like his mom's.

It made him feel sick. Like the kid he'd been when he'd cried in the hospital, the only one in the pediatric ward not surrounded by adults who loved him when he'd been injured.

A mistake.

A bad decision.

It all added up to the same thing. He wasn't wanted.

"I gotta go," Griff said, shaking his head, though the messy thought refused to move.

Lydia reached out for his arm. "You should wait to talk to Autumn. She'll be out soon."

"I can't." He shrugged her off in the same gentle way he'd eluded Ember. When you're as big as he was, you knew how to stop from hurting others inadvertently.

Funny how he couldn't stop himself from hurting, though. Not when the word 'mistake' was battering around in his head like a pinball on speed. He heard it in his mom's voice, a little bit screechy, and a whole lot of painful.

For all his life he'd gotten in the way of her plans. Was he getting in the way of Autumn's, too?

Christ, he needed a drink. Or five.

"The pier isn't for sale," Autumn said, looking from her father to Mr. Carlsson and back again. "I'm sorry for your wasted journey."

"Of course it's for sale." Her dad did that lying laugh again. It grated her nerves like cheese. "As I explained,

Autumn has gotten attached to this place. Who wouldn't? It's a beautiful property in a beautiful town." His steely eyes slid to Autumn's. "Hence the agreed price."

"Dad..."

"Actually, could you give us a minute?" her father quickly said, striding over to the door and pulling it open. He beckoned at Josh, who was standing with Lydia and Carla of all people. Autumn frowned, wondering where Griff was.

"Josh, can you take Mr. Carlsson on a tour of the pier?"

"Now?" Josh asked, frowning just a little.

"Yes. I want to talk to my daughter alone."

"Oh, sure," he smiled agreeably. "Let's go."

Autumn watched as they left, her arms folded tightly across her chest. All the adrenaline shooting through her veins seemed to evaporate, making her body feel leaden and achy. She collapsed into a chair, frowning as she tried to work out how the day had morphed from triumph into disaster.

She should have been up front with her dad about the pier not being for sale. It was her own stupid fault that this had happened.

"Why didn't you tell me you were coming?" Autumn asked him.

"Because I wanted to surprise you."

She wasn't going to hit something. Not even if her fists were aching to feel the wood of her desk. "You should have called. You've just wasted twenty-four hours for nothing. And I haven't even gotten started on Josh being here. Why the hell have you involved him in this?"

"Because he has good contacts, and he wanted to help. He feels bad that you bought this place while you were drinking away your sorrows." Her dad frowned. "You should have told me all about that from the start, by the way. I could have stopped the sale."

"I didn't want you to. I wanted to buy the pier." She blew

out a mouthful of air. "And I'm glad I did, because it brought me back to life again. Made me realize I can make it on my own. Without Josh and our business. And without *your* help."

His face fell, and she winced. That hadn't exactly come out right.

"If you don't sell, it's going to be impossible to manage this place from New York. Which means you'll have to employ somebody to do it for you, and that'll eat into your profits even more." He leaned forward and cupped her face. "Think about what you could do with the money if you sell. I'll help you set up a new business if you want." He blinked at her expression, hastily pulling his hand away. "Or I can let you do it yourself," he added quickly. "But it'll give you the freedom to choose."

She took a deep breath, steeling herself. "I don't know that I want to come back," she said, not quite able to meet his eye. "I like it here."

He didn't respond for a full thirty seconds, and her nerves felt every one of them. She could hear the blood rushing through her ears, matching the beat of the music from the stage.

"Is it about that man?"

"Why does it have to be about a man?" She shook her head. "It's about me. What I want. What makes me happy."

"You left because of Josh. And now you want to stay here because of this captain. That doesn't sound like you're using your business sense to me." He sat on the edge of the desk in front of her. "You've had a hard couple of years, sweetheart. I know how tough the divorce was on you. Plus losing the business. And I can see the lure of escaping somewhere new and leaving all your troubles behind. But if you stay here, you'll wake up one day and realize what a huge mistake you made. You're my daughter. I know you better than anybody does."

His voice quieted. "And I really want you to come home. I miss you."

Her eyes welled up. "I miss you, too."

"Then sell the pier. You could fly home with me tomorrow, and leave all this behind. Let me take care of this for you."

Her stomach dropped at the hope she saw in his eyes, because to her the situation felt hopeless. No matter what she did, somebody was going to get hurt. Her dad, Griff, and even herself. She hated that thought.

"I can't," she whispered, giving him a watery half-smile.

"Why not?"

"Because I love Griff. I want to stay here with him."

Her dad shook his head. "That's not love. It's infatuation."

"How would you know? You haven't even met him."

"I don't need to. I know *you*, sweetheart, and that's enough. I know how ambitious you are. Or how ambitious you used to be, before you came over here and seemed to give up. I know how much you loved working in Manhattan, how much you enjoyed running a big business." He leaned toward her, and touched her face again. "The Autumn I know would never be happy living here for the rest of her life."

"Then maybe you don't know me at all," she said softly, a tear sliding down her cheek. She wiped it away with the back of her hand and stood, looking at the door. "I need to get back out there and check that everything's okay." And she wanted to talk to Griff, too. "You can stay here if you want, or come and enjoy the charity day."

"I'll come."

"Okay then."

It was almost a surprise the pier was still full of people when she stepped outside. It felt like she'd been in the office for hours, long enough for the sun to go down and come up again. Lydia was leaning on the rail, her face serious as she caught Autumn's glance.

"You okay?" she asked, looking warily from Autumn to their father.

"Yeah." Autumn gave a quick nod. "Um, where did Griff go?"

Lydia took her arm and pulled her away from their dad. "It's all my fault, she whispered, walking Autumn over to the side of the pier. "Well, it's Dad's fault really, for bringing Josh. He's such an asshole. I never knew what you saw in him."

"Did Josh say something to Griff?" Autumn felt her stomach churn.

"He was just being his usual self. Making things ten times worse than they already were." She took a deep breath. "He told Griff you only bought the pier because you were drunk. That it had been a mistake."

"How did he know that?" Autumn felt her breath catch in her throat.

Lydia bit her lip. "I told Dad, who must have told him. I'm so sorry, I should never have said anything. But Dad's always talking about you as if you're some kind of perfect daughter. I wanted him to know you're human, but you're also perfectly able to manage your own problems." She sighed. "I know I've made things ten times worse."

Autumn squeezed her eyes shut. "All right," she said softly. "So that little sordid secret's out. It's okay, isn't it? What else did Josh say?"

"Nothing. But Griff left looking pissed. That's when Dad asked Josh to take the buyer on a tour of the pier."

"He looked pissed? Why? Because I actually do stupid things when I'm drunk?" She didn't understand. Not at all. Why was it even an issue?

"I don't know. I asked him to wait for you." Lydia's voice

was small. "I'm so sorry. I'm such an idiot. I should think before I speak."

"No, you shouldn't. I like you the way you are, loose lips and all." Autumn hugged her. She'd fallen out with enough people already, there was no way she was going to let this come between her and Lydia.

"Thank you," Lydia mumbled into her shoulder. "Now go and find Griff. The two of you have some talking to do.

27

It took almost thirty minutes to make her way down the pier, thanks to all the people who wanted to talk to her about the charity day, and a few snafus that required her attention. With every minute that passed, Autumn felt her anxiety increase, especially when Griff didn't return the messages she quickly tapped out on her phone.

Was he really that angry about her getting drunk?

She weaved through the crowd, her head turning from side to side as she sought him out. It was infuriating – he should be easy to spot, but she couldn't see him anywhere.

Then her gaze landed on his boat. The gangplank was down. She tried to remember if it had been that way earlier. Taking a deep breath, she walked onboard, feeling the gentle bob of the anchored boat as the waves lapped against it.

"Griff?" she called out, feeling a strange shiver snake down her spine. "Are you here?"

She was about to turn back when she heard a sound coming from the front of the boat. She walked past the cabin, and the ladder that led to the wheelroom. Her eyes landing on him sitting on a bench, a glass full of something amber held to his lips as he looked out to shore.

She could see the outline of his muscles through his thin t-shirt. Was it only this morning she was running her hands all over them?

"I've been looking for you," she said softly.

He stood as soon as he heard her, the glass still in one hand. There was a blankness in his eyes. "I've been right here." He lifted up a bottle that was resting on the bench beside him. "Did you know this whiskey's been here since my dad ran the boat? He must have forgotten to take it with him when he left." He shook his head. "About the only thing he's ever given me. I kept meaning to throw it out, but maybe I knew it'd come in handy." His words were slurred. Enough for her to know it wasn't the first glass he was drinking.

"Can we talk about what just happened back there?" she asked. "Maybe go to my office?"

"Why? You want to sell me a pier?" The roughness of his voice sent shivers down her spine.

"No. I want to explain."

He looked down at his glass. "There's nothing to explain. If you want to sell the pier, that's fine. It's what you intended to do all along." He lifted the whiskey to his lips and tipped his head back, emptying the glass before pouring himself another.

"Can you slow down?" she asked, shaking her head as he swallowed another mouthful. "This is supposed to be a happy day."

"I'm just trying to see how it feels. How drunk do you have to get to buy a pier?" He shrugged, that steely glint still in his gaze. "Two drinks? Three? Five? How many until I become somebody completely different for a few weeks."

"You're making an idiot of yourself," she hissed, grabbing

his arm. "Can we please talk about this somewhere less open?"

"Why? You want to tell me about your ex? I didn't know you'd invited him to the charity day." He gave her a sour smile. "Maybe you should have warned me."

"I didn't know either." She let out a sigh. "I'm sorry... I should have..." her voice trailed off. What should she have done? She had no idea. All she knew was she hated the way he was looking at her.

Like he was angry and hurt and every emotion in between.

She was acutely aware of how alcohol and boats didn't mix. It made the hackles on her neck rise up. "Come on," she said again, reaching for his arm. "Let's go."

"What is it with women and my arm," he muttered, pulling away from her. "You chicks have a thing about it."

"Chicks?" She straightened her spine. "Seriously?" Damn, he was aggravating. "Maybe it's you who's got the problem. If you just came with me when I asked, I wouldn't have to drag you."

"I've come with you enough." His voice was low. "Every night for the past few weeks. Remember all the times I held you in my arms afterward? All those long conversations about my family and your divorce? I don't remember you once mentioning you only bought the pier because you were drunk."

"Why should I mention it? It's not a big deal."

"It's big enough for your ex to know about it."

She took a deep breath. "What did Josh say?"

Griff looked down at his drink, staring at it as though it had all the answers. "It doesn't matter," he muttered, then lifted the glass to his mouth.

"It obviously does," she whispered as he swallowed

another mouthful. "I know he told you about me buying the pier when I was drunk. What else?"

"There's more?" Griff shook his head. "What, did you buy the Empire State Building, too? What else does Josh and your sister know that I don't?"

"Nothing! And Lydia's my family. Of course I'm going to tell her everything."

"Because family's more important than anything else, right? More important than me." His words were becoming more slurred.

"I didn't say that."

"You didn't need to." He tipped his head back and finished the whiskey, slamming the glass on the bench. "I get it. Your family matters to you. More than I do." He stood, and she was hyper aware of his height. He wasn't steady on his feet like he usually was. One tumble and he could hurt himself. "Maybe that's why Josh and your Dad have no idea I even exist. I'm nothing to you, am I? Less important than this damn pier."

"You should go home," she told him. "Sleep it off. Before you do something you regret."

He looked her in the eye, and it made her heart jolt. There was nothing there. No kindness, no understanding. Just blankness, like he'd closed down the shutters and left his body to do the work.

"You want me to leave?" His voice was icy.

"Yes... no... I just don't want us to be talking like this while you're drunk. And on a boat, too. You know how dangerous the ocean can be."

"Did you throw your dad off the pier?" he asked her. "How about Josh, is he gone?"

"No I didn't. And I've no idea where Josh is."

"I guess I know where I stand. Below your family, below

your ex." He gave her another sickly smile. "Sorry if I'm messing with your style, Miss Paxton."

"I never said that."

"Nope. But I can see it in your eyes. What was I, a distraction? A bit of rough for the rich girl?" He raked his hand through his hair, and it made him stumble to his left.

"Don't bother answering," he muttered. "I'm leaving." He stepped forward, this time not meeting Autumn's gaze.

"I'll call you later," she whispered.

"Don't bother. You'll be too busy with your family. And your ex, no doubt." He blinked.

She tried to take a breath, but her chest felt too tight. "So what happens next?" she whispered.

He shrugged, his dark eyes finally meeting hers. "Nothing," he whispered. "Nothing happens. I'll go home, have another drink, and remember why I don't do relationships. Because they fucking suck."

He'd almost made it to the pier entrance before he let out a growl of anger. Every bit of him hurt. The healing bruises on his skin, the muscles he'd used to build the stage, but most of all his chest.

It felt like his heart might explode out of his ribcage.

There were people everywhere, brushing past him in their excitement to get on the pier. To eat funnel cake and ride the rollercoaster, or listen to the band whose music was echoing from the stage.

And yet he'd never felt so alone. Or like such an asshole. He wanted the pain to go away. Wanted to take her pain away, too, but it was impossible. He'd messed it up, the way he always did.

"Griff?" Ally called out from the Déjà Brew stall. "You

okay?" The makeshift shop was surrounded by customers desperate for a caffeine fix.

He nodded. "I'm good."

"Where you going?"

"Home."

She opened her mouth to say something else, but he turned and walked away. He didn't want to talk to anybody. Not now. He had a feeling if he opened his mouth again he'd only hurt someone else.

He needed to get away and close the door on the world. Maybe then he could think about what he'd just done.

Because right now, it felt like he'd ruined everything.

"He didn't mean it," Lydia said, passing Autumn another tissue. "He was blindsided by Josh and Dad arriving, that's all. It was his ego talking, and we all know that guys' egos are full of bullshit. Give him a day to sober up and he'll be begging you to take him back."

"Maybe I don't want him back," Autumn said, shaking her head wearily. Every muscle in her body ached. It was like she'd spent the day climbing Everest rather than overseeing a charity event. The pier closed an hour ago, laughing visitors leaving after the final concert, as the fairground rides switched off one by one. And now the pier was empty, save for Autumn, Lydia, and Ally who'd snuck into her office with a bottle of wine and three glasses. Ally was pouring them out as Lydia helped mop up Autumn's tears.

"Griff's a complex guy," Ally said, passing the wine out. "He's like an iceberg. That top ten percent is calm and easy-going as hell. But it hides all the crap he's been through in his life." Her eyes caught Autumn's. "And he's been through a lot."

"I know." Autumn blew her nose loudly. "But he shouldn't take it out on me."

Ally smiled. "You're one of the only ones he shows the ninety percent to. That means he trusts you." She pulled out the chair next to Autumn's. "But that doesn't mean he should get away with it. You should definitely give him hell, nobody should talk to you like that. But maybe you can understand why he's the way he is. He's built up this armor to protect himself."

"Then you stripped the armor away," Lydia said, patting Autumn's hand. "And he panicked, like a wild animal."

"That's a pretty good description of him," Autumn muttered, remembering the hardness in his stare. "It was like he'd closed in on himself and was lashing out without thinking." Another tear rolled down her cheek. "And it hurt."

"Of course it did." Lydia hugged her. "You poor thing."

"So what are you going to do?"

"Go home and go to bed, I guess." Autumn looked at Lydia. "All your things are at Griff's, but I don't think I can go there. Can you go pick them up in the morning and bring them back to the cottage?"

"Of course. But you'll have to face him yourself some time."

"I can't. Not yet." Not without it hurting too much.

"What'll you do if you two never make up?" Ally asked. "Would you still stay here?"

Autumn ran her finger around the top of her glass. She hadn't touched a drop. The thought of it made her stomach tight. "I don't know," she admitted. "But it would be difficult if I did. Griff's a tenant and I'll have to work with him every day."

Her mouth was dry at the thought. Could she deal with seeing him every day knowing she couldn't touch him, go home with him, laugh with him? So much of her time in

Angel Sands had been spent with him, first as friends, then as friends with benefits, and now as...

Nothing.

The blankness made her heart ache. And the tears started to pour all over again.

"I'm sorry, just ignore me," Ally said quickly. "You don't have to worry about any of that now."

"Of course she doesn't." Lydia checked her watch. "Hey, when was the last time you ate anything?"

"I think I had some funnel cake late this morning," Autumn croaked.

"You should eat. You must be starving."

"I'm not hungry." Autumn shook her head. "I think I'll just go home and sleep. What time is dad's plane home?" Her dad and Josh had beaten a hasty retreat to their hotel rooms at the Silver Sands Resort when it was clear Autumn didn't want to talk to them. Mr. Carlsson was already on his way back to L.A.

"At lunchtime tomorrow." Lydia shrugged. "I'm supposed to fly out in the evening, but I can change it."

"No need to change anything," Autumn told her. "I'll be fine. And you've done enough for me already."

"Yeah, because all of this is my fault." Lydia gave her a sad smile.

Autumn smiled tenderly at her. "No it isn't. We all know you can't keep a secret. You're an open book, and that's part of who you are. It's not as though it was some terrible thing, anyway. I got drunk, made a mistake, and then tried to fix it." She shrugged.

"I love you," Lydia said, her own eyes watering. "So much. And if Griff has any sense, he'll realize how much he loves you, too, and come crawling on his knees to beg you to take him back."

Autumn almost laughed at the image of Griff crawling

anywhere. Only almost, though, because her heart was so bruised it hurt to do anything other than breathe.

It was time to go to bed and sleep, because she had no idea what else to do. Maybe tomorrow would be a better day.

His head was pounding like somebody had taken a pick axe to it from the inside out and was determined to make a tunnel to the outside. It was only made worse by the shrill ring of his cell phone. A glance at the screen told him it was Jackson. He refused the call and tapped out a quick message that he was fine and he'd call him in the morning.

Jackson's reply flashed in front of his eyes. *Fine. Hah. Whatever you say, pal. But yeah, call me tomorrow.*

After he'd left the pier, Griff had headed straight home, and moped the evening away on his couch, staring out of the window of his apartment at the ocean as though it held all the answers.

If he'd been sober, he'd have climbed into his truck and driven out of town. Far enough that the sound of the people on the pier didn't pierce his ears wherever he went. But he wasn't sober, and his friends were all busy with their families, so instead he'd stood in the shower until his skin puckered up, trying not to look at the pretty bag of toiletries Autumn had left propped on his bathroom counter.

Okay, so he looked. And in his inebriated state he might have unscrewed her shampoo and breathed it in, the smell of her hitting him viscerally as he thought about those words he'd said.

Cruel words.

Words that had made her eyes water and her lips tremble.

Words he could *never* take back if he wanted to.

And now here he was, nursing a hangover from day

drinking and wondering how the hell things went wrong so quickly.

From the moment he'd seen Autumn's father and ex, he'd felt the hair on the back of his neck stand up. In their fancy, New York suits, their hair perfectly styled and gelled, they were the opposite to him. It made him feel lacking, and he hated that. As though he wasn't good enough for her.

Yeah, well he'd proven that from the way he'd treated her.

Truth be told, he *wasn't* good enough. He'd spent a childhood learning all about that. Not good enough to earn his father's attention. Not good enough to feel his mother's love. He was an irritation who occasionally came in useful.

He looked at himself in the bedroom mirror, leaning his brow on the cool glass, and hating the reflection staring back at him. His heart physically ached, like it was going through some kind of major crisis. If he wasn't so damn healthy and fit, he'd be worried he was having a heart attack.

There was a loud banging at the door of his apartment, and his sore heart leapt a little. Was it her? Had she realized what a damn idiot he was? His breath caught in his throat as he raked his hair back from his face and strode out of the bedroom into the hallway. He didn't bother to check the peephole, too desperate to get the door open.

"Lucas," he said, trying to hide his disappointment when he saw his friend standing there. "Everything okay?"

"That's what I've come to ask you. We've just finished at the pier and I realized I hadn't seen you for hours. What's up, man?"

Griff stood to the side so Lucas could walk in, before he closed the door behind him.

"You know what happened between me and Autumn?"

Lucas gave him a short smile as they walked into the living room. "It's a small town and everybody has a loud mouth. So yeah, I have some kind of idea."

Griff collapsed onto the sofa, and Lucas took the chair opposite. "I messed up."

"So I hear." Lucas blew out a mouthful of air. "What were you thinking?"

He wasn't. That was the problem. His lizard mind had taken over, whispering in his ear with a hissing voice that it was inevitable that she'd leave. He wasn't good enough for her, the same way he'd never been good enough for his parents.

This was why he didn't do relationships. He always messed things up and got hurt. Even worse, he ended up hurting other people.

Autumn. Carla. He had a whole list of them.

"She bought the pier when she was drunk."

"So? We all do stupid things when we're drunk." He gave Griff a pointed look. "What does that matter?"

His heart was throbbing again. "It means she didn't decide to come out here. It was a mistake." His voice cracked. "That's what she told her sister."

"So? People are allowed to change their minds." Lucas's voice was thick with incredulity. "Autumn loves you. You only have to see the way she looks at you to know that. Like you're some kind of giant knight riding on a dragon to save her."

"A dragon?"

Lucas shrugged. "I figure you'd squash a normal size horse."

Griff would have laughed if he was capable, but the sound was trapped in his throat. "Did you see her ex? And her dad? They're both here to help her sell the pier so she can go back to New York."

"And does she want that?"

Griff blinked. "Why wouldn't she have told me about it if she didn't?"

"I don't know. This is all stuff you need to ask her, not me. But none of it makes any sense."

Griff dropped his head into his hands, his hair falling over his fingers. "She won't talk to me. Not after the things I said."

"What did you say?" Lucas asked, folding his arms across his chest.

"I told her to go back to New York and forget me."

"You really are an idiot, you know that?"

"Thanks for reminding me." Griff gave him a humorless smile. "And even if she wasn't going back before, she will now after I've been such a douche."

"The world doesn't revolve around you, you know? And for the record, her dad and her ex are flying back to New York tomorrow. *Without* her."

Griff lifted his head. "She's staying?"

"That's what I said, numbnuts." Lucas pressed his lips together in a firm line. "I suggest you crawl over to her place first thing tomorrow and start begging for her forgiveness. Because I've never seen you as happy as you've been in the past few weeks. Or so at ease with yourself. The two of you work." He cleared his throat. "Or you did, until you went and fucked it up."

"She'll never forgive me."

"She won't if you don't ask."

He slumped against the wall. "Yeah, well maybe she shouldn't. She deserves somebody better than me."

"Who the hell is better than you? Jackson?" Lucas laughed. "Or the asshole she divorced before she came out here? You want to see her with one of them?"

"No!" The thought of it made Griff want to hit something. Or someone. Preferably the smug asshole who broke Autumn's heart.

"Then go and talk to her. Tell her why you pushed her away. Apologize for it, make some damn amends. And if she still wants nothing to do with you?" Lucas shrugged. "At least you tried."

Griff exhaled. "Yeah. You're right." There was one thing he was sure of, he couldn't let her go. It hurt too damn much. He needed her like he needed air.

Lucas looked like he was going to say something more, but then his cell rang. Griff recognized the tone – the same one Lucas got whenever the station put out an emergency call to all of its firefighters.

Pulling his phone from his pocket, Lucas glanced at the screen, frowning as his eyes scanned the message. Lucas slowly brought his gaze back to Griff, the expression making the pit of Griff's stomach churn.

"There's a fire," Lucas said, his voice strained. "At the pier."

And just like that, the bottom fell out of Griff's world.

28

Autumn was sleeping next to a starfished Lydia when a loud shriek pierced her dream. An overwhelming volume of sirens cut through the silence of the night, making her heart hammer against her ribcage. She sat up and looked around, suppressing a chuckle when she saw her sister's undisturbed slumber. Blue lights were flashing through the window behind her like a frenzied disco.

Curious, she climbed out of bed and looked through the thick glass at the back of the house, blinking as the fire engines whizzed past. They continued north along the road until they were out of her sight, the high pitched alarms fading into the night.

In her bare feet, she padded out of the bedroom and into the living room, perplexed when she could see an orange glow flickering through the window facing the beach. She licked her dry lips and pulled at the curtain, her feet frozen to the spot as she saw where the color was coming from.

The pier was on fire.

Large flames were licking up against the darkness of the sky, the grey smoke curling and dancing in the night time breeze. She wrenched open the door, and the sound of the blaze hit her. Little pieces of ash were drifting past the cottage.

Without thinking, she began to run, her bare feet pounding against the cool sand. Her breath was short, panicked, and with every stride she completed, the heat of the air increased.

It was every owner's worst nightmare. The reason insurance was so damn high on the wood-and-iron constructions. In spite of the frothing ocean beneath, pier fires were a dime a dozen. Their materials were combustible, the construction and electrical wiring often out of date, and more than anything, they were hard for firefighters to access, meaning it took longer than usual to douse any flames.

She was panting, her legs flying as she got closer still. Firefighters were pulling hoses from the engines parked at the base of the pier, their movements fast but considered, as they entered the burning edifice.

As she got closer, she could see the fire was consuming Delmonico's and her office. Everybody had left, hadn't they? She remembered Pietro saying goodnight before she'd sat down with Ally and Lydia in the office. He'd locked up the restaurant and all his staff were gone.

The fairground rides had been taken down and put back onto the trucks that had driven them away. The stage was still up, but she didn't care about that. Her eyes darted this way and that as she scanned the pier, her chest screaming from the speed she was running.

Then her gaze landed on the *Ocean Explorer*. Griff's boat. He'd left the pier hours ago. Please god, don't let him have come back for any reason. She blinked, her eyes watering from a combination of the smoke, salty air, and fear.

The smoke was so thick as she reached the end of the pier, choking her lungs as she tried desperately to stop breathing it in. When she reached the boardwalk she slowed, lifting her gaze to the orange flames as tears rolled down her face.

The heat scorched her nose and throat as she hurried along the wide concrete path. A crowd of onlookers had gathered, held back by caution tape the firefighters had placed. A few of them turned to look at her, blinking as she walked toward them. She looked down and remembered she was only wearing a thin tank and a pair of tiny sleep shorts, with nothing on her feet.

With her hair tangled and knotted, she must' look like a crazy woman.

What sounded like thunder rumbled ahead of her, even though there were no clouds in the sky. She looked to see Griff running at twice the speed she had, his face twisted with emotion as he reached her.

"Thank god," he said. "I thought you might be in there." He pointed at the burning pier.

She blinked back stinging tears. "I thought you might be, too."

He looked like he was going to hug her, but then he stepped back, shaking his head to move his hair from his eyes. Standing with the blazing fire reflected in his gaze, he looked every inch a wild man.

"Do you know if there's anybody stuck on the pier?" she shouted over the noise of the flames and the firefighters, fear clenching her chest in a vice grip. "I know Pietro went home, and everything looked empty when I left tonight, but..." she trailed off as she turned to look at the blaze again. Please God, don't let anybody get hurt.

"Not that I know of. I came with Lucas and he's been briefed by the team. They think it was empty."

"Thank god," she whimpered, her legs trembling. Her whole body quivered, as though the ground beneath her was vibrating. Her teeth started to chatter. Griff was looking over her shoulder at something, and she followed his gaze.

"Oh Griff, your boat," she said, clamping her hand over her mouth. It wasn't simply her pier that the blaze was destroying. Those flames were eating up Griff's livelihood, and the Delmonico's, too. Her body shook uncontrollably as she watched the firefighters train water onto the flames, trying to beat the blaze into submission.

"Forget about the boat," Griff said, his brows pinching together. "It doesn't matter."

"Of course it does." A sob escaped her lips. "It was your grandfather's fishing boat. You told me that. And Delmonico's. All that history being destroyed." Her teeth chattered as she spoke.

"You're cold," he said, his voice strangely calm. "Here, take my shirt." He deftly unbuttoned it and lifted it around her shoulders, but the shivers didn't ease at all. She was finding it hard to breathe. Any air she managed to inhale felt like fire against her throat. Her chest rose and fell quickly in an effort to get the oxygen she needed.

"I think you're in shock." Griff put his hands on her arms, rubbing them fast to try and get some warmth into her, but nothing in her was responding.

In spite of the heat radiating from the pier, she felt so cold. As though ice had replaced the blood in her veins, and was freezing every organ. The tremors in her body increased, making her shake like crazy, her legs barely able to keep her standing.

A moment later, they buckled beneath her, and she was falling to the concrete. That's when she felt them – those strong, sure arms, wrapping themselves around her and saving her from impact.

He lifted her against him with a whoosh, her frozen skin pressed against his heated chest. She turned her face against him, her skin desperate for warmth, as she tried to keep breathing.

"Stay with me, baby. It's going to be okay," he murmured into her hair. She tried to mumble that she wasn't planning on doing anything else, but the words froze against her tongue. The last thing she heard before everything turned black was Griff's worried voice.

"Any paramedics here?" he shouted out. "I need a goddamn medic right now."

"Is Autumn okay?" Ally asked Griff as she and Nate carried crates of coffee over to the fire crews and onlookers.

Griff was sitting next to the ambulance. Inside, the paramedics had managed to warm Autumn up with a heated blanket that was still enveloping her. She was awake and talking to them, though the shivers hadn't quite gone away.

He could hear her telling them she was wasting their time. They had much more important people to take care of, that she would be fine if they let her leave.

Griff's lips twitched, relief flooding through him. "Yeah, she sounds better. They're getting her warm and she's bitching, so that's good."

Ally laughed, looking relieved. "She's had such a bad day. With her dad and then you." Her voice was pointed. "And now the pier. No wonder it got to be too much."

"Yeah, well a lot of that is my fault." He pressed his lips together. "I was a dick."

"Glad you realize that." Ally gave him a tight smile. "Here, have a coffee. You look like you could do with a warming up yourself."

From a brief chat he'd had with Lucas, the fire was under control, but still burning. The worst of it had hit the restaurant and the office, but there was smoke damage to everything that wasn't burned. Not that he gave a shit. Everybody was safe and that's all that mattered.

Just thinking about Autumn being in the office only hours before made him want to throw up.

He should have been with her when she found out about the fire. If he hadn't been such an ass, he would have been. She and Lydia were supposed to stay at his place, after all.

Lydia...

"Have you seen Autumn's sister?" he asked Ally, his brows dipping.

"No." Ally shook her head. "She left the pier when we did and headed home." Her eyes widened. "You think she's still asleep at the cottage?"

"She could be."

"I'll get somebody to go and check on her." Ally nodded at him. "You stay here with Autumn."

"Wasn't planning on going anywhere else."

"She loves you, you know?"

He swallowed hard. "No, I didn't know." But it warmed him more than the coffee cupped between his palms. "I know I love her, though." And that the thought of losing her made him feel sick. "If she'd been on the pier when..." his voice cracked, and he looked down.

Ally set the extra coffees down and slid her arm around his shoulders. "She wasn't," she said softly. "She's fine. You told me yourself. Don't start beating yourself up for things that aren't your fault." She bumped her shoulder against his. "Beat yourself up for being an asshole instead."

He huffed out a laugh. "Thanks."

"Hey, I just say it as I see it." Ally stood and grabbed the tray of coffees. "You guys have some talking to do."

"Yeah, we do. But not now." He glanced into the ambulance again. "Now I just want to make sure she's okay."

Ally's face softened. "She's a lucky woman. We all care about her."

He couldn't help but feel like he was the lucky one. From the moment Lucas got the call about the pier, Griff had been beside himself with anxiety. The two of them had run from his apartment to the pier, and as soon as he saw the blaze he'd wanted to run to the office to be sure she wasn't there.

It had taken all of Lucas's strength to hold him back.

Then, when he saw her running along the beach, her body orange from the reflected flames, a sense of relief had washed over him. So strong he'd almost laughed out loud from it. All he'd wanted to do was scoop her up and take her far away from the danger.

But that wasn't Autumn. She didn't run away from things, she confronted them. He could learn a thing or two from that.

"I don't think we're going to be able to keep her in there much longer," one of the paramedics told him as they climbed down from the ambulance. "And she refuses to come to the hospital to get checked out. Do you have somewhere you can take her and keep her warm?"

"Yeah." Griff nodded. "I'll take her home."

"Good. Her temperature's almost back to normal, and there are no other signs of distress. She needs to get some sleep, but it'll be better if you're there in case of any trouble. If she gets cold again, call nine-one-one right away."

"I will." He nodded. "Thank you." Taking care of her was all he wanted to do.

Tonight and forever.

He'd lost her once today. He wasn't planning on doing it again.

Autumn sat up suddenly, panic taking over her body. *There'd been a fire!* She tried to scramble out of bed only to find a strong, warm hand restraining her.

"It's okay. You're okay," Griff murmured as he leaned over the bed from where he was sitting on a wooden dining chair. Had he been sitting there all night? It looked uncomfortable as hell. He must have knots in the knots of his muscles.

"What's happening with the fire?" she asked him, looking down at her body. She was wearing one of his t-shirts and a thick pair of leggings.

"It's out. Lucas called about a half an hour ago."

She let out a sigh of relief. "Did he say what the damage is?"

"The restaurant and the office are gone, but the front part of the pier is unharmed. They'll inspect it later this morning. We should know more then."

Autumn nodded, feeling her eyes well with tears. "And your boat?"

"It's damaged. I don't know how badly."

"Oh god. I'm so sorry." The tears spilled over as she reached out to touch his arm.

He covered her hand with his own. "It's okay. Nobody was hurt, and that's all I care about right now. Insurance can sort out the rest."

"I'll need to call mine first thing. I should probably make a list." She looked around. Why had Griff brought her here instead of taking her home? "Oh damn, I left my purse at home." Another thought occurred to her, and her mouth dropped open. "Lydia," she whispered. "I left the door open. She's still there." She tried to scramble to her knees. "I need to get back."

"Lydia's here." Griff inclined his head to the bedroom door. "She's sleeping on the sofa. And... uh, somebody else is here to check on you, too."

Autumn frowned. "Who?"

He cleared his throat. "Your dad. He came as soon as Lydia called him."

"Dad's here?" She glanced at the door, not sure how to feel about that.

"He's worried about you," Griff said. "We all are."

"Don't tell me Josh is here, too."

He gave a little laugh. "I think he knew better. Or your dad did. Whatever. He's leaving first thing for New York."

Autumn felt the tears welling again. Where the hell were they all coming from? She didn't cry. She hadn't even shed a single tear when her divorce came through. Yet here she was, a snivelling mess.

If she wasn't so exhausted, she'd be embarrassed.

"You probably think this is payback for me buying the pier when I was drunk."

"I don't," he murmured. "I think it's crap and it never should've happened to you. You've been through enough." He looked at his hands. "There's so much I want to tell you, but it's about an hour until dawn and you should get some sleep. We have a hell of a lot to do once the sun is up."

She raised her eyebrow at his use of 'we', but didn't comment. Now wasn't the time. There was one thing she wanted to know, though. "These clothes. How did I get into them?"

"You want to know if I stripped you and took advantage?" Griff raised an eyebrow. He sat back on the chair and she missed the warmth of his hand against her hip.

"I'm sorry. I was just wondering..."

He smiled. "It's okay. Lydia helped you get into the shower. Those leggings are hers. I gave her the t-shirt so you'd have some modesty when you were in bed. I figured you wouldn't want to wake up in here naked."

She remembered the way she'd woken up naked yesterday

morning, his lips dragging against her skin. Before any of this happened. The thought made her heart ache a little more. She wrapped her arms around her abdomen, but it wasn't enough to stop another shiver wrack down her spine.

"You're cold. Get back under the covers and get some sleep." He nodded at the door. "I'll let your family know you're okay."

"But you're coming back, right?"

"I got nowhere else to go." He shrugged as he headed out. "Lydia called the sofa, and your dad's made his home on the love seat.

She could have pointed out that he had a spare room, one that still had Lydia's things lined up neatly next to the bed. But she didn't want to, because the thought of being alone made her breath catch in her throat.

He was back within a minute. "They're both half asleep. I told them you're okay, but going to try to get some more rest."

"Thank you."

He flashed her a half-smile. "No worries." He sat back down on the dining chair. His body made it look like a piece of dollhouse furniture.

"That looks uncomfortable."

"I've slept in worse."

She licked her dry lips, trying to find the right words. "You could sleep in here if you like? The bed's big enough."

His wary eyes met hers. "It's okay."

No, it wasn't. It felt far from okay. "I want you to sleep here," she admitted. "Please."

His brows lifted. "You sure?"

She nodded. "I want you for your body warmth."

This time his smile was full on. "Why didn't you say so?" he asked, climbing into bed beside her. She felt the mattress dip under his weight, then his arms slid around her as his chest pressed against her back.

"This okay?" he asked softly.

"Yeah," she breathed. It was more than okay. She opened her mouth to say more, but a combination of his warmth and his protection made her feel tired again, and she felt exhaustion over take her.

They'd talk later in the morning. Hopefully things would be clearer then.

For now, she'd just escape into the blackness.

29

The next time Autumn awoke it was Lydia she saw next to her. Her sister was in the dent Griff had left behind, her arm flung over her head as she lay on her back, unashamedly snoring. Autumn's lips twitched at the sight, at the same time her stomach dipped at the realization that Griff wasn't next to her. The urge to curl up in his arms felt stronger than ever.

She rolled over and sat on the edge of the bed, circling her shoulders to loosen the knots there. The unbearable shivers had gone, and the constant icy feeling of her skin had disappeared with it, but her muscles still told the story of last night.

"What time is it?" Lydia croaked, groaning as she sat up. "Oh hey, are you okay? No headache or shivers or anything?"

"Nope." Autumn turned to her sister. "How about you?"

"I'm exhausted." She yawned as though to demonstrate the truth of it. "One minute we were curled up in bed together, the next I'm being woken up by Ally and getting dragged outside. Now I know how my first boyfriend felt when Dad found us in bed together."

Autumn would have laughed, but she remembered that night so well. The poor boy hadn't stood a chance.

"Talking of Dad, is he still here?"

"Yeah. He's in the living room. Griff left to meet his friend Lucas at the pier. They're inspecting the damage."

Autumn scrambled to her feet. "He should have woken me up. I need to be there."

"He only left half an hour ago. I promised to tell you as soon as you woke up. We can head over there now." Lydia swung her feet to the floor. "Just as soon as you put some clothes on."

Autumn blinked and looked down at her tatty leggings. "I don't have anything to wear."

"Yeah you do. Your things are still here, remember?" Lydia pointed to the open bag on Griff's ottoman as she stifled a yawn. "Let's shower and clean our teeth, then we can head over, okay?"

The pier looked worse than ever in the morning light. The end was charred, the red painted iron buckled from the heat of the blaze. Griff's boat was floating there, the port side black from smoke. Autumn pressed her lips together, determined not to cry again. She'd shed enough tears for a lifetime.

A group of people were huddling around the boardwalk, talking as they faced the pier. She recognized Frank and Deenie, Lorne from the surf shop, and Ally's husband Nate, along with the firefighters who worked at the ASFD under Lucas's captainship.

As soon as they saw her, Autumn was swallowed up in a succession of hugs, each one of them telling her how sorry they were.

"We'll do whatever it takes to get the pier up and running

again," Frank promised. "We've already started a fund for the repairs."

"I'll put a bucket next to the register," Deenie told her. "Everybody will. It'll be okay."

"That's so kind of you, but I have insurance." Autumn attempted a smile. "Maybe we can raise money for the Delmonicos and Griff instead. They're going to lose a lot of money until everything's repaired."

"We're a generous community," Frank said, patting her arm. "You'll all be taken care of."

She could see Lucas and a few of his firefighters at the end of the pier, so she said her goodbyes before she headed up there. It was only when she climbed the steps that she realized Griff was with them, too. He swallowed hard when he looked at her.

"So, what's the damage?" she asked, trying to keep her voice light.

Lucas shook his head. "It's not great news. The end of the pier is a write off. It's going to have to be rebuilt from scratch."

She breathed in sharply. "Okay. How about Griff's boat?"

Griff shook his head. "I can get another." Their eyes met and she felt her chest tighten.

"I'm so sorry," she whispered.

"It's not your fault."

"Do we know what caused it?" she asked Lucas.

"It looks like it started in the kitchen. The investigators are in there now, but we won't get their report for a while."

"In Delmonico's kitchen?"

Lucas nodded. "Yeah. Looks like a classic electrical fault, but we can't say for sure until the investigation is complete."

"Thank you for what you've done," Autumn said softly. "All of you. For getting here so quickly and making sure nobody was hurt. That's the important thing."

"I called my insurance," Griff told her. "And yours, too. They'll be sending an adjuster out as soon as possible." He ran his thumb along his jaw. "Now I just need to go tell Pietro the bad news that the fire started in his restaurant."

"I should tell him. I'm his landlord," Autumn said, dreading the conversation.

"We'll go together," Griff said firmly. "You don't have to face it alone."

She nodded and he took her hand, squeezing it tightly. It was strange how people who'd only known her for weeks were supporting her.

Strange and beautifully heart-warming. It was taking a lot of effort not to cry again.

By five that afternoon, she was dead on her feet. After meeting with the Delmonico family, she'd hurried back to the pier where her claims adjuster was waiting to inspect the damage. It was the first time she'd walked on the burnt and buckled construction since the fire, pulling on safety boots and a yellow hat as Lucas and his team instructed.

It had broken her heart to see her beautiful pier so damaged. Only yesterday it had been strung with bright lights and floral garland, and full of people who oohed and ahhed at the black and white posters she'd put up. As they carefully made their way toward the charred ruins of what was once Delmonico's, a sob caught in her throat.

All that history obliterated in one night. And on her watch, too. It was the first time in over a hundred years that Angel Sands wouldn't have a pier. And it was her fault.

The adjuster made notes and took photographs as they walked, Lucas standing on his other side as he pointed out where they believed the fire had begun. In the far corner of what used to be the restaurant she could see tiny pieces of paper dancing around in the breeze. On closer inspection they saw what were the remains of Delmonico's menus.

"I think I have everything for now," the adjuster told her after three hours of inspecting the ruins. "I'll write my report this week."

"But she'll be covered, right?" Lucas asked.

"Unless anything unexpected is found, then yes." He looked at Autumn. "You have the top level of insurance. That's good. So many people don't think things like this will happen to them."

"I have my dad to thank for that." She gave a little laugh. "Always expect the unexpected."

When the adjuster had gone, she'd hugged Lucas again and thanked him for all his help, before she walked slowly back along the beach toward the cottage. It was less than twenty-four hours since she'd run like crazy the other way, her eyes trained on the orange flames that were consuming the pier.

Now everything felt different. *She* was different. Sadder, more lost. All the things she thought she could count on were gone.

"You're back. We've been looking for you," Lydia said as Autumn walked through the door. She was sitting in the tiny living room, her dad opposite her as he worked on his laptop.

"I've been with the adjuster."

"All this time?" Lydia's eyes widened.

Her dad looked up. "He's been thorough. That's good. Did they say when you'll get some payment?" he asked.

"Hopefully I'll get something next week. That should allow me to contract the repairs out." Autumn slumped in the empty chair, letting her head tip back. "But it will be months before we can open again. Maybe years."

Her dad caught her eye. "You could use the money for something else."

She blinked. "Like what?"

"Take the payment and come back to New York. Invest in some real estate there."

With a jolt of frustration pulsing through her, Autumn caught his gaze. "I'm not leaving the pier in ruins. And I wouldn't come back to New York, anyway. I've already told you that."

He shrugged. "It was worth a try. But if you're staying, then maybe I can help you."

"How?" she asked warily.

"I've spoken to someone who has an empty restaurant about twenty miles from here. He's open to renting it to your tenants on a temporary lease until they can move back to the pier." He clicked on the laptop and turned it around to show her the screen. A low-level modern building with a backdrop of palms filled it. "What do you think? He's agreed to charge no more than you were. It's a win-win."

For the first time that day she felt a shot of hope. "It's a good idea," she conceded. "Thank you. I'll let the Delmonico family know."

Lydia's phone buzzed and she lifted it from the coffee table. "Oops, that's Griff. I was supposed to tell him when you got back."

"Griff has your number?" Autumn asked, as Lydia quickly typed a reply.

"Yeah. We swapped them this morning when he left to go to the pier. He's there now, finishing up with his own insurance guy."

"Is he okay?"

Lydia laughed. "That's exactly what he asked about you. I feel like some kind of interpreter. How about you ask him yourself. He's a ten minute walk away."

She was right. With everything she'd done today, there was still unfinished business. This morning when they'd sat and told Pietro about the fire starting in his restaurant, Griff had squeezed her hand tightly as Autumn tried not to cry. Then he'd walked with her to the pier and sat down on the edge of the boardwalk with her until the adjuster arrived.

He'd been ever present in her day, yet there was so much they hadn't said. Yesterday's argument had felt as devastating as the fire in many ways. She'd believed in him. She'd thought he believed in her, too. And then his words had cut her like a knife.

Maybe the problem was she'd never believed in herself. She should have told him about the stupid drunken pier purchase as soon as they'd grown closer. He probably would have laughed, instead of seeing it as something she was hiding from him.

She should have told him about her dad and Mr. Carlsson, too. Not to mention Josh.

The truth was, she wasn't used to having a relationship of equals. She'd had to fight to have her voice heard – first with her father, then with her ex-husband. So when she'd had an opportunity to show Griff her weakness, she'd been afraid he'd use it against her.

But that wasn't fair. He'd never tried to be anything more than her friend, her lover, maybe more. She'd tarred him with the same brush she'd always used, and then look what happened.

She'd messed things up.

"Are you going or what?" Lydia asked, her eyes dancing.

Autumn stood and rolled her aching shoulders. "I guess I am." She turned toward the door, then looked back at her father. "When are you going home?" she asked him.

"Tonight. Unless you preferred I stay. I can book another night at the hotel."

"It's okay. But thank you." Her smile was wan. "There's nothing else you can do. I just need to wait for the insurance company to make their decision."

He stepped forward and took her hands in his. "I've made mistakes, but I've always loved you, sweetheart. And there'll always be a home for you in New York." He pressed his lips together for a moment, then smiled. "But I can see that you want to stay here."

"I do." She nodded. "This is my home now." She still didn't trust him as far as she could throw him, not after the trick he'd pulled yesterday. But he was her dad, and he'd taken care of her – in his own way – for as long as she could remember. Maybe the distance between them would do them both some good. Give him time to work out that she didn't need him to solve everything for her, especially not when it was on his terms.

"I'll probably be gone before you come back," Lydia told her, hugging her tightly. "Keep me posted on the pier, okay? And about Griff. I want to know everything."

"I know you do." Autumn closed her eyes as she hugged her sister tightly. "Are you sure I can't take you to the airport?"

"I'm hitching a lift with Dad. Saves on the gas and the environment."

"Unlike catching a plane to Hawaii," her dad said dryly. Lydia rolled her eyes.

"Take care, sweetheart." Her dad gave Autumn a smile, as though he was waiting for Autumn to make the first move. She sighed, then hugged him tightly.

"Safe journey," she whispered.

"If you need anything, or if you change your mind..." he trailed off when he saw her expression. "Well, you know where I am."

"Sure do."

"All right then, you need to go," Lydia said, grinning as she gave Autumn's ass a shove. "I'll make sure the place is locked up before we head out."

"Thank you." Autumn flipped her hair over her shoulders and walked out of the cottage, turning to give them a final wave.

It was time to do some talking.

30

Griff was sitting on the sand when he saw her walking toward him, her hair lifted by the breeze, dancing around her face. He had his phone in his hand, replying to a message from Lucas who was asking if he wanted to talk. He quickly typed out a reply.

Thanks, man. Maybe later. There's somebody else I need to talk to first.

"Hi." Autumn sat next to him, her bare legs stretching out on the sand. They were bronzed from her time living in Angel Sands, but he could remember how pale they'd been when she first arrived.

He liked them both ways. The exotic and the familiar. That's exactly what she was to him.

She leaned her chin on her hand, staring out at the ocean.

"How're you doing?" he asked her softly.

She slowly brought her gaze to his. "I think I'm okay. The adjuster meeting went better than I expected. Thinks we can get the claim through pretty quick."

"That's great news. Will you start repairing the pier right away?"

"That's the plan." Her lips were pink, her eyes clear in spite of the past twenty-four hours. God, he wanted to touch her. "Did you think I'd take the money and run instead?"

"Not for a minute." He shook his head. "I know you too well for that."

"My dad wanted me to. Until he saw my expression."

Griff chuckled. "I'd have liked to see that."

"How about your adjuster? What's the news on the boat?"

"They want a second opinion on if it's repairable. There's some specialist place up the coast that restores old boats – they're arranging for them to take a look."

The skin between her brows pinched together. "Won't repairing it take a long time?" she asked, tracing a circle in the sand with her fingertip.

"It'll take as long as it takes. There's no hurry. I can't exactly use it until the pier is ready."

Her finger froze, mid-circle. "You can find somewhere else to run your business. There's a dock at the Silver Sands Resort, they might be able to help. Or you could go to the marina." The thought of him losing all that money made her want to be sick.

"It's okay," he said, his voice soft. He put his hand over hers, his palm warming her. "I figure it's time to take a really good look at the business while the boat is repaired. Somebody clever told me I should diversify, make more plans. I can do that and crew on some friends' boats to tide me over until the Explorer is ready."

"Not on Sam's boat, though." Her worried gaze met his.

He laughed. "No. I prefer to stay above the water line when I'm onboard."

"It could be months until the pier's ready. Years, even. The season will be over. You'll have lost at least a year's income."

"I'm not worried about that," he told her, his gaze sure as

it connected with hers. "All the best things are worth waiting for. And working for."

She swallowed, her mouth suddenly dry. "I should never have lied to you about the pier. And I should have told you about the buyer being interested. And I'm sorry I didn't." Sliding her fingers between his, she curled her hand around his. "If you hadn't guessed, I have a lot of trust issues."

He gave her a rueful smile. "I didn't give you a lot of reasons to trust me. I jumped to all the wrong conclusions and treated you like shit. And I'm so desperately sorry for that." He lifted her hand to his lips and kissed her palm. "The things I said..." His voice trailed off as he tried to find the right words. Maybe there weren't any. "I was an asshole." That was the crux of it.

"Yeah, you were. But you were a hurt asshole. I should have told you before you found out from someone else." She swallowed hard, trying to find the right words. "Can I tell you a little about my marriage? Maybe it'll explain why I find this so difficult."

He cocked his head to the side. "Yeah. I'd like to hear it."

She tilted her head, looking up at him. "So, I told you before, Josh and I had a real estate business. A really successful one we'd built up from scratch. And I thought we were a team, each of us playing to our strengths, but it turned out Josh didn't agree."

Griff said nothing, his deep eyes steady as he looked at her.

"He'd have meetings and not tell me. Make deals without us talking them through. Ones I wouldn't have risked, or where I didn't trust the people involved." She sighed. "And when I asked him to run things by me first, he'd just laugh. Told me that I brought the contacts and he brought the brains. I needed to let him do what he was best at without questioning him."

"What an asshole."

She nodded her agreement. "And then one of my friend's husbands called me one afternoon and asked me to meet him in a coffee shop." Her hand was still curled in Griff's. "He works for the FBI. Wanted to give me a heads up that Josh was involved in something he shouldn't be. And because the business was involved, that implicated me, too. They suspected he was helping people launder money by renting them office space, but they were still trying to prove it."

Griff swallowed hard. "What did you do?"

"What any wife would. I asked him about it. And he told me I shouldn't get involved." She ran her tongue across her bottom lip. "That's when I knew I needed to get out. I'd spent a lifetime doing what my dad told me to do. I thought my marriage would be different. But it wasn't."

There was a tic in Griff's jaw, as though he was biting down too hard. "Was he investigated?"

"I'm pretty sure what I said spooked him." Autumn shook her head. "But I can't imagine he'll walk the straight and narrow for too long. He's an opportunist. In some ways that's what I found interesting about him in the first place. He was different to me. Maybe too different." She blinked, still gazing at the ocean. "The divorce took a long time to negotiate. The business was worth a lot of money. But I didn't know how much of it was dirty. I guess I still don't. So I asked him to buy me out."

"Did he offer you a fair price?"

She chuckled. "It depends on what you mean by fair. I was willing to take below market to get out of it. I wanted my name off everything. But I had my dad in my ear, asking me why we couldn't work it out. He likes Josh a lot. Said he reminded him of himself when he was younger." She grimaced. "He even offered to buy Josh out so I could keep the company."

"Did he know about the bad deals?"

"I didn't tell him. And now I can't because I signed an NDA."

"A non-disclosure agreement?" He lifted an eyebrow. "Yet you're breaking it to tell me." His eyes were soft.

"That's because I trust you."

Her words lit a beacon of hope inside him. "Even after everything I've done?" he asked, tracing the lines on her palm with his finger.

"Yeah. You're like a brick wall. Things go into you but nothing gets out. I've noticed how people confide in you. Ask for your help. And if we're going to have a relationship, I don't want there to be secrets between us. None at all."

He cocked his head to the side. "You still want to have a relationship with me?" A half-smile played at his lips. The sun was reflecting in his warm eyes, but she still saw something there. Hope. Desire.

The same feelings that warmed her own skin.

"I've always wanted that," she said softly. "Even when I pretended to myself that I didn't and no strings attached seemed like a good idea."

"I mess up. A lot." His voice cracked. "That's something you should know about me."

"And when you mess up, you fix it. That's something else I know."

"I spent my life believing I wasn't wanted," Griff told her. "And I wasn't. Not for the longest time. I was an inconvenience. Something that took my parents away from screaming at each other. A flesh and bone reminder that they had obligations other than to themselves." He swallowed hard, looking down at her hand cradled in his. She reached out with her free hand to rake her fingers through his thick hair. He sighed, closing his eyes for a moment.

"I hurt you because I was afraid of being hurt like that

again, and that was wrong," he told her, breathing out as she continued to massage his scalp. "I'm like a wounded animal. I strike first because I'm so damn scared I'm not wanted. And I'm so sorry I didn't give you the space to talk when I should have."

"You're wanted," Autumn whispered. "I want you very much."

Something flashed behind his eyes. It made her legs shake as he stared at her, his lips parted, his jaw set. He leaned his head down until his brow was touching hers. "Not as much as I want you. Can you forgive me for what I said yesterday?"

"Yeah." She breathed. "I already have."

He closed his eyes for a moment. "Thank god." Then his lips were on hers, their warmth sending pulses of electricity through her body. He reached around to cup the back of her neck, sliding his other hand to the small of her back so he could angle her just right. She looped her arms around his neck, kissing him until her toes were curling with delight.

When they parted, they were both breathless, their eyes shining brighter than the sun above.

"I love you," he whispered, pressing his lips to her warm throat. "I promise to never hurt you again."

Just then, a little child kicked a ball in front of them, wobbling on his feet as he ran after it, his mom following close behind. The ball bounced against Griff's feet, and the boy stopped dead, looking up with wide eyes at the man-giant in front of him.

Griff winked and kicked the ball back. The boy picked it up quickly, snatching it against his chest. He still couldn't take his eyes from Griff, though. Funny how he had that affect on children. They were awed, but not afraid.

"How many do you want?" she asked, laying her head against his shoulder.

"Balls?"

She laughed. "No, children."

He kissed her temple, sliding his arms around her. "One, five, twenty. I've no idea."

"But you want children one day?"

"Yeah. If you do."

She turned her head to the side, smiling into his eyes. "I do, too. One day."

Griff stood, pulling her up and sliding his arm around her shoulder. "In that case, we have some practicing to do," he told her.

She laughed as they walked along the beach, the warmth of the sun reflected in the heat radiating inside her. He was a giant, he was vulnerable, but he was all she ever wanted. For so long she'd been a shadow of herself, torn by those who wanted pieces of her.

Here in his arms, it finally felt like she was whole. She lifted his hand to her lips and kissed his palm, feeling the rough skin against her mouth. "I love you," she whispered. "So much."

His eyes crinkled. "Come on. Let me take you home."

EPILOGUE

If there was one thing Autumn had learned since she'd moved to Angel Sands, it was that time here ran at a different pace. Maybe it was the lack of distinct seasons that made things seem slower and more laid back. In New York, it was either too hot to work or too snowy to get into the office, with only a few days in spring and summer that felt just right.

Sure, the temperature in Angel Sands dipped a little in the winter. Griff would pull a half suit on over his body when he left early in the morning to meet his friends for a surf before work began. And Autumn would slide a pair of jeans on to wear with her tank or t-shirt. If it was really cold she'd pull a thin sweater on, too. But for the most part, each day felt the same as the ones before and after.

There was a comfort in that. Unless you were desperate for your pier to be repaired, that was. The six months she had planned for the rebuilding had stretched into nine, then twelve. More than long enough to have a baby, as Ember had pointed out.

But now it was ready, and her heart was hammering against her chest as she looked around it. Not only was the structure itself rebuilt with deep green painted ironwork and light varnished wood, but there was a brand new restaurant and office, along with two shops that she'd rented out before the construction was even complete. Each building was painted in a different pastel color; green, blue, pink, and yellow. They looked like the ice cream Delmonico's served in tall glass bowls, with swirls of cream and curled chocolate on top.

And at the end of the pier, floating proudly in the water, was Griff's rebuilt boat. He'd renamed it, too, making Autumn christen the side with a bottle of champagne before he revealed the gold paint. *Forever Autumn.*

"I've heard of guys getting tattoos of their girlfriend's name on their arms, but this is the first time I've seen a boat named after one," she'd told him, trying to swallow down the tears.

He'd kissed her softly, brushing the hair from her face as he cupped her chin. "I like it," he whispered. "Now I'm branded by you."

She walked steadily up the pier, toward her office which was now two stories. The top floor was where she worked, and the bottom was outfitted with sofas, along with a huge mirror on the wall where a bride-to-be and her party could be primped and preened by her beauty team, before heading out to the pier to say her vows.

Rapping on the door before opening it, Autumn smiled when she saw Brooke sitting there, her hair being curled into barrelled ringlets as she sipped a glass of champagne. She'd been so sweet about the delay to her wedding, and refused to even consider moving venues. *"I'll wait until the pier is ready,"* she'd told Autumn. *"However long it takes. I can't imagine a better place to get married."*

Ally was sitting next to Brooke, having mascara carefully applied to her lashes. Ember was on the sofa with Arthur, who looked adorable in a tiny suit and bow tie. He had a car in his hand and was running it over the cushions, making engine noises through his lips.

Caitie and Harper would be here later. Though Caitie was working hard on her water phobia, she knew her limits. So the two of them were getting ready at home, and would arrive for the ceremony, where Breck and James would be waiting for them.

"Everything okay?" Autumn asked her friends.

"It's wonderful," Brooke said, grinning at her from the mirror. "I feel like a princess."

"You look like one, too," Autumn told her. Brooke's dress was hanging up, a delicate ivory lace bodice that would cling to her body, then fan out in layers to the ground. Ember and Ally would walk down the aisle in front of her, along with Arthur who was in charge of the rings, or at least would be holding the ring bag in his hand. Brooke's fiancé, Aiden, would be waiting for her with their son, Nicholas, who was standing up as his best man.

"You have an hour until the ceremony's due to start," Autumn told them, checking her watch. "Are you ready for a snack?"

"From Delmonico's?" Ally asked. "Hell yes."

"I think she's going to need it to soak up the champagne," Brooke said dryly. "Speaking of which, would you like some?"

"I'll pour," Ember said, rising up from the sofa. Her hair was already finished, but her face was bare, waiting for the make up artist to finish with Ally.

"I'm okay, thanks," Autumn said, before Ember could walk any further. "I need to keep a clear head so that everything goes to plan."

"But you'll have some later, won't you?" Ally asked. "Once the party begins you should relax and kick back with us. I'm planning on dancing all night." She shimmied her shoulders to prove the point, earning her a smear of mascara on her cheek. "Oops."

"We'll see." Autumn grinned at them all. "I'm going to check on the guys now. Make sure they're almost ready."

"You can guarantee they've all been drinking," Ember said, kissing Arthur's cheek. "Six men on a boat is asking for trouble."

"At least we know where they are," Autumn pointed out. It had been Griff's idea to use the boat as the groom's base for the weddings they were planning to have on the pier. "I'll ask Vincent to bring some food over on my way out. I'll be back in about a half an hour, but call me if you need anything, okay?"

"Sure." Brooke smiled warmly at her.

Autumn let herself quietly out of the lounge and walked over to the restaurant. They'd tried to keep the construction as faithful to the original as possible, knowing that Pietro's grandfather had built it with his own hands. But the materials had been upgraded – the wood used was less flammable, and the kitchen had been fitted with high-end appliances. When Delmonico's re-opened a couple of weeks ago, people had traveled from far and wide to attend the party.

The kitchen door opened before she could get to it, and Vincent came out carrying delicious pastries topped with whipped cream. "Hey, I was just taking these over to the lounge."

"Great." Autumn smiled. "You read my mind."

"You want to try one?" he asked. "I know you love my cannolis." He pushed the platter toward her, and her stomach turned.

"I'm too nervous to eat," she confessed. "Maybe later."

"We'll have some more for the buffet," he told her. "The food is going to be magnificent."

"I knew it would be." Her stomach was still churning. She

tried to smile to hide the nausea. "I'll come and see you after the ceremony, okay?"

"Sure thing." He winked and carried on to where the bride and her party were waiting for him.

It was so good to see Delmonico's up and running again. Or *Delmonico's on the Pier* as it was called now, because they'd kept the restaurant location Autumn's dad had found them further up the coast, as well as returning to this one. Carla had been promoted to manager there, and Autumn had heard through the grapevine she was flourishing – and that she was in a relationship with one of the chefs, who was equally as smitten.

Talking of smitten, Autumn turned her gaze to the boat rising gently up and down in the water at the end of the pier. As though he could sense her getting closer, Griff was standing at the entrance plank, a smile playing at his lips as he watched her approach.

"Hey, baby." He walked toward her, curling his arms around her waist. "I've missed you."

"It's only been a couple of hours since we left home," she said, smiling at his neediness. It reflected her own.

"Yeah, well I'm counting the hours until we're back there. Maybe we should sell the pier and boat and become hermits."

"You'd go mad after two days."

"Nah, I can think of things we could do." He brushed his lips against her ear.

"Then you'd drive me mad," she said, a shiver snaking down her spine.

"That's the plan," he whispered.

"How are Aiden and the groomsmen doing?" she asked him, trying to ignore the way her body responded to him. He only had to look at her in a certain way for her legs to turn to jelly. Good thing he was strong enough to carry her.

"They're fine," he said. "We're having a beer and the guys

are roasting him. Usual pre-wedding fun."

"Just *one* beer?" she asked, raising an eyebrow.

"As you insisted." He winked. "How long do we have until you need them outside?"

"It's an hour until the ceremony starts, so they need to be ready in half an hour."

Griff ran his finger down her back, making her skin tingle. "That's plenty of time," he said, his eyebrow rising as he smouldered down at her.

"For what?"

"I think you know."

She laughed. "Where are we going to go? My office is being used, and so's your boat." And they'd already christened them both in their delight at having everything repaired.

"That's a good point." He glanced at his watch. "Do we have time to make it home?"

"Not anymore." She'd moved out of the beach house months ago, and was immediately replaced by a new tenant. She and Griff had stayed in his apartment for a while, until their new house a mile up the beach was ready for them to move into. It was beautiful, with wide glass doors that opened onto a terrace overlooking the ocean.

And it had a closet dedicated only to shoes. They might have christened that room, too.

"Griff, your beer's getting warm," somebody shouted from inside the boat.

"I guess I should go back in." He brushed his lips against hers. "I'll see you at the ceremony. And all night. I plan on dancing with you a lot."

"I'll see you then," she said, smiling softly. And when the moment was right, she'd tell him the secret she'd been keeping all day. She was pretty sure it would make him happy.

They'd reached the part of a wedding reception where too many drinks had been swallowed down, and too much dancing had been done, yet nobody wanted to go home and have the magic end. Griff had spent most of the evening with Autumn, spinning her around the dance floor, laughing as they watched Brooke's great Aunt Shula flirt with all the eligible bachelors, then kissing her until they were both breathless.

Griff leaned on the bar and ordered two glasses of champagne. He wanted to drink to their future, to their businesses, but most of all, he wanted to drink to the realization that he couldn't live life without her. He didn't *want* to.

But he did want to ask her to be his wife.

He patted his pocket to check that the little box was still there. He'd chosen the ring the last time they'd visited New York. Autumn had been out for coffee with an old friend, and he'd taken Lydia to the jewelers for her opinion, and they'd chosen the beautiful square cut diamond that had been in his pocket or his sock drawer for the past month.

It was time to put it where it belonged. If she'd have him.

"You done it yet?" Lucas asked as Griff passed his table of friends. Lucas was the only one he'd confided in, apart from Lydia, who asked him the same question every week without fail.

It would be a relief to tell her yes, he had.

"Just on my way," Griff murmured to Lucas.

"Good luck. She's a lucky woman."

"I'm the lucky one." Of that he was sure.

He found her leaning on the painted blue railing, staring out at the dark blue ocean, her face illuminated by the string of lights swaying in the breeze above her.

"Hey, I've been looking for you," he said, passing her a glass of champagne. Autumn stared down at it as though she couldn't work out what it was. "It's for a toast," he told her.

"What toast?"

"That's what I'm getting to," he said. His stomach did a little flip. Were those nerves? He never got nerves.

Though he'd never asked the woman he loved to marry him before, either.

"Before you do, there's something I need to tell you," she said quickly. She was biting her lip the way she always did when she was worried.

He smoothed a lock of hair from her face. "What is it, baby?"

"I can't drink this." She passed him back the glass.

He sniffed it in case it was off. Then he looked back up at her, a question on his face.

"Do you remember how I promised to never keep secrets from you?" she asked. She looked as nervous as he felt.

"Yeah." He nodded, perplexed.

"I've kind of been keeping one all day. Since this morning. Though I've suspected a little longer." She ran her hand down her front, lingering on her stomach. "I'm pregnant. Or *we're* pregnant. How the hell does this even work?"

Griff opened his mouth but nothing came out.

"Oh god, you're angry, aren't you?"

He shook his head. "Not angry. Just confused. How did we..."

"I think it was when we moved out of your apartment. Remember we wanted to say goodbye to the bedroom?"

Yeah, he remembered. He still had dreams about it. "We didn't use something then?"

"I'm guessing not." She looked at the champagne glasses he was holding. "I'm guessing we're going to be toasting a different future now. Or you are. I can just watch."

That's when it hit him. Autumn was carrying his baby. Warmth washed over him like a wave and he grinned like crazy. "We're having a kid?" he asked, putting the champagne glasses down on the wooden plank at his feet. His eyes were wide as he held his hand to her stomach. "Seriously?"

She put her hand over his, pressing it against her abdomen. "There's nothing to feel yet. But there will be."

"Yeah, there will." He felt like he'd grown ten feet taller. He wanted to shout it out to the world. That this beautiful woman was his, and she was carrying his baby. God, it didn't get any better.

"What was it you were going to tell me?" she asked him as he caressed her belly.

"What?"

"You said you were getting to something when you gave me the champagne," she reminded him. "What was it?"

The ring! He ran his hand down his pocket. It was still there. Still waiting. The same way it had been all day.

"I wanted to ask you something. And I need you to know it's not because of the baby, as freaking excited as I am."

"Okay." She gave him a confused smile.

He pulled the box from his pocket, then dropped to his knee, his face in line with her chest. Angling his head, his gaze met hers.

"Autumn Paxton, you're the most amazing woman I've ever met. You're the first thing I think about in the morning, and the last thing at night. I didn't know what real love was until I met you. And you're the only woman I'll ever want to spend the rest of my life with." He opened the box, and the ring glittered beneath the string lights. "It would be the greatest honor if you'd agree to marry me." He leaned in to kiss her stomach through her satin dress. "If you'd both agree to it," he said, his voice cracking.

Her eyes glinted as she reached for him, a half-laugh, half-sob escaping from her lips. "This isn't just because of the baby?" she asked as he stood and pulled her into his arms.

"How could it be? I had no idea." He pulled the ring out

of the box and she held her hand out, swallowing hard as he pushed it onto her finger. "I know I said I never wanted to settle down, and I know you're wary of ever marrying again, but I want to be your husband, and I gotta tell you, I'm desperate for you to be my wife."

"I want that, too," she said, rolling onto her toes to kiss him. "So much."

He kissed her back, marveling at how soft her lips were. Then he touched her stomach again, amazed that a tiny life was growing in there. A little baby they'd made together.

A child who would always know how much it was loved. A child who would *always* be wanted, taken care of, adored.

For years he'd thought he'd never have that. Never have this overwhelming love that he both gave and received.

It was a brand new life – one he'd never dared to dream of. And he couldn't wait for it to begin.

He brushed the tears away from her cheeks with his thumbs, pressing his lips to her nose. "I love you, baby," he whispered to her, then looked down at her belly. "And you, too, baby."

Autumn laughed through her tears. "And we love you, too. So much."

Then she kissed him hard, as though she could never get enough of him.

"Come and dance with me," he murmured against her lips. "We've got some celebrating of our own to do."

They really did. As far as he was concerned, he'd be celebrating forever. Because his life was finally what he'd wanted it to be all along. Happy and complete.

Thanks to her.

THE END

DEAR READER

Thank you so much for reading Griff's and Autumn's story. If you enjoyed it and you get a chance, I'd be so grateful if you can leave a review. And don't forget to keep an eye out for CHASING THE SUN, the next book in the series, coming in JANUARY 2021

I can't wait to share more stories with you.

Yours,

Carrie xx

ABOUT THE AUTHOR

Carrie Elks writes contemporary romance with a sizzling edge. Her first book, *Fix You*, has been translated into eight languages and made a surprise appearance on *Big Brother* in Brazil. Luckily for her, it wasn't voted out.

Carrie lives with her husband, two lovely children and a larger-than-life black pug called Plato. When she isn't writing or reading, she can be found baking, drinking an occasional (!) glass of wine, or chatting on social media.

You can find Carrie in all these places
www.carrieelks.com
carrie.elks@mail.com

ALSO BY CARRIE ELKS

ANGEL SANDS SERIES

Let Me Burn

She's Like the Wind

Sweet Little Lies

Just A Kiss

Baby I'm Yours

Pieces Of Us

Chasing The Sun

THE HEARTBREAK BROTHERS SERIES

Take Me Home

Still The One (Coming Aug 2020)

THE SHAKESPEARE SISTERS SERIES

Summer's Lease

A Winter's Tale

Absent in the Spring

By Virtue Fall

THE LOVE IN LONDON SERIES

Coming Down

Broken Chords

Canada Square

STANDALONE

Fix You

Made in the USA
Monee, IL
17 December 2020